Springtime
of the
Spirit

Springtime
of the
Spirit

Maureen Lang

TYNDALE HOUSE PUBLISHERS, INC., CAROL STREAM, ILLINOIS

Check out the latest about Maureen Lang at www.maureenlang.com.

TYNDALE and Tyndale's quill logo are registered trademarks of Tyndale House Publishers, Inc.

Springtime of the Spirit

Designed by Beth Sparkman

Edited by Sarah Mason

Published in association with the literary agency of WordServe Literary Group, Ltd., 10152 S. Knoll Circle, Highlands Ranch, CO 80130.

Scripture quotations are taken from the *Holy Bible*, King James Version.

ISBN 978-1-61129-491-0

Printed in the United States of America

Dedicated to my three brothers,
David, *Mark*, and *Patrick*, and my brother-in-law, *Jim*,
each of whom at one time or another inspired
political "discussions" in my family.

For this model of political passion,
I extend my heartfelt gratitude.

Acknowledgments

As with all my books, only my name shows up on the cover. In fact, my stories would barely be recognizable without the encouragement and insight of my two editors, Stephanie Broene and Sarah Mason. For this one especially, I am deeply grateful.

Germans who lived during those first ten postwar years talked
of them afterwards as a time full of dangerous strains,
yet too of hope and promise—a springtime of the spirit.

TERENCE PRITTIE, *Life World Library: Germany,* 1961, 1968

And what doth the Lord require of thee, but to do justly,
and to love mercy, and to walk humbly with thy God?

MICAH 6:8

A Summary of Terms:
By **bourgeoisie** is meant the class of modern **capitalists**,
owners of the means of social production and employers of wage
labour. By **proletariat**, the class of modern wage labourers who,
having no means of production of their own, are reduced
to selling their labour power in order to live.

F. ENGELS, NOTE TO THE ENGLISH EDITION OF 1888,

The Communist Manifesto BY KARL MARX AND FRIEDRICH ENGELS

Once there was a country that wanted a turn being a great and mighty empire. They thought their freedom was at stake when the countries around them matched their race for armaments. To protect that freedom and to make a try for their mighty empire, they ordered their army—an army with a glorious history of excellence—to fight.

Despite all assurances that they would surely win, this country was defeated after all. And its people, shocked at losing a war they'd been told would be won, ripened for revolt against the leadership that had brought them not only the loss of so many men, but the scorn of the world.

Some were willing to allow more sacrifice, but no longer from the workers and soldiers who had already given so much.

Some wanted a better nation through finding a better part of themselves.

This is the story of two such people.

Part One

NOVEMBER 1918

1

One step, then another. He'd started out with his eyes forward, chin up, but all he could see now were the tips of his boots.

Christophe Brecht was inside German territory, the train having taken them back over the border, away from the trenches that had marred France for the past four years. The ground his boots pounded now belonged to the fatherland.

Home.

The only sound was that of his men marching beside him— not that their tread could be called marching. Most looked as tired and worn as he, barely able to take the next step. They were still covered in the mud of no-man's-land, thick from boots to knee and in varying layers up to the helmet.

Did any of them remember how it had been when they marched—yes, really marched—in the *other* direction? Songs and praise echoed from every avenue, and flowers showered them from smiling women, with proud pats on the back from fathers and old men.

The city that had sent them so gloriously off to battle was still beyond sight. Those not wishing to go all the way to Munich had been made to get off the train already, close to but not at their requested destinations. The train lines were in disarray after handing over half of Germany's locomotives to the Allies—too much disarray to answer individual needs.

But Christophe wasn't far from Braedon, his small hometown some distance west of Munich. He shoved away old thoughts of how this day was supposed to be. No victory parades to greet them, no flowers. No woman to kiss him now that he was home. Just silence.

He stared ahead under the autumn sunlight. His vision was clear, something the army had taken advantage of when they'd trained him to be a sniper in the last chaotic weeks of the war. Despite his earlier promotion from Hauptmann to Major, they'd stuck him where he was needed most, no consideration of his rank. Not that he hadn't been a successful sniper, but what he'd counted success only days ago now seemed something else altogether.

Very likely many of the men beside him couldn't see the details he could—signs on the series of poles before them: splashes of red, in flags, in backdrop. Signs he hadn't seen the likes of since before the war. Back when people still talked about politics, when the German voice wasn't the single one it had turned into during the war.

Then he saw it. An older poster, a bit tattered by the wind. The Kaiser's face, easily recognizable with his mustache and uniform. A call to arms.

Christophe tore his gaze away, to the sky, back to his boots. He'd answered that call; so had each of those who trod at his side. A call that had ended this way.

Rumor had it the Kaiser had fled Germany in disgrace. Good riddance. If what they said about the armistice was true—that Germany was to be given sole blame for the war— then the world hated them. Hated all of them for how the

Kaiser and his cronies, both aristocratic and military, had pushed them into this war.

Hated them almost as much as Christophe hated himself for all he'd done while in it.

His pace picked up before he knew it; blood pumped as wildly as it had during any fight with the British or French, in offense or defense. He reached for a rock and hurled it at the Kaiser's image. It landed with a thud directly between the eyes.

Another rock, then suddenly more than just his own, along with a grunt here and there, a muffled cry. Were they his? No. A few men broke ranks and hurled themselves at what was left of the poster.

All his life Christophe had needed something to cling to. His parents, a schoolmaster, the church, his commanding officer. In the trenches, other soldiers. And Christ.

Hate filled him now—something he didn't want but couldn't rid himself of. He clung to that.

Christophe kept hold of the rock in his hand. No need to throw it—the poster had disappeared.

❦

"And so, fellow Germans! The calendar may say autumn, but in fact we are in the springtime of Germany. The winter of an unjust war is behind us. New life buds for all of us. Are there storms in spring? Yes, but the squalls bring us the energy we need for change. We can build our country anew and model for all—for ourselves and for our neighbors, with the world's eye on us—that we speak as one voice, a voice of men, of women, *all of us* together as one people without differences."

Annaliese barely paused, although the crowd was already

beginning to cheer. She read the same fervor on every face; it was like a wave passing over those gathered, binding them together, uniting them.

"They'll hear us speak of protecting and not exploiting our fellow citizens. They'll hear of our compassion for those in need, feel it in the plans to protect even the least in Germany. They'll hear our demands for the equal distribution of food!"

Cries of affirmation forced a pause.

"We'll no longer be burdened by the yoke of a monarchy or kept under the thumb of warmongers, but we will be free—yes, really free—to live in the peace for which our men fought. Peace! Freedom! Fairness! And bread!"

Annaliese Düray reveled in the jubilation, in the immediate approval of her call. They outmatched her voice, which was a considerable thing because her voice—especially on this platform—was bigger than she was. Hands raised, she lifted her cry even louder, proud of the timbre she'd inherited from her one-time schoolmarm mother. Not the strident screech of some women but midtoned, boisterous, easy on the ear even at this volume. "Peace is ours! And so is the future! If we rally behind the party!"

"Anya . . . Anya, come along now."

Leo Beckenbauer's arm went around her waist and he ushered her from the crowd. Two others carved a path between the brick wall of the *Apotheke* behind them and the crowd before them, and off they went, the exuberance still echoing in her ears.

"Did you see them, Leo?" she called, breathless. "And more were coming! We should stay—"

But he pressed forward, and there was little she could do except follow, with Leo next to her, bodyguards in front and behind them. Each one was a brother to her, united not by blood but by something deeper, a passion ardent enough to stir all Germany to embrace a better future. One that would bond them with others throughout the world.

They evaded the few people who followed by turning into a narrow gangway between the back of the *Apotheke* and the shop next door. Only four blocks to the back of the butcher shop Leo's father once ran, the temporary headquarters for those whose ideals about the future matched their own.

Not a block away, Annaliese heard the echoes and cries of another rally, led by a voice she recognized as belonging to another party. The Communists—a party not likely to support the recently appointed Bavarian Prime Minister Eisner the way she did. Eisner had been appointed by revolution, with a quick and systematic takeover—and not a single shot fired. Such a takeover would have been far different had the Red Communists been in charge, even if they did want some of the same things Annaliese's own party wanted. Eisner had agreed to a quick election just weeks from now, proving his confidence that he had the will of the people behind him, even though a half-dozen other parties demanded their voices be heard, too.

But in this neighborhood, one voice rang loudest, and that was Jurgen's. A Socialist one.

She saw the exchange of glances between the men around her, starting with Leo, who looked at Ivo, who looked at Huey. Huey was an ironworker and Ivo a woodworker—or Ivo had been, until the war had claimed most of his fingers. Despite any hint of a disability, he was as tall as he was stalwart, just like Huey. It would take little more than a word from either one of them to disperse a competing crowd in their territory.

"I could have stayed this time, Leo," Annaliese said once they entered the back of the darkened shop. Though the kitchen hadn't boasted a single slab of meat or even the stingiest of sausages in well over a year, the slight residue of blood and spices still tickled her nose when Leo closed the door behind them.

Leo went to the table, where a stack of papers awaited him. "You know how Eisner likes it; you and Jurgen are to keep their thoughts on Eisner's council so the vote will be won. You'll spend time more freely with the people once Jurgen is back beside you. He *is* Eisner's council around here—or at least the best known of the council members."

Of all the voices struggling to be heard these days, other than Eisner himself, it was Jurgen who attracted the biggest response from nearly all corners of their broken society. His promises to meet everyday needs did not fall on deaf ears, because his was the voice of the workers and the peasants themselves—of all those who'd never had a voice before.

Jurgen liked to tell Annaliese she brought the women's voice to him, but Annaliese knew better. People came because they wanted to see Jurgen, to hear him, to witness the spark in his eye as he promised them what they wanted most of all. Each came with one need or another, but Jurgen promised that the council had the answer, no matter the question.

And Leo had access to bread. Bread few could afford in the quantities their office provided through donations and collections at street rallies. They could afford collectively what individually they must do without. Starve alone or unite and eat. Practical evidence of the effectiveness of the council's goals.

"Oh! This must have been delivered while we were gone."

Annaliese scooped up the package left on the wide butcher's table beside the stack of notes Leo tended. "And just in time for tomorrow's council meeting."

Ripping away the string and paper, she held up the jacket for Leo to see. It was exactly as she'd told the tailor to make it: broad across the shoulders, with a touch of padding to make those shoulders appear fully capable of holding the world's woes, just as he needed them to. And not black, but blue— dark, though, because anything too bright would be out of place in their tattered world. Yet blue would cast his elegant eyes in the best light.

But Leo was shaking his head. "He'll look like a capitalist."

"No jacket will hide Jurgen's working-class background. It's in the width of his shoulders, the strength and size of his hands. In this, he'll look the way every man wants to look. Strong. Fatherly yet handsome; a leader. And the color will reveal the poet in him."

Leo aimed a skeptical brow her way. "Fatherly? I wasn't aware that's how you viewed him."

She ignored the comment; it wasn't the first time Leo had tried coaxing free her infatuation with Jurgen. "It's important that he not look like a military man, even if we do want the military behind us. We've seen enough leaders in uniform. And he won't wear the top hat of a capitalist, either, or the shoes of a monarch. He'll wear trousers like anyone else, only this jacket will show he can take on another's burden without the excesses of an exploiter."

"Yes, well, he's doing that, isn't he?" Leo fingered the sleeve—durable fabric, plain but for the dark blue color. "Well chosen, Anya. You're young but smart; I've said so right along."

Annaliese smiled at the praise, especially coming from Leo. Jurgen might be the one to receive public praise in the name of Eisner's council—or the blame from those who disagreed—but anyone who worked beside them knew whatever Jurgen believed, Leo had believed first.

2

At last Christophe stood outside his home. From here he could almost make himself believe it looked the same. He had to ignore a few cracked tiles on the expansive roof, and there were weeds in the flower boxes his mother once kept. The door needed painting again, something his father never would have tolerated had he still been alive to make sure it was taken care of.

Christophe pushed the door open, and it squeaked on its hinges. Even in the dim light, Christophe could no longer fool himself. Everything had changed. No one was here. No family, not even a housekeeper or maid. He walked through the parlor and the dining room, noting that much of the furniture was gone too. In the kitchen, cabinet doors stood agape, revealing nothing but empty shelves. Everything held the gray film of dust, from the curtains at the windows to the kitchen table left behind, even down to the floorboards under his feet.

An item beneath that dust caught his eye, there next to the sink. He picked up the envelope, blowing away the coating and only faintly pleased to see his name scrawled across the front. He ripped it open.

My dearest brother,

I pray one day you return from the war to hold this letter in your hands, and I send my deepest apologies that I cannot be there to greet you.

It is my fervent wish that we will see one another again, but I fear that will never be. I am going all the way to America, where hard work will reward me in ways it can no longer do here. The sacrifices have been too great and the hunger so fierce, I no longer believe we are winning this fight the way the papers say that we are.

I go to our uncle in Milwaukee. He's made arrangements for me to travel as a Swiss citizen so I won't have any trouble being admitted. Perhaps you will follow me there, if you wish to.

I'll write to you if ever there is peace for Germany again. I think of you fondly. Always. Your loving sister,

Nitsa

Christophe crushed the paper in his hand. His eyes stung hot and wet and he busied himself by brushing aside some of the dust from the tabletop, then straightening the paper, smoothing it so it would slide once again into the torn envelope.

He slipped it into his pocket, even though part of him was tempted to do worse than crumple it. Why did Nitsa have to leave? She knew he would be coming home, didn't she? Coming home as their brother, Hann, never would? Couldn't she have waited? To be here so he wouldn't have to see . . . this . . . alone?

He turned around again, the empty silence broken only

by his quickened, angry breath. He had thought he would die along with Hann, that day they'd fought together in the second great battle at the Somme. But Christophe hadn't died; somehow life had gone on for him, even when he hadn't wanted it to.

His parents were gone too, dead from the heartache of losing their youngest son, from fear of losing Christophe, and from the rest of the horrors war brought with it. Malnutrition and dangerous substitutions in the food supply might have been the cause assigned by a doctor—at least for his mother, who'd never been strong. But his father? What should he call malnutrition of the spirit? Christophe didn't know. He knew only that it could kill someone. It took a year from the day his mother had died, but kill it had.

And now he'd lost Nitsa, too.

He would have stumbled to a chair, but there wasn't one, so he sank to the floor, all passion, all strength, abandoning him. God was here; Christophe knew that still. He wasn't alone. And yet he could only sob for all the war had stolen from him.

◦◦◦

"What we want is universal brotherhood. Germany should stand for that, after all."

"We shouldn't let the bosses and the owners have so much, and us so little!"

"We want bread for our families!"

"And care for the sick!"

Annaliese drifted through the room, assessing the mood, hearing the breathing, smelling the anger as voices rose with the acuteness of the various needs and opinions.

Jurgen himself stood, towering above the others, even those on the platform beside him. Where once a sales counter had displayed German delicacies, there now stood a table and chairs for the men who would lead the way to a better future, who defined what their message was to be.

"Gentlemen . . . and ladies," Jurgen said with a familiar smile that seemed so natural on his handsome face. His eyes skimmed the crowded room, and Annaliese stood still, waiting until they landed on her, even though there were at least a half-dozen other women present. All wanting the same two things she did: a voice . . . and Jurgen.

She saw the blue of his gaze even in the dimming light. It passed over the other women before touching her, too.

But then kept going.

Of course; he had an audience to address. She hadn't expected him to single her out. Hoped, perhaps, but not expected.

Soon this room would be too small to hold them. Their numbers grew every day; even now, more men waited just outside the door. This was their core support, those who did far more than just gather to witness Jurgen's public addresses. He spoke in support of Eisner, who'd brought Socialism to power in Munich for the first time. Jurgen was the link between them, having the ear of both Eisner and the people. A link that would bring the votes Eisner needed in the coming election.

Jurgen held up a pamphlet in one hand, a copy of something they'd circulated throughout Munich. Something he'd drafted with his eloquent pen, the same pen that had once created poetry in celebration of women and nature but now offered promise for Germany. Words to spur Germany into looking forward and not back, offering security for those who'd been exploited too long.

"The enemy is no longer Britain," he said. "It's tyranny. And it's here, inside Germany. It's in Britain, too, and France, and everywhere the wealthy misuse their workers." Affirmation echoed from one end of the room to the other. "Our voice is growing. We're being heard. Being heard by *all* the people, from the hardest worker here in the city to the field-workers on the farms. We've all seen what tyranny can do. We've seen what war can do. We've seen the rich still able to buy what they need while we resort to whatever means we can to keep scraps on the table. Now it's time for us—the factory workers and the soldiers who gave so much—to join together with farmers and anyone of lesser means and take part equally in the benefits this country and this earth have to offer. With your help, we can bring the change Germany needs. Each of us in the area of our strengths, working together for one another."

Cheers bubbled, quietly at first, before Jurgen even finished.

"We've had enough of power in the hands of a few wielded over many. We do have a voice, and we'll make it heard in the election. If we stand together!"

Raucous salutes burst through the room and no doubt beyond, because even from here, Annaliese heard those outside join in the noise. They couldn't have heard a word but were eager to join those who had, trusting them and trusting the leadership that inspired them.

"But what about winning? Can Eisner win what some say he took?"

"There are more of us than there are of the rich. Eisner will win!"

"Eisner needs to win to stay where he is!"

Jurgen held up a palm again, nodding in the general vicinity of the question's origin. "We want a fair vote; all of us do. And it's true this election is coming sooner than we'd like, before the prime minister and we in the council have had a chance to prove our ways. But it's another product of war, this rush to democracy, this need to have a formal voice to use in the armistice talks. Ours isn't the only voice demanding to be heard. Our message is new, and the people need more time to hear and understand. Which is why we need all of you—men and women, too, now that they have the vote—to support the prime minister and those of us on his council. It's the only way we can fight the tyranny of the monarchy, of capitalism, of warmongers who sent us to war in the first place."

More cheers, followed by more rallying from Jurgen, until surely the crowd was as frenzied and parched as Annaliese. She watched him for a moment, mesmerized by his passion, caught up in what he believed, then slipped out the door. She passed through the people unnoticed, unrecognized as the one who had spoken just yesterday, gathering her own flock, many of whom were here today. With her blonde hair covered in a dark felt cap, a brown jacket over the white blouse she wore at all her rallies, and without the platform making her so much taller, she escaped attention.

The street was full to the end of the block. She walked around, pleased to see more people scattered even around the corner, those who were interested yet perhaps discouraged by the competition to hear a speech meant for the small group inside the building. Maybe some were only looking for the bread Jurgen sometimes had a way of producing. Finding her way to the rear of the building, she nodded to Ivo, who stood guard but let her pass. Ivo, who always had a smile for her, he with a missing tooth and mangled hands but a twinkle in his eye. Jurgen would be finished soon, and bodyguards would whisk him away. Along with her.

The wait was longer than she expected; Jurgen must have been enjoying himself more than usual to draw out his speech so long. But how could he not? She'd learned for herself what it was to have the crowd joined with a speaker, united in message, in dream, in spirit. Heady fruit indeed.

When Jurgen finished and joined them in the rear of the shop, Leo led the way to a truck waiting at the end of another block. It was hardly a plush mode of transportation, but few vehicles were left anymore, so even this old ambulance truck pockmarked like no-man's-land itself was a precious commodity.

Annaliese handed Jurgen a flask of water mixed with only a touch of wine. It made the water more palatable, but the limited supply forced rationing.

He never drank plain water, not since the day just a month ago when factory workers, inspired by a sailors' revolt in Kiel, had liberated him from a prison right here in Munich. He'd spent the past year of his life as a political prisoner for protesting the war through the poetry he'd written and circulated. Wine, he'd once said, was what he missed most about freedom. It stirred the poetry in his soul, and without that he was nothing.

They drove through a neighborhood full of parks and trees, to what once had been a fine residence for a single family. Rumor had it the entire family had died of the influenza. It had been cleaned out and converted to several units, one of which Leo shared with Jurgen. For the past month or more, Annaliese had been housed in another flat above, while one of the bodyguards, Huey, and his wife lived across from Annaliese.

"You should rest your voice," Annaliese told Jurgen when he invited her to Leo's flat rather then letting her go upstairs to hers. "For tomorrow's march."

Turning to her, he caught her hand and pulled her close. "One of these days, Annaliese, you will learn to take care of more than just my voice."

His smile lingered in her direction, and for a moment she wanted to forget the rallies, forget his need for rest. It was a curious thing, this desire he often expressed to be with her. It fed her fascination with him. In the month since she'd found her own voice in the political group known as the USPD, the *Unabhängige Sozialdemokratische Partei Deutschlands*, she hadn't been able to tell if she wanted Jurgen the way he seemed to want her . . . or if she only wanted his message.

She moved his hand from her hip, placing it on the railing beside them, careful not to smile. "Perhaps. Someday. But aren't we supposed to be concentrating only on our country these days? Individual concerns don't matter so much, but as a whole we can do great things for all. . . ."

He smiled at her quotation of one speech of his or another, or perhaps an encapsulation of all, even if she did use it to counter his flirtation.

Then she went up the stairs, conscious that he watched her. She didn't breathe until inside her apartment, where she waited to hear his door close behind him, his voice mingling with Leo's.

He wasn't easy to resist. Jurgen was tall and handsome, with light hair and cerulean eyes that seemed to look inside every person he saw. Yet the sand of his hair was touched with gray, his eyes edged in feathers of maturity. Even so, his back and hands were strong from his family's peasant background, and his mind stronger. He'd given much to Germany already in his poetry, his months in prison, and now in his passion for serving on the council. Any woman would be eager to be with such a man, to see to his needs both public and personal . . . as she'd witnessed a number of them do already.

She just wasn't sure she wanted to become one more.

3

Christophe tried the gate but it was locked. The mere jingle, however, ignited a charge from two tall Doberman pinschers that must have been patrolling the wooded grounds. Christophe pulled his hand from the gate and stepped back, having witnessed at the war front how belligerent such guard dogs could be. Their wide, square chests heaved out a series of strong warning barks from the other side of the iron fence.

So this was how the Düray family greeted their invited guests these days.

A call from the shadows had the dogs heeling within a moment. But this man wasn't Manfred Düray—Christophe saw that in an instant. He was someone Christophe had never met before, and he carried a gun. In the dimming light of the evening shadows of the woods, someone else might have missed that he'd secreted the weapon in the deep folds of a tattered, army-issue overcoat.

"Christophe Brecht?"

He nodded. "Isn't this where the Düray family lives?"

The man reached for the lock. "Yes, they are here. They're waiting for you."

Without another word to either Christophe or the dogs,

the sentry led the way. The Düray family Christophe had known all his life hadn't been living here when he'd left for the war. Since then they'd moved into the finest home in the area, one that had sat empty when the old count had died and left no heirs.

Christophe had no idea why he was here, particularly if the rumors he'd heard in town were true. Giselle Düray was dead, and she was the only possible connection he might have had—ever dreamed of having—to this family.

The home was cast in a cottage style, though no one would call it that. Two stories and two wings made the home too large. From the tall gate to the zealous dogs, there was nothing unassuming about a family who lived here. Not anymore.

As predicted, a maid answered the door. Once Christophe was handed into her care, the guard behind him disappeared, and along with him the dogs.

"Follow me, please."

Christophe did, through a wide, impressive foyer boasting a staircase intricately carved no doubt by the finest German craftsmen. She led him through open double doors to a parlor, in which sat two couches facing one another in front of a man-size fireplace. Beyond plush chairs and occasional tables sat a polished grand piano, resting in the light filtering through the outdoor trees.

"Herr and Frau Düray will join you shortly."

Then the maid left Christophe alone.

He looked around the room, noting the finery. Porcelain bowls and vases, a crystal lamp placed near the window to scatter a shower of colorful beams across the room. His gaze stopped at a family portrait hung above the fireplace, an appealing glance into lives of elegance. Christophe recognized Herr

Düray immediately, with his mustache so like their Kaiser's—their former Kaiser, he should say.

Frau Düray was seated beside him in the portrait, the detailed weaving of her gown precisely drawn, her hair upswept, a single jewel at her throat emblazoned with light.

Two daughters stood behind them, and Christophe's eye was drawn inevitably to Giselle. Captured in the beauty that would be hers forever now, without witness to age or decay. Her hair, like her mother's, had been twirled up for the occasion—though he remembered it falling beyond her shoulders, a slight breeze making it dance. Those were her eyes on the canvas, lightly drawn, and yet he remembered them grown wide in laughter, not quite so sedate.

Was this the girl who had first claimed his heart? He knew it was, and yet even before her death, he knew she wouldn't be the only love for him. Hadn't other women tempted him much the same? some German, some French?

His gaze was drawn to Giselle's sister then, the younger of the two. Her hair was long and light and full of waves, the kind of blonde that caught anyone's eye, as bright as a child's. Perhaps she was even prettier than Giselle, or so thought the artist from this rendition.

"Christophe Brecht."

He turned at his name, spoken curtly, more like a roll call than a greeting. The oddness of the man's tone was softened a moment later by the woman at Herr Düray's side, who came forward, hand outstretched.

"Thank you for coming, Christophe. And welcome home!"

"Thank you."

The maid had followed with a tray that she set on the table between the couches.

"You'll have coffee, of course."

"Or would you prefer something stronger?" Herr Düray asked.

"No. Coffee." He was surprised they had more than coffee to offer, with how scarce food was in the village. Even scarcer than it had been at the front, when they'd occasionally been able to raid an enemy trench that hadn't been limited by the blockade that still strangled Germany.

Christophe would have liked to say he couldn't stay, but what should he tell them he must attend? Since his return days before, and the end of the war only weeks before that, he had nothing to do. The army commission his parents had arranged was at an end, he was too old to return to the university even if he wanted to, and numerous shops, including his father's, were closed down. What sort of employment awaited him? Even the factories were still in chaos from strikes and the planned transition from war production to less-urgent supplies. There were few jobs to be had for a man, even if every woman who'd found a job during the war relinquished it to stay home.

"I'm sure you must have stories to tell from your time away from home," Frau Düray said as she poured. Her hand trembled and some of the coffee splashed to the saucer. "But then I'm sure you mustn't want to speak of it."

"No more than we should like to hear of it," Herr Düray put in. "You served your country well, young man. Let that be enough said."

Christophe accepted the coffee, curious why they'd summoned him if they didn't want to hear of his experiences. The rest of the villagers who'd welcomed him home had let him talk, and somehow he'd found comfort in it, even if everyone knew it had all been for nothing.

Short of asking why they'd invited him, he could think of nothing else to say. Except one thing. "I was sorry to learn of Giselle. I offer you my deepest condolences."

Frau Düray's hand trembled again, heard in the clash between her cup and saucer when she set aside her beverage. "Thank you," she whispered.

Although he'd been told Giselle had died, he still wondered how it had happened. A neighbor had said she'd been found three months ago, at the back of the Düray factory following an explosion. An accident, he'd called it, but said in such a way that Christophe was inclined not to believe it. No one answered his questions, and he could hardly ask now, though he was certain her parents at least would know the truth.

"We, too, would like to offer you condolences, Christophe, on the loss of your brother. It must be difficult for you to be home now that your parents are no longer there either."

"Nor my sister."

"Oh? Has she gone somewhere?"

Vaguely surprised at the question, he nodded. "My sister went to our uncle in America."

"Good," Herr Düray said. "That is very good for her."

"Though I'm sure you must miss her," his wife added gently.

Christophe nodded again even as he was surprised Herr Düray thought it wise to leave Germany. Hadn't Germany— even in war—served him well? The roof over his head said that much was true. Perhaps nothing had been easy these last four years, not even for those who profited most by the goods being sold.

Frau Düray looked at him with obvious kindness and sympathy, unexpectedly reminding Christophe of the loss of his own parents. The feeling stabbed at his heart, and even though a moment ago he'd wished to cut short the visit, he found himself now wanting to stay.

"Our daughter spoke of you fondly," Frau Düray went on. "We always knew you were a fine young man and would come home a hero."

"The heroes are on the other side. The winning side." Herr Düray leaned forward, shoving aside his coffee on the table before him. "That's what the foreign papers say, while ours are silent. Our own government doesn't think we have ways of reading those papers." He leaned back on the cushion again, rubbing his face. "But you did your duty, same as I. When the war began, we were both heroes, you for your service and I for my supplies. Do you remember? That it turned out this way . . . it makes neither of *us* a failure."

Christophe didn't repeat what others said, that he'd done his duty because he had no choice. But the Düray factories did have a choice.

"The first time our daughter mentioned you," Frau Düray said softly in contrast to her husband's gruffness, "we knew you were one to watch with pride. We were convinced you would bring honor to our town by your service to Germany. Because you're an honorable man, much as your father was."

Her words sharpened his ache for family and he found himself glancing again at the portrait above. Such a fitting example of the family unit, each one touching another. Herr Düray's hand covered his wife's; each daughter had a hand on the shoulder of the parent in front of them. Connected, cohesive. He wanted to say indestructible, separated only by the death that had taken Giselle away, but wouldn't remind them of their loss again.

"We plan to retool the factory, of course," Herr Düray was saying. "Back to metalworks for everyone's use. Pots, pans, tools. Useful, important items. It won't be long before the factory is outfitted for peacetime again. Plenty of jobs for soldiers like you. New management, new product."

Frau Düray spared a quick glance in her husband's direction before continuing. "But in the present time, while the factory is being refitted, as my husband says, you'll be having some time on your hands, won't you, Christophe?"

He set down his cup, eyeing not Frau Düray but her husband, who seemed to be growing agitated, judging by the look on his face. A sort of detachment had developed, as if his mind were elsewhere, in a place he didn't want to be.

"So you invited me here to offer a job, Herr Düray?"

"They hate us, you know," Herr Düray said without looking at either his wife or Christophe now. "It's why we've had to hire the guard and bring in the dogs. I cannot even enter my own home without fearing one of the dogs will attack me. How should they know they owe me for their meals? that I provide them their shelter?"

"My dear, please . . . let us come to the point." Frau Düray glanced at her husband again and Christophe sensed she was in a race with Herr Düray's hold on dignity. "Christophe, the reason we invited you here today was to offer you a job, as you've guessed, but perhaps not the kind you're thinking."

"What sort of job?" Even he heard the skepticism behind his question.

"I wonder if you might consider going to Munich for us? That's where our daughter is, you see. We wonder if you might be able to bring Annaliese home to us. The city is so dangerous these days, you know. Between the sicknesses and the street violence the papers talk about. It's no place for her, and we worry so. . . ."

"Annaliese?" His gaze went to the portrait again. "She is in Munich?"

"Yes! She refuses to send word to us, even to tell us she's all right."

"Do you think she's come to harm?"

"We pray every day for her safety. But truth is, we don't know."

"I came through several cities on my way home, Frau Düray." He wouldn't tell her all the details—he didn't like thinking of them himself—but he could tell her the best of what he'd seen and leave out the worst. "People are celebrating the end of the war. Perhaps she is caught up in the busy city life."

"But she must come home, Christophe. To her family!"

"If she doesn't want to, how do you suppose I should persuade her? Is she of a majority age? able to make her own decisions?"

Frau Düray reached out a hand for one of his. The look on her face held such despair he couldn't help but take hold. "Christophe, she's the only child left to us and not even eighteen. The truth is, we plan to follow the path your dear sister has taken, to America. We cannot stay—but we cannot possibly leave her here alone. Will you fetch her and bring her home so we can convince her to come with us? We'll be happy to compensate you generously."

Though she still clutched his hand, Christophe let his gaze leave her face for Herr Düray's. Did he agree with the plan to leave Germany? When he had plans of refitting the factory, offering jobs to returning soldiers like Christophe?

"She'll listen to you," Frau Düray went on. "She's always held you in high regard. As Giselle did."

"Munich is a big city. How would I find her if she doesn't want to be found?" He tried pulling his hand away, but Frau Düray held fast.

"We can guess where she might have started out, and it was only two months ago. Surely if you went there, to one of the inns where we stayed when visiting Munich—the only inns she would have been familiar with—you would learn something about where she went off to. I'm sure of it!"

Christophe was anything but. "Perhaps if you were to go to Munich yourselves . . ."

She pulled her hand away as if he'd scalded her, her blue eyes wide. "Oh, no, no, Christophe! It's frightening enough here, among neighbors. But there? We wouldn't go. We couldn't."

Although he'd seen the unrest himself, knew it was as bad as the newspapers made it sound, should he assure them no one would know them in a city as big as Munich, despite the recently overtaken government? Surely their identities as capitalists—and worse, warmongering capitalists—wouldn't be obvious by their name or manner. Although . . . with the quality of their clothing, he knew they wouldn't blend in with the masses filling city streets, the only safe group of citizenry these days. And those not very safe at that.

In truth, soldiers were the only ones no one seemed to hate anymore. The Socialists wanted the soldiers' confidence and cooperation, and the government wanted their arms. The Communists might hate them for having fought at all, but they wanted the soldiers' armaments too. He knew if Herr and Frau Düray wanted someone to go into Munich—a city torn by all those grabbing for power—it would have to be someone like him.

He would certainly be safer than either of them. And what else did he have to do, anyway?

Perhaps it was the right thing to do; Annaliese might be exactly where she wanted to be, in no danger at all. But what harm would there be in finding out for certain? God seemed to be whispering that into Christophe's soul even before he uttered his response. He'd given Christophe no other direction in a very long time. And God's urging, unlike the Dürays', was impossible to ignore.

"I don't want your compensation, Frau Düray. But I'll go."

4

Annaliese fingered the brooch in her palm. It was small enough to conceal in almost any pocket of a jacket or a skirt. She'd done it often enough, mindlessly toying with it while tending to something else, proofreading pamphlets dictated by Jurgen or writing content for some of her own. Answering letters she'd begun receiving almost daily, ever since she'd spontaneously joined one of Jurgen's speeches almost two months ago. A speech he'd welcomed her to share, once he saw her message reflected his.

She touched the brooch sometimes when sharing the platform with him. Only Annaliese knew she concealed a jewel virtually no one in or connected to the crowd listening to her could afford. Its very existence was the antithesis of everything she espoused these days. It was the symbol of what she'd turned her back on, everything she'd left behind. Her parents' money, her parents' greed. They'd given her a brooch similar to this one, which she'd had no trouble selling, promptly donating the money to the cause for world unity. For a better future for all, one of fairness and equality.

The brooch she held now hadn't been hers. It was Giselle's.

She rarely took it out except in the privacy of her own room. Here, she could look at it and remember how Giselle had worn it pinned in the center of her collared blouses the way their mother always had, how the black onyx had winked in the light but had never matched the sparkle of her eyes.

"Annaliese."

The sound startled her, so unexpected was her own name when Giselle's had filled her heart and mind. She nearly dropped the brooch but caught it back and slipped it into her pocket before going to the door.

Leo stood there, not quite as tall as Annaliese. He had dark, receding hair and a slight paunch he'd somehow managed to maintain through four years of blockade and deprivation. He was not the kind of man most imagined when thinking of a charismatic leader—and never claimed to be—but was, without doubt, the right man to stand behind any leader.

"Are you ready?"

She nodded and would have stepped into the hall, but he did not move away from the threshold.

"I'd like to talk to you before we leave. We have time. The streets are crowded today; we'll have no trouble gathering listeners."

The last month had been a whirlwind of action, working for a wage when they could, igniting one rally after another, taking advantage of the crowds in the street who fled the influenza or searched for food or work. It was easy to gather a crowd when they reminded everyone—starting with the police on the street—that they deserved a better life.

Annaliese stood still, waiting.

"Inside, please. And close the door."

Her mother would have fainted if she knew a man, even one as harmless as Leo, wanted to speak to her without a chaperone inside her small flat, but the thought had little impact on Annaliese. She closed the door behind them.

"You know, don't you, that this continued denial of your affection for Jurgen is distracting him from our work."

"How odd, since most of his speeches remind others this is not the time to indulge in petty self-interest. It's time to rise above, to be selfless—"

"That's enough. I suggest you support him in any way he needs if you're invested in everything you claim to believe. Things are changing so fast in this country that it's difficult for any of us to hold on to what we have. You're making him take his eyes from the race and put them on you."

"I've never done a thing to encourage him. He only wants me because he hasn't had me. Have him ask any one of the others. They've been compliant enough so far."

"So it's jealousy preventing you from going to his bed? A petty, self-centered wish to have him all to yourself or not at all. Like a *wife*, when all of us know marriage is one more vehicle for the government to control us."

"Call it what you will. I have my own reasons. If he wants proof of my loyalty, tell him to listen to my speeches."

For a moment Leo's eyes sparked; his color heightened. Never in the weeks since she'd first met him had he looked at her in such a way. He had become, after all, her protector and adviser, too, from the moment Jurgen had spotted her in the crowd and invited her onto his platform. Leo might have sent such a fierce look in the direction of countless others, but never to her.

And then, as quickly as it appeared, Leo took control of

it. Banished it with a smile. "This is why you make such a fine pair, the two of you. Each as stubborn as the other." He walked past her toward the door but turned abruptly only inches from her face. "I warn you, Annaliese, he will not be put off forever. What he wants, he gets. And for the good of Munich—indeed, all Germany—he should have it. Sooner rather than later. He may be as important as Eisner."

"Parade the others in front of him, Leo," was all she said before walking into the hall.

The smaller beer halls could no longer contain the kinds of crowds Jurgen drew, particularly when other speakers joined him—including Annaliese. And so they met on the streets, even now in December. The leaflets telling everyone about the rally listed only Jurgen's name, but most of the rally attendees knew her anyway. That's all they knew: Annaliese, as if that were her first name and last, like Jurgen. Even she knew him by only one name.

She had followed Jurgen's example by design. While her father's munitions factory outside the city might be a little fish compared to those here in Munich, she didn't want to take the risk of linking her name to his. She needed to be trusted by the very population she most wanted to serve.

For nearly an hour, she and Jurgen spoke and cheered with the masses, but it wasn't her own words or even Jurgen's that held her attention. Leo's words replayed in her mind. How easy it was to be united with Jurgen on a platform. To be stirred by his smiles, to feel the current that sparked between them when he held up her hand. They presented a connected pair and, in so doing, attracted both the men and the women who cheered before them.

Somehow it was more than the appearance of unity that seemed to bind them today. His message was more personal, more in tune not only with the needs of the people but with her own. Individual goals seemed selfish sometimes in light of the needs of so many—and yet beside him, speaking to those whose trust he'd inspired, she couldn't help but feel set apart, distinct even from the other women who wanted to be near him, who had already been near enough to be cast aside. They were there in the crowd, she knew, but it was she whose voice echoed his, she whose hand he held, whose knuckles he kissed in the affirmation of the cheering crowd.

And she whom he wanted.

Was it only her mother's latent warnings about being pure that had kept her away from Jurgen since she'd met him all those weeks ago? or a leftover touch of the faith Annaliese had abandoned when she walked away from her parents' home?

Perhaps she needed to abandon the remnants of their rules and let the passions she'd found here in Munich dictate her behavior. Did her actions really matter, after all, if she didn't hurt anyone? She'd thought everything mattered, once, if not for the moment, then for later. Some things had eternal consequences, or so she'd been told.

But here, now, everything she believed told her *this* was all she had. Life must be made better for everyone because life—*this* life—was their only chance.

Looking at Jurgen, standing beside him in the light of his power and charisma, she found it impossible not to want him. For now. He had his choice of any woman in their crowd, yet he'd chosen her.

What was the harm, anyway?

"This is a photograph of Annaliese Düray. Her family often took rooms here, whenever they were in Munich."

"Ah, yes, one of the Düray daughters." The woman behind the counter glanced up and tsked at Christophe, frowning and shaking her head, her double chin wobbling. "Is it true they lost one of their daughters to an accident in their factory? Ach, such a shame, such loss."

"But this is the younger daughter, Annaliese. She's here in Munich. Do you know where I can find her?"

The woman stared at the picture again, still shaking her head until Christophe repeated his question.

"She's not here, not anymore. She was here for several days, but that was . . . oh, two months ago, at least."

"And where did she go? Did she leave an address should she have any mail?"

"No, no . . . Oh, but wait. There is someone who might help you." She started to say something but suddenly drew in a breath as if a thought had frozen her words. "Whom did you say you were, sir?"

"Christophe Brecht. A friend of the family."

"And have you some proof of that? Why should I help you to find her? The family has always been very kind to me and generous. They've lost one child already. I don't want something to happen to the only one they have left."

"Herr and Frau Düray sent me to Munich to find Annaliese. To bring her home."

She tsked again. "So she's run off and left her parents. Such a shame, when they have only her now. Such a shame."

"Did you say there was someone who might be able to help me find her?"

"Well . . . yes, I suppose you might ask the widow, Frau Haussman. She held the room next to Fräulein Düray, and the two of them were friendly. It's possible they've kept in touch."

"How can I find her, this Frau Haussman?"

"I'll send someone to her room," she said as she waved to a bellman nearby. Then she looked again at Christophe. "You wait."

And so he did, pacing between the window and the glass door of the plush lobby. He'd been tempted to follow the bellman to the widow's door but thought better of it under the hotel matron's scrutiny.

When finally the bellman returned, he only shook his head and said no one had answered.

The woman behind the desk sent Christophe a sympathetic smile. "Frau Haussman often goes out for lunch, but I suppose she'll be back before too long. You can wait in the café. It's there, just beyond the double doors. Best stay inside today. There are a number of rallies going on again, and they're getting more boisterous every day, all that shouting and carrying on about the election next month." She frowned. "They're all promising a better future, but I don't know how every group can say that when all they do is argue about how to do such a thing."

Christophe walked away, passing by the café. Instead, he went back to the street. Activity in this city was more frantic than he'd seen elsewhere, with flyers littering the streets, shops still closed, factories shut down. Wide avenues were jammed not with shoppers but with food lines or men protesting, marching, or simultaneously cheering and jeering at various rallies held in nearly every park or street corner. Not a smile to be found, just shouting and bristling.

And Annaliese was here; she chose to be. He'd thought of little else in the past few days since agreeing to search for her. He recalled her tagging along behind Giselle wherever she went; back then he'd been fond of her, although Giselle had seemed to think her a nuisance.

Annaliese hadn't been at either of the other hotels her mother had suggested and no one had seen her, though a waiter at one of the hotel restaurants had provided a list of possible restaurants the Duräy family might have frequented, popular places with many of the regular guests. Christophe had chased all around the city but was running out of places to look.

"Take one of these, comrade," said a man who thrust a leaflet at him.

Christophe barely glanced at it. He shoved it into his pocket, along with several others he'd been handed that day.

A motorcar skidded by, leaving a cloud of street dust behind. After that a cart pulled by a donkey ambled along, separating two bicycle riders with packets stacked above their rear wheels. Farther down the block, his ear caught the sound of a woman's voice. Loud, boisterous, followed by cheers from a crowd more mixed than any of the others he'd seen. Mostly men, but some women were there too.

He walked along the edge, impressed by the size of the gathering and the fact that it was a woman who drew them together. Attentive faces stared as she touted a better future—the same message everyone offered these days, so he soon stopped listening. The future could hardly be worse than the past four years, so what good were such words? What they needed were open factories with paying jobs. They ought to stop the strikes and these protests that blamed everyone from the government to the military to factory owners; then everyone could get back to work.

He walked on, turning back now so he wouldn't be far from the hotel. He would meet Frau Haussman and see if she could be of any help.

He was directed to a woman who sat in the vestibule of the hotel, a little white dog at her feet yapping his guardianship. When Christophe approached, she looked at him welcomingly despite the dog, which she pulled close and settled on her lap.

The widow was younger than he'd expected, but then there were so many widows in Germany these days. She was finely dressed, and though she wouldn't be called pretty, she had a unique look that wasn't altogether unappealing. Her nose was prominent but straight; her eyes too small and yet bright, as if details wouldn't go long unnoticed. He briefly introduced himself and then asked her about Annaliese as he showed her the photograph.

"Yes, that's Annaliese, isn't it? Not the best likeness; she's so much prettier in person." She looked toward the door. "If only you'd caught me sooner, you could have accompanied me to her rally. I've just come from there."

"You've just seen her at a rally?" He looked again at the quality of her clothing; most of the rallies held throughout the city attracted working-class listeners, not anyone dressed as finely as she.

"Yes, she was magnificent as always. So impassioned, so selfless. She inspires the rest of us toward the greatest hope and generosity."

"Do you mean to say she spoke at the rally?"

Frau Haussman laughed. "Of course! If you go three blocks to the right, you might still catch the remnants of her group. I don't know when she'll be speaking again, but I can assure you it'll be soon. Just look for the leaflets from the USPD."

Christophe bowed with a thank-you, then hurried from the hotel, all the while pulling flyers from his pockets and discarding ones that said nothing about the USPD. The moment he spotted one with the picture of a woman, he stopped to study it.

It was taken from too great a distance to be identifiable, yet there was nothing in the photo to make him believe it couldn't be her. The name on the leaflet belonged to someone else, however, an invitation to hear someone named Jurgen promising *Freiheit, Frieden, und Brot*—freedom, peace, and bread.

Had it been her, the woman speaking at the rally he'd passed not an hour ago? If so, he could surely find her before this day was out.

5

"There was something different about you today, *mein Herz*." Jurgen brushed the top of Annaliese's arm, a spot halfway between her elbow and shoulder. Hand in hand they'd led a procession through the streets, from the city center up to the Friedensengel. What better place to conclude their march and then disperse, full of hope, than at the foot of a statue commemorating peace?

Now they sat in the back of the truck, on benches that only recently had been padded to offer a more comfortable ride.

She might have admitted there was indeed something different about the way she felt today. But since she couldn't define it for herself, she only smiled, letting him hold her gaze and ignoring Leo's approving attention.

"There is another meeting this evening," Jurgen said. "To prepare for the council tomorrow. You needn't attend, but if I knew you waited for me, the meeting would go by all the quicker."

"Why don't I attend, too, then?" She didn't have the direct access he had to those on the new council—those who had been allowed to take power after last month's revolution. Only weeks ago, she'd been in the hotel while armed soldiers had driven through the streets of Munich and stationed themselves in front of nearly every public building. That was all it took for the government to surrender and warn the Bavarian royal family it could no longer protect them. They'd fled, putting an end to the Wittelsbach dynasty. Those behind the guns proclaimed Munich a republic of the Free State of Bavaria. On that day councils of workers and soldiers had proclaimed Kurt Eisner not only their leader but the new Bavarian prime minister.

It was an easy bandwagon to jump on, at least for idealist poets like Jurgen, power forces like Leo . . . and the guilty, like Annaliese herself. Eisner would make right the wrongs Germany had inflicted on its people, which was why, ever since that day, she worked so hard to make sure he won the election.

But as much as Jurgen told her he wanted women to have a voice, even claiming Germany had made the right decision by allowing women a vote, he had never agreed to have Annaliese or any other woman sit in on the meetings with those connected to the council. It had rankled her on other occasions, but tonight she wouldn't let it.

"It isn't yet time for your place on a council. But soon." He raised one of her hands and kissed her fingertips. "You'll have a powerful voice for women on their own council."

Before long they were at an abandoned factory warehouse. It provided more than enough room to house a press for the flyers and pamphlets they produced, a roof and cots for bodyguards who weren't on duty, as well as a private place to meet. It wasn't as convenient as the butcher shop–turned–headquarters, but it was far larger.

"I will see you soon," Jurgen whispered, then leaned close,

hesitating only long enough to catch her eye and smile before pressing his lips directly to hers and letting them linger.

Annaliese watched him alight, staring after him until the doors to the truck had been shut. Leo went with him, and so when the truck lurched forward on its way back to her flat, with Huey driving, she was left alone in the back.

She let her fingers brush her lips. Perhaps what would happen between her and Jurgen was inevitable. They'd been moving toward each other ever since the day she'd heard him speak. Certainly she'd imagined being with him before today. She knew what would happen if she followed her desires and let herself into the flat he shared with Leo instead of going up to her own apartment. Leo would surreptitiously disappear. And then Jurgen would kiss her again . . . and more.

Why shouldn't she want such a thing to happen? She was a woman now, able to face her desires, make her own decisions. Decisions that could be made without childish embarrassment, her parents' cautions, or the faith they'd tried to instill in her.

She wasn't going to run away from what she wanted anymore.

"Sign here. I've printed your name below, as you can see."

Christophe eyed the man behind the desk inside the butcher shop. He had a German education, after all, and if they'd done anything right before the war, it had been education. Why would he need help filling out the most basic form? If this party offered anything of value, even the soldiers, workers, and peasants they claimed to represent would continue to be offered free education.

He signed his name.

"I'm interested in speaking to a leader in the party." Christophe held out a leaflet. "This woman in particular. Annaliese Düray."

"Contact with members of the party is available through letters of support," the man said, producing an envelope from a pile on the desk. Just the size of a German *Mark*, no doubt to encourage donations as well as letters.

Another man Christophe had casually noted in the shadows stepped forward. He was large, taller than Christophe himself. Bulkier. Missing a few fingers, but still formidable.

"What is your business with her?"

"I am a friend of the family."

"She has no family."

Christophe smiled, though inside he cautioned himself. He hadn't seen so many guns in such a small room since he'd been in a bunker at the front. "Everyone has a family," he said. "I do. Don't you?"

The man looked in no mood for friendly discussion. He folded massive arms on his massive chest, the gun tucked under his arm, and stared at Christophe as if contemplating the fastest way to crush him.

"Where are you from?" he asked suspiciously. "The Communists?"

Christophe had only a vague familiarity with the multitude of political arguments raging through Munich these days, but he wondered what prompted the question. Were his clothes so tattered? He'd given away his coat and hadn't shaved in a few days, both good reasons he might be associated with such a group.

"I just signed a paper to join *this* group—"

"And why is that? To meet a pretty girl?"

"I've spoken to a number of people who attend these rallies on a regular basis—" six, not counting the first, Frau Haussman—"and not one of them claimed to know Annaliese by anything other than her first name. They verified only that this picture was she. How could I have known her full name if I'm not acquainted with her family?"

"What is your name?"

"Christophe Brecht."

"I will tell her you support our cause, and if she knows your name, she will leave word here when you can see her. Come back tomorrow."

Christophe didn't protest. He'd had four years of confrontation and wasn't going to risk another for politics . . . or for a young woman who might not want what he had to offer—her parents' attention. Obviously Annaliese was healthy and not in any danger—at least beyond the danger she chose to put herself in by being a leading figure in a politically volatile world. The Socialists were the ones in power for the moment.

But if she was willing to risk her life for German politics, he doubted she'd be interested in fleeing to America. At least not anytime soon.

6

How many times had she been in Leo's flat since she'd come to Munich? Too many to recall, usually to share a meal or to discuss the election or the needs of the people. They often met in the dining room, not for a banquet of food but for a smorgasbord of ideas.

The lines between individual liberty and security of the masses, both personal and financial, might be gray in some circles but not here. No topic was banned, though most often they discussed such things as the real meaning of freedom, the ideals of universal unity and fairness, or the pitfalls of capitalism and hazards of profit in light of those ideals.

Annaliese had kept silent during some of the early conversations, though she'd come to Munich with many of her own opinions about the menaces of greed and the evils in capitalist businessmen. She soaked up the knowledge and passions around her and somehow, with less and less coaching about what she should say, not only were her street speeches drawing more and more attention, she'd joined in a few of the discussions in this very room. Unlike Bertita, Huey's wife. She was the only other woman who lived under this roof. Bertita quietly did the cooking and the cleaning, the laundry and the mending, but Annaliese knew she kept an ear on what happened. Perhaps as avidly as Annaliese herself. More than likely Bertita knew, at this moment, that Annaliese waited for Leo and Jurgen to return.

But Bertita couldn't know that the politics discussed in this room was the last thing on Annaliese's mind right now. She sat alone on one of the chairs near the window so she would spot the truck when it pulled up to bring Leo and Jurgen home. *If* Leo came along; she suspected he might find something else to do this evening.

Which might pique Bertita's curiosity, if she knew Annaliese and Jurgen would be alone in the same way Leo often left him with a woman of choice.

Annaliese's mind raced. She *had* been alone with Jurgen before, but never like this. Expectations of the evening thrilled and frightened her all at once. Right or wrong no longer mattered, not the way it once might have. What mattered now was what she wanted. Her only question was if allowing herself this freedom would help or hurt her future.

She wasn't naive enough to think what happened between her and Jurgen tonight would mean anything to him. Though she had met him less than two months ago, she knew his taste for the women he'd been with rarely lasted. Lovemaking, to him, was like creating one of his poems—flaring up with passion, loving the words into place, only to have other words, other women inspire him. She couldn't envision his desire for her to be any different. She would face the same fate, a similar season of favor that would bud, flower, and fade.

Surely since she was aware of that, expected each step of the pattern, she wouldn't end up with the remnants of tears on her face every time she saw Jurgen after he no longer wanted her.

A rumbling in the street caught her attention, and the heart that had been dancing about in her chest all evening now whipped to and fro, unfettered. He was here.

She'd expected only one set of footsteps on the stairs, but as she neared the door, she heard two. So, Leo must not have believed she would go through with it, after all.

When she opened the door, it wasn't Leo at Jurgen's side. It was Ivo.

Jurgen walked past her, casually removing his hat and jacket as if coming home to her happened every night. When she looked at him, secretly uncertain—should she greet him with a kiss?—he only cocked his head Ivo's way.

Ivo looked surprised to see her. He removed his hat and didn't meet her eyes. "I came to tell you there was a visitor at the center today, looking for you."

She waited. That was nothing new.

"He knew your full name. Annaliese Düray. Claimed to be a friend of your family's."

"Oh?" Now her heart started beating in a new way, pounding painfully. Anyone who knew her family was probably not a friend—to her or to the cause she'd picked up in Munich. "Did he leave a name?"

"Christophe Brecht."

Her knees might have been wobbly from the moment the truck pulled up to the door, but now they nearly failed her. Christophe! Looking for her, after all this time? Her gaze went beyond Ivo to the hall, foolishly hoping he might have followed them all the way here, demanding to see her. But of course there was no one in the hall.

"You know him," Ivo stated, watching her.

"Yes."

He looked from her to Jurgen, whose back was to them. Then he twisted the soft hat in his hand and looked once more at Annaliese. "I told him to come back tomorrow, that you would leave word with me. Do you want to see him?"

Of course! Yes! He'd come calling for her. For *her*! Yet she pulled the reins on her wild thoughts. Christophe couldn't be the same person she'd dreamed about as a child. Hadn't his letters to Giselle taught her that? All she said was "Yes, Ivo. Did he say when he would return?"

"No. I told him only to come tomorrow."

"Tell him I'll be there at one o'clock—if he comes before then. Otherwise . . . I will be there myself, won't I?"

He nodded and his gaze stayed on her a little longer than necessary, as if curious about something on her face. What did he see? That the name had ignited all kinds of emotions—so many she couldn't easily sort them out? That not only had Christophe been the first boy who'd ever filled her mind, both day and night, but he'd also been the first who'd ignored her? Who'd wanted her sister instead of her?

Who had played a part in Giselle's death, whether he knew it or not?

She shouldn't see him. She should leave word that she never wanted to see him or speak to him. Leave word that he was less than welcomed, he was hated.

But suddenly even the lines between love and hate seemed blurry.

Ivo closed the door behind him, and Annaliese rubbed one hand over the other, staring at the doorknob. What could Christophe possibly want?

"Would you like a glass of wine, *mein Herz*? I have a bottle I've saved."

She looked over her shoulder, momentarily surprised not only by the question but by Jurgen's presence. He held up a bottle that was already half-empty, along with a glass. Suddenly everything was fuzzy, not just how she felt about Christophe Brecht or her memories of him. What she was doing here, now, was every bit as confusing.

And wine certainly wouldn't help to make anything clearer. "No . . . thank you."

He laughed and filled the glass anyway. "I think you need it. Here, take it."

She did but did not drink it.

"Jurgen," she said slowly, watching him fill a glass for himself. She was grateful, for the moment anyway, that he would be busy consuming the beverage instead of demanding anything from her. "Why do you want me? Instead of the others, I mean?"

He laughed again. "I knew you would want to talk, *mein Herz*, which is why I cut short the meeting before I tired of talking. Although you will excuse me if I hope we do not discuss things for too long?"

"But my question, Jurgen. Why do you want me?"

He lifted his brows. "How could I not? We work side by side, with the same passions and goals. I find you lovely, and a man cannot ignore that forever."

"Those reasons have more to do with you than me. Why do you want *me*?"

He neared her and with his free hand stroked her cheek gently. "Because I cannot resist you. Isn't that enough?"

Her mind went back to another day, when she was little more than a child and Christophe sat beside her on a park bench, overlooking one of the lakes in their village. He'd told her what it was like to be in love, to see someone in a crowd and feel linked—an invisible bond but immovable, unchangeable, impossible to deny. Everyone else could disappear with a single exchange of glances, like magic, leaving two people alone together even while surrounded by others. It was part of the connection, the excitement that came with learning, then knowing, such mundane things as a beloved's favorite food or book, with dreaming together and . . . What else had he said? Praying together? Such an intimate thing, he'd claimed.

That was when she'd hoped Christophe would love her like that someday, but he'd been talking about Giselle.

And none of what he spoke about, not even a trace of the love Christophe had described, was here in this room tonight—even without the distraction of any other people present. She and Jurgen might have a bond on the platform, but it was the same bond she shared with every other listener.

"I need to go upstairs now, Jurgen. Alone."

"What?"

Annaliese settled the wineglass on the table nearby, turning away from him and walking toward the door. With one quick movement he slid his wineglass onto the table somewhere near hers—a dull clink sounded when the two collided—and before she'd reached the doorknob, he stood between her and it.

"Why do you want to go? Have I said something wrong?"

She shook her head. "It isn't what you said. It's what I'm remembering."

"I don't understand."

"I'm sorry," she whispered. "I shouldn't have waited here tonight, to make you think I might do something I cannot do, after all."

He put his hands on her shoulders, and she was grateful

his touch was light. "It's why you need the wine, *Liebchen*. To relax you."

"I'm not ready, Jurgen. You wouldn't want me to do something I might regret. Wouldn't that make you regret it too?" She touched his chest, where his heart would beat beneath her palm if she rested it there long enough to feel it. She did not. "You have a good heart. I know you want what's best for others. And what's best for me is to go upstairs."

Instead of letting her go, he leaned closer and his mouth claimed hers. His lips were warm, soft, tender. Accomplished at making her want more. Slowly his arms went around her and she wanted to lean into him, to give in to his closeness. Maybe . . .

And yet she couldn't.

She pulled away, reaching past him to take hold of the doorknob. "I'm sorry."

Annaliese was relieved when he didn't stand in her way.

7

The sun was high but the air cold, and Christophe turned up the collar of his old suit jacket. It was neither his finest nor his warmest. The warmest coat he'd owned had been issued by the army and had seen four winters in France, four of the coldest winters of his life. But the day before yesterday, when he spotted an old man just coming away from the food lines, Christophe knew even with a temporarily filled belly the man wouldn't be warm for long. The army-issue coat had nearly been too heavy for the man's frail body, but he'd been grateful nonetheless.

It had been easy to give away. Maybe some of the memories would go with it.

This jacket was inadequate, but at a brisk pace Christophe barely noticed. He pushed open the now-familiar shop door under the butcher's sign draped with a flag depicting men and women reaching upward—no doubt toward the better life their politics promised. Politics and politics alone. From what he could tell of the flyers he'd seen, they weren't reaching for God. The only kind of faith their pamphlets preached was faith in unity.

Inside, there was considerably more activity than yesterday

when he'd signed up for his tepid membership in their party. There was still a man behind the desk who started to address him before another man stepped forward, the man who'd been so protective of Annaliese yesterday.

"Good day!" He held out his hand, all stiffness of yesterday abandoned. The hand he extended wasn't an invitation to a handshake; Christophe noted he held what few fingers he had left close to the palm, as in a mangled fist. Rather the gesture was an invitation to enter deeper into the room, past the desk in front of him. The man cocked his head toward the other half of the room, and Christophe looked that way.

Nearby, two other men worked folding flyers, stacks of them. Others bundled papers or performed various clerical duties. Beyond them in the foremost corner, sitting amid the light streaming in from the window, sat an artist at an easel with a woman in a black skirt and white blouse bending over him. Her back was to him, but based on the picture and the familiar color of her light blonde hair, Christophe guessed it was Annaliese. At last.

He nodded a silent thank-you to the man who'd pointed her out.

"Yes, I see your point," she was saying to the artist while they both stared at a rendition of a woman with two children at her side. "But it isn't only children women must worry about. This is the second poster you've drawn emphasizing just one role women fill. We do worry about the protection of children and their education—but so much more. Why not draw an equal number of women at work to show that our contribution is equal—or can be? or the one I mentioned yesterday: women beside men at the ballot box?"

Even from behind, Christophe could tell the artist hadn't

caught her vision. He pitied the man; her idea was sound, but the reality of women working outside the home—and even voting next month—was something they would all need time getting used to.

"Annaliese?"

He saw her stiffen and wondered for a moment if she would turn around. Most likely she didn't recognize his voice; perhaps she wouldn't even remember him.

"It's me, Christophe Brecht. Do you remember me?"

At last she turned, and he wished he were better at reading faces. All he saw was how pretty she was. Her skin was pure and white with a touch of pink highlighting her cheekbones. Her hair was piled up and he wished it were down, the way it had been painted, because it was full of waves. But of course she'd been younger in the portrait, the child he remembered her to be.

It was her eyes he wished most to read; although she stared at him—not just glanced, but stared—he couldn't tell if she was happy or sad to see him. Not indifferent, which he might have understood. No, there was emotion behind that stare, but he couldn't determine what it was.

"Yes," she said slowly, "I remember you. I wondered how long it would take you to show up here."

"You expected me?"

"Well, I thought you might already have a place in the party. Here or perhaps with the Communists."

That was the second time he'd been taken for a Communist. He could understand why she might think him a member of her party already—a number of those who'd given him information about her independent Socialist party had been soldiers, so he knew it was a popular movement among them. Perhaps the Communists were just as popular with soldiers.

He shook his head.

She looked at his inadequate jacket. "I see you no longer wear your uniform. Weren't you a Hauptmann in the army? You might have removed the rank but kept the jacket."

He hadn't come to discuss politics—or to tell her he'd been a Major for over a year. "I wasn't able to come home until recently, but army life is behind me."

She stepped closer but kept the table between them, gripping its edge as if she needed its assistance. "And are you living in Munich now?"

He shook his head. "No, I went home."

"I'm sorry about your brother. It was hard on Nitsa—harder I think than even losing your parents."

"And I'm sorry about your sister. I didn't know . . . not until I came home. It's been so long since I'd heard from her, but I always imagined her home. Safe with the rest of you. Or as safe as anyone could be, considering everything."

Her knuckles had gone white at the mention of Giselle. Annaliese looked away, and he noticed her profile was so different from what her sister's had been. Annaliese had a small nose, delicate chin. Giselle had had a wider forehead and a slope to her nose he doubted he would ever forget.

"Thank you for stopping by to see me, then."

He stepped to the side, putting himself in her line of vision. "I came because your parents asked me to find you. They'd like you to come home."

One brow rose as if he'd spouted something ridiculous. Perhaps he had. In that moment it made sense to him. Here she was, working for a party that was as anticapitalist as her father was capitalist. A warmonger, the village called him—and so would anyone in this butcher shop–turned–party office. He was hated, so hated he'd had to buy the dogs and hire a guard for fear of his life. Enough hatred to inspire his upcoming flight to America.

Did Annaliese hate him too?

Christophe might not have been able to read her reaction to his arrival, but he could read her reaction to his words easily enough. She wanted no part of the reason he'd come.

He might be taller than the last time Annaliese had seen him, he might be older and even sport a new scar across one eyebrow, but he was every bit as handsome as the moment she'd first noticed him as more than just another boy in her village. The moment her child's heart had listened to him describe what it was like to fall in love, when she herself had thought she wanted to love him someday, when she was all grown up and the five years' difference in their ages would no longer matter.

When, she wondered for the hundredth time, had Giselle fallen in love with him? He knew when he'd fallen in love with her—he'd as much as told Annaliese that day on the park bench.

But what had he meant when he said it had been such a long time since he'd heard from her? Perhaps, to someone in love, it had only *seemed* a long time. Giselle had done what she'd done just four months ago. Before that, she'd written to him. Hadn't she?

Annaliese sent a quick glare his way, wondering what he

would do if she accused him right now in front of everyone in this room. Those letters—his letters—had been to blame for what Giselle had done. But Annaliese knew she wouldn't accuse him. This man standing before her, who only shook his head with no further explanation about whether or not he was a Communist, might not see things as he'd seen them when he wrote those letters. She would keep her secret and not tell him anything at all about Giselle. He didn't deserve to know, anyway. The knowledge gave him too much importance.

Annaliese repeated his words in her head. What had he just said? Her parents had sent him to Munich for her? to bring her home? She nearly laughed. Not only at the irony of him *doing* anything for them, but of him being *willing*.

"You of all people should not want to do their bidding, Christophe. Once a soldier, always a soldier."

He reached for one of the flyers on the table between them. *Kameraden!* it said in bold black lettering. *Freiheit, Frieden, und Brot.* He pointed to the words. "Isn't this what you believe? That it's time for peace now?"

She took the flyer from him, replacing it on the stack. So he was ready to put it all behind him, the passion he'd written of in those letters. The passionate hatred of anything fueling the war.

Well, she wasn't.

How she would have loved naming all the reasons she knew peace was impossible between her and her parents—and in particular between her and her father. Christophe should still understand that, even if he only wanted peace now.

He hadn't been in the village when one by one their neighbors lost interest in the war except for the agony it brought.

When people stopped talking to her family, when the block-ades that were still in place slowly cut off the flow of food to starvation levels but somehow, from somewhere, metal was delivered to keep the munitions factory going. And her father brought in more money—enough to leave the village for that house, that big, awful house that was a testimony to the lives his weaponry had cost.

"Yes, it certainly is the time for peace," she said, mindful of the fact that no one in this room—not a single one pretend-ing to be too busy to hear—knew of her close connection to a warmonger. She needed to see this man out, not just out of the office, but out of her life. "You may tell my parents I wish them well. Good day to you, Christophe."

She started to turn away but he held up a hand as if he would touch her, causing her to stop where she stood.

"Is that all you have to say to me, an old friend? Just good day? What about your parents?"

She faced him, but no other words came to mind. Not here. Not now.

"I'm a member of the party," he said. "Your party."

If that was supposed to impress her, it didn't. The letters he'd written had been full of passion to change Germany, many beliefs that were right in line with her party's—and even more radical, farther to the left, where only Communists and Spartacists could stand. "Why are you here at my parents' bidding, then?"

Someone stepped closer, behind them. "Did you say you're a member of our party—the USPD?"

Leo's voice; he was one person who didn't care if others knew he was eavesdropping.

"Yes," Christophe said, standing at what would have been

attention if he still wore his uniform. Thankfully, he did not salute.

"You were a soldier?"

Evidently refraining from that salute had made no difference in giving him away. Christophe nodded.

"Welcome! We can use a man like you, tall and strong and trained. Tell me, what is it you most want for Germany?"

"Peace," he said without the slightest hesitation. "A lasting peace."

"Good! That's very good! It's what we all want. You know, don't you, that coming from a soldier, these words mean more to everyone else? to everyone filling the streets these days, wanting the same thing? How long were you at the front?"

"I was in France nearly the full four years. Assigned over occupied villages at first, before I had . . . more specialized training."

Annaliese wondered why he'd paused and what *specialized training* meant. But she had no time to ponder that as she watched Leo pull Christophe farther into the office, going so far as to pat him on the back as if they were already partners in vision.

"Come in, come in, and talk to us. You're here in the middle of the day. Does that mean you've not yet secured work? It's hard these days. You might find your hours well spent here if you can support yourself for a while."

Neither looked her way. She saw Christophe take a seat near the desk Leo most often occupied. She followed but did not sit; instead she leaned against the wall, watching. Unsure what to think, how to feel. It had been only a few months since Christophe had written his last letter to Giselle, at least the last one that she knew about. The end of the war might have mellowed him, but surely he hadn't abandoned everything he believed in so short a time. If he had, she would demand he tell her why he'd inspired Giselle to do what she'd done.

She might enjoy watching him receive such news: that if it weren't for him, Giselle might still be alive to accept his attention.

But first she would observe him, because even though he was willing to listen to Leo, it was obvious he'd lost the passion he once had. This calm, self-assured man before her didn't seem at all like the frenzied man who'd written from the battlefield.

The poster artist caught her eye, waving her near, but Annaliese ignored him. This was one induction conversation she wasn't going to miss.

8

"What do you think we fought for, soldier?"

Christophe settled back in the chair, noting that the other man didn't seem interested in his name, just his role as a former soldier.

"We were told we fought for freedom," he said slowly, "but after a while, the reasons for the war were as muddy as the trenches."

"Exactly! And now is the time to restart our society; don't you believe it to be so? We have an opportunity few other countries have. An opportunity to develop this country into something better than it was before. But we must do it together."

From the corner of his eye, he saw Annaliese's shadow. Her arms were folded, and even from the farthest corner of his peripheral vision, he could tell she was skeptical. But about what? Surely not of what this man spoke. Suspicion of Christophe himself, then. But he sensed more; it felt like animosity. He hadn't expected that. What had happened to the affection her parents thought she had for him?

He caught the gaze of the man before him, clearly impassioned and eager for Christophe to embrace the cause, too. An idea, a hope. Christophe barely listened until a phrase caught his ear.

"The monarchy is dead, and good riddance. It was antiquated before this war began. Along with it will go all of the old ways. We're equal, after all. Aren't we?"

Christophe hadn't thought much about the aristocracy of Germany, except for the Kaiser. It was his face Christophe still remembered and hated for urging them all into the war that became a debacle for the entire world.

"We believe in the most basic fairness for all," the man went on, "in the most practical of ways. We want nothing more than the best interests of people like you and those who served at your side. We're stronger with a united voice, along with the workers who supported you here at home. I can see you're the kind of man who's interested in such things, aren't you?"

Christophe nodded. How could he not be? "I can't deny that if everyone beyond this room respected the equality you talk about, the world would be a better place. But fairness is a hard thing to practice, isn't it? Owners and workers don't always agree about what seems fair."

The man smiled even as his eyes narrowed. "It's ownership and profit that corrupt the basic generosity of spirit we're all born with. I daresay it is wealth itself that produces poverty. A country is worth only what it produces, but for generations it's been acceptable for the poor to sacrifice to the rich by the sweat of their brow. Now it will be the other way around, until we all unite under equality. Once we see everyone being treated equally, earning equally, each of us will be inspired to work equally, to be part of such a great and equal society. Christophe—is that what you called yourself a moment ago?"

He nodded, although beyond the question about his name, the man's words sifted together, making little sense to Christophe.

"What we do here is more than revolution to change Germany, Christophe. There is a natural sense of brotherhood in all of us, no matter where we were born. Did you notice it, even in the trenches? how unnatural it was to be shooting at those just like you on the other side instead of working together toward a better world? And yet the capitalists convinced us we were threatened. What better way for them to fill their coffers than to produce material destined for destruction—so we must need more and they must produce more? It was a never-ending cycle designed only to line their pockets."

Christophe glanced Annaliese's way, seeing she was already staring at him. Did he need to assure her he wouldn't betray her secret? If indeed it was a secret that she'd been raised in a home where the risks, profits, and losses of capitalism were breathed in like the air around her. Hadn't he been raised with the same ideals as Annaliese? His own father had clung to the golden rule of capitalism: what was good for others was good for him because trade begot trade. Though his haberdashery had shut down because of the blockades and lack of imports, it had provided well for Christophe's family before that day, just like the business in Annaliese's family. They'd *both* been raised on the capitalism this man blamed for the war. Christophe had never thought one person's gain was another's loss, which seemed to be what Socialists thought.

Still, he could see the good in this man's goals, and it had been too many days since Christophe had thought about something other than himself, his hatred, the defeat. The loss. He should care about things like fairness and equality, at least.

"I like aiming toward brotherhood," Christophe said. "It reminds me of the first churches, when people shared everything to take care of one another." *And didn't promise soldiers their battles would be won.*

"Those churches knew what people today have forgotten," the man in front of him said. "Didn't you mention once, Anya, that if there is a God, He must have envisioned a world without classes? He would see the heart and not be distracted by the quality of our clothing or the positions we hold."

She stood straight, hands falling to her sides. Christophe wondered if he'd imagined a flash of . . . something in her eye. Annoyance? She wasn't at all what he remembered of the cheerful, somewhat-shy girl he once knew. She'd grown bristles.

"I mentioned it as something my mother once said," she told them. "Personally, I don't believe there is a God at all. Entirely faithless, like you."

No, this was not the Annaliese he knew. Not Giselle's sister, whose faith had matched his own. But then, perhaps Giselle's faith had changed too. It had been so long since he'd had any contact with those left at home, he couldn't know.

The man in front of Christophe looked around the room, raising a hand as if to include anyone else there. "Oh, we have faith, Anya, and plenty of it. It's faith in our fellow man here. But we also want to appeal to those of every faith . . . or no faith at all."

He stood then, placing a hand on Christophe's shoulder. "We're having a march in the morning. Jurgen is our spokesman in support of Prime Minister Eisner for the election in just a few weeks. It would be an honor to have you march with us. We need more men like you, with a background people admire. You might consider working with us." He looked from Christophe to Annaliese. "Anya is one of our most popular speakers."

"So I've heard," Christophe said as he stood.

"You've been to our rallies?"

"Not yet."

"What was it that drew you to our party specifically, then?"

Christophe had never been one to lie, though if there were ever an opportunity for doing so, it would have been now. "I wanted to see Annaliese and thought joining the party would provide the quickest way of doing that. And," he added, because there was more truth than that, "because in the last four years I've been forced to believe killing is right. I want to believe in something better than that."

The man laughed as if Christophe's honesty was refreshing. Then he leaned closer, his gaze intent. "You're what I hope walks through that door every day, young man. A slate upon which to write the truth. You're looking for it, and we have it."

He grabbed a pamphlet from the desk behind them. "Here, take this home with you. And this." He pulled another from a different stack. "Read these and see if you agree that what we want will make Germany a better place. And isn't that what we all want? We've been disgraced, betrayed by the monarchy, and handed over by the High Command. Now it is our turn to lead. The people's turn."

The words were as firm as any general's, though Christophe thought neither lofty generals nor common people would welcome any link to the other, even one of comparison.

"I'll read them." Then he turned to Annaliese. "Perhaps I might speak with you before I go?"

"Actually, I think she's needed," said the man behind the desk, who also stood. His gaze went past them, to the artist in the corner, who was waving their way. "But if it's a quick word, that might be all right."

Christophe nodded and followed her halfway toward the artist. "Will you meet me later, when you're finished here?"

She didn't look at him. "I'm busy until very late."

"Your parents," he whispered, "want very much to see you. They're leaving Germany and want to see you about it. To talk to you."

At least now she looked at him as if to see if he was telling the truth. "Leaving?"

"Yes. For America."

Her lips tightened. "Good."

She tried walking away, but he caught her wrist. He hadn't meant to touch her, but he couldn't think of any other way to stop her without raising his voice loud enough for others to hear.

"You won't see them?"

Annaliese shook her head, tugging at the wrist he still held firmly.

"I thought everyone in this room believed in the brotherhood of man. How does that not extend to your parents?"

"Leave me alone." She ripped her hand from his and allowed no more than a glimpse into her eyes before turning away. But it was enough to see something he hadn't noticed before, something that made him want to refuse her demand. She wasn't angry with him for his persistence. It wasn't anger he saw. It was pain.

She kept her back to him once she reached the artist at the window.

Christophe was sure she wouldn't give him so much as another glance. Yes, she certainly had grown bristles, and they grew on a strong backbone.

He left the party office feeling every bit the failure. There was no getting used to defeat.

9

"We're no longer under the thumb of the industrialists, not with our voices echoing from one corner of Germany to the other. Even now, men of our council are working for an eight-hour workday and for wages to be more evenly distributed."

Annaliese paused for the cheers, holding up her hand to stay the noise in favor of them hearing more. "We're willing to do what Germans do—we value work and production and discipline. We're willing to do our part and end the strikes, work toward production so we can share the fruits of our labor. For a better Germany—a fairer Germany!"

More cheers. She sensed the crowd's increasing energy, half in approval of her words, half in anticipation of seeing Jurgen. She saw their faces, not as one mass of people but as countless individuals with lives of their own, with dreams and fears and hopes and worries. So many needs that could easily be met if only they worked and shared.

She was nearly ready to hand them over to Jurgen . . . and then she saw Christophe.

How long had he been there? Sticking to the edge, the outskirts of the crowd, where loners tended to be—those independent ones who never came, like others did, in hordes.

There he was, his eyes so fixed on hers it was as if the rest of the rallygoers had disappeared.

The way he'd once told her it would be if ever she fell in love. Their gazes would meet, and everyone else would disappear.

But no, that was only her interpretation.

Instead of speaking anymore, she waved an arm Jurgen's way. He looked only momentarily surprised that she was finished, so eager was he to take over. Grabbing her hand in the way he liked to do, sharing the cheers with her, he joined in the call for unity that had been their habit ever since she'd first raised her voice on his platform.

But she hardly listened when he took over. Not that she needed to; she knew exactly what they were fighting for, what they hoped to accomplish by letting the Socialist government keep the place it had taken weeks ago, this time by vote. So she went by rote, cheering when the crowd cheered.

If Christophe intended to speak to her, he would have to wait. They marched as usual through the streets of Munich, their sheer numbers punctuated by the signs they carried identifying their party and by the songs of unity they sang. She walked beside Jurgen, glad for his public smile, no hint of the awkwardness she'd felt in front of him just after her refusal the other night. They stood hand in hand as if nothing could ever come between them.

United in the cause they both believed in.

❧

Christophe followed the crowd, only a few paces behind Annaliese, stunned by what he'd seen. Had he once thought her shy? vulnerable? She was anything but that up on a platform. She was self-assured, fiery, thoroughly captivating. Selfless in her message, convinced of the validity of her argument—so much so that Christophe thought he must surely agree with her.

And why should he not? The pamphlets he'd read last night were noble if anything, claiming society was only as good as its care for the least of those within that society. Lofty dreams, perhaps, but so superior to what he'd been living these past four years that he couldn't help but want to believe it too.

Hearing what both Annaliese and the man called Jurgen had said this morning, he could be persuaded into thinking they *were* right. They did have at least one answer for Germany.

Germany had given the upper classes a chance to rule. The monarchy had utterly failed, and the elite in the military, too. Christophe had seen firsthand just what a mess they'd made and how costly were their mistakes. Letting the people have their turn couldn't possibly bring any greater disaster than had already been wrought.

But something else made Annaliese's argument more powerful to Christophe. She loved them; he could see that in her eyes, hear it in her voice. That was what touched him from the moment he'd heard her voice up there. How easy it could be to love others through her, too. He knew he should, and he wanted to, but knew whatever love he'd once had for mankind had been used up when he'd watched too many of them die. Killed too many of them himself. How could he love that which he'd been made to destroy?

Her words rang through his mind, mingling with other words he'd always believed to be true. God loved them—loved them even when Christophe could not. And yet how many times had he reminded himself what God required of him? To act justly, to love mercy, to walk humbly with God.

Wasn't that everything Annaliese proclaimed? Maybe not to walk with God, but the rest? She wanted justice for all—from the top of the society to the bottom. For mercy to make up whatever differences inevitably surfaced.

She might not have known it or wanted to acknowledge it, based on what she'd said in the party office the day before, but Annaliese Düray was preaching straight out of God's Word.

The march continued on through the streets, block after block, Annaliese walking hand in hand with the man who seemed every bit as enigmatic to the crowd as she was. Christophe had to acknowledge they were well paired, at least in spirit and talent. They had a connection; he'd noticed it the moment the two of them shared the platform and exchanged one of many smiles. Together, they represented men and women, young and mature, both attractive in their single-minded passion, sincere in their concern for those in need. They made their arguments all the more powerful because of their connection to each other, more than doubling what one alone could have done.

Annaliese might have found the very place God wanted her to be. Such a thought made his heart skip a beat. Perhaps God Himself decreed that she be the voice of the masses, the voice of the workers that others like her father supposedly used to fuel their own capitalistic greed.

A touch to his elbow distracted him from his focus on Annaliese.

"Christophe! Were you at the rally?"

He turned to see the man he'd spoken to yesterday, who'd

been absent from the stage but obviously present behind the scenes.

"Yes, I was there." He wanted to smile, to say something about how the speeches—particularly Annaliese's—had stirred even him, but he wasn't yet sure if the source of his excitement was the speech or the speechmaker. Annaliese had grown so independent and passionate—something he hadn't expected from a member of such a proper family as the Dürays.

"You'll stay after we disperse, won't you? I'd like to introduce you to Jurgen."

"You might start by telling me your name," Christophe said as they continued on, stopping traffic, attracting attention from those on the street. A trumpet player in front brought people to the windows of their homes and more marchers from the side streets.

"I'm Leo," the man said. "Leo Beckenbauer."

Christophe gave a small nod for a greeting, then let his gaze return to the back of Annaliese's head. "She has a voice to remember up there, doesn't she?"

"Yes, she's very talented."

"God-given talent, I would say."

"You seem to have a lot to say about God," Leo said. "We could use that, you know, even if some of us don't personally share your beliefs. It's important that we reach all of the people, including those who use faith in different ways."

Christophe laughed. "You speak of faith as if it were a hairbrush or tooth powder, an understandable—if dull—sort of habit to get me through the day."

"I meant no disrespect. To speak for everyone, we need representatives from all corners, to appeal to more people. Could you work with others who don't hold to some of your beliefs?"

"I have for the past four years."

Leo smiled. "Then come and meet Jurgen after the march, and let's talk about how we can work together, shall we?"

The march ended at the Marienplatz, the large city square where the glockenspiel—which had survived the war, the blockades, and even now continual marches from opposing sides of political upheaval—chimed midday.

After a brief, barely heard introduction between Christophe and Jurgen, Leo disappeared just long enough to herald the one type of vehicle Christophe never wanted to enter: a trenchside ambulance. More of his friends had died in the back of one of these trucks than Christophe wanted to count.

But Annaliese jumped in, along with Jurgen and Leo and a bodyguard. Christophe had no choice except to follow.

He sat across from Annaliese, who seemed as intent on avoiding eye contact with him as he was on establishing it.

"So you have experience at the front?" Jurgen asked. The older man was sitting beside Annaliese and, for the moment, wasn't holding her hand as he'd done throughout the march. Somehow Christophe was relieved by that, even if he did suspect their public connection must include a personal side.

Christophe nodded.

"Leo says you might want to help in our fight for a better future."

"I don't know enough to say how involved I'd like to be. For now, it appeals to me because it's the opposite of the hatred I've seen other places, even in myself." He wasn't used to expressing himself this way—least of all in front of someone from his own hometown—but words fell out anyway, ideas he hadn't expected to share. "I believe what you say about Germany being in a unique place, about being able to change our future from the past. Your pamphlets say you want to protect the weak, give work to the strong, stop those who might take advantage of others, and demand fairness for everyone. I have plenty of questions about how best to do all that. But I know one thing: I'm as tired as any German of being lied to and forced to fight against an enemy that I'm not even sure was there before we first marched out."

He saw Jurgen and Leo exchange approving glances, while at the same time Annaliese now looked at him as though she hardly knew him—or couldn't believe what he said.

But maybe this *was* what he wanted. He'd had enough of the desolation that came with defeat. It was time to hope for something better, to brush off the ashes and see what goodness lay beneath. To find the better part of Germany—and the better part of himself.

Still, he couldn't figure out the intently suspicious look on Annaliese's face. What had he ever done to inspire such obvious mistrust?

"What we want," Leo said, "is for the people of lesser means to be heard. Everyone is sick of war, both rich and poor, but especially the poor because we've been made poorer. We all need a voice, and the councils we helped establish all over Germany are the real voice of the people, not the National Assembly left over from the last regime. The new prime minister here in Bavaria must be allowed to stay in place to enact the changes we talk about every day."

From what Christophe had learned since reading the pamphlets circulating in Munich, every party thought they had the answer. "But the People's Councils haven't been in power long—barely more than a month. Before them, the monarchy and the military were in place for generations, and they failed.

Why do you think the councils will do better, with so little experience?"

"I'll grant you they haven't been in place long," Leo said, "and the election is a risk. But what choice do we have? If we don't allow an election now, there will be anarchy in the streets."

"It may come to another revolution," Jurgen said softly. "Depending on how corrupt this election turns out to be."

Christophe shrugged. "If it's another bloodless revolution, it won't matter."

Leo scraped his palms on his knees, swiftly, as if Christophe's words had irritated him. "It does matter. It matters a great deal."

"But what's to stop the councils from the same kind of dictatorship the Kaiser had before, when he ignored the assemblies put in place to check him? Doesn't Germany need checks and balances like other countries—like America, for one?"

Jurgen leaned across the aisle, attracting Christophe's attention. "The councils *are* the people. They can hardly dictate over themselves, can they? We want the fairness that's been beyond our grasp all these years. To make sure even the weakest among us has a voice. We want nothing more than justice for those who don't have power like the strong and wealthy."

"Some of your fellow soldiers are joining the free corps," Leo said. "Have you heard of them?"

Christophe nodded. "They used to tell us in the army that anyone in the free corps was untrained. I would say that must not be true anymore, with so many soldiers returning home and joining in."

"Yes, that's right. Do you think you might be interested in helping us increase our forces—a sort of free corps of our own?"

"All of the parties have their own guns," Jurgen added. "We have a few men already, but none are officers. Is it true you were a Hauptmann?"

He nodded, wondering if there was any reason to correct him. Did it matter anymore that he'd left the army as a Major? "It seems to me this is what brought us trouble four years ago," Christophe said quietly. "Different groups racing to build up their arms."

"That may be true," Leo said, "but the sad fact is we have no choice if we want our message to be heard. Armed members from other groups stir up trouble and discourage people. To frighten them from voicing support elsewhere. We've no choice, if we want to ensure freedom, except to be equal to the other groups of the city. Don't we?"

With all eyes on him, Christophe knew they wanted him to agree, to support them. But guns . . . he was sick of them, especially when they were used in the name of freedom.

He found himself looking at Annaliese, wanting to know what she thought of such an assignment. Was she in for all that? guns and all?

"We have no intention of using the armaments against our fellow man." Annaliese had directed her statement at Christophe but now turned to Jurgen. "Tell him."

"It's true," Jurgen said. "Our aim is for peace, of course. But we live in troubled times. An armed population is a dangerous thing, and until we can remove those arms, our men must be armed in defense."

In the thick of battle, it was impossible to tell who was

on the offense or the defense. Death came to both sides. Yet Jurgen's words were true too. They did live in troubled times. For some reason unknown to Christophe, God had appointed him to live in such a time as this.

"What exactly would you have someone like me do?"

Just as the truck pulled to a stop, Jurgen reached across to offer Christophe his hand. "Come inside the party office," he said with a smile.

Christophe knew following them inside right now was a decision he hadn't planned to make, but at that moment it seemed the only thing to do. Maybe the training the German army had used against men could somehow be used to save some. Maybe—just maybe—this was exactly what God intended when He'd sent Christophe to find Annaliese.

In any case, this was the only connection he had to Annaliese, and he wasn't yet ready to break it off.

10

Annaliese refused Jurgen's offer to have Ivo see her home. And miss what plans they had in mind for Christophe? Unthinkable.

And so she stayed, although she said little. For the rest of the day, Jurgen and Leo tutored Christophe on the state of affairs, their voices competing with the sounds of visitors in and out of the office, those who came with questions or support, others who came to inquire about the bread they sometimes had.

Leo detailed for Christophe the more localized scramble for power ever since the Bavarian castle had been abandoned. Ties to the seven-hundred-year-old monarchy had died a quicker death than anyone might have predicted, and even here in Munich the population was ripe for a people's government, a people's army. Never once did Leo or Jurgen bring up words like Communism or bolshevism, and when Christophe did, they both shook their heads.

No, the rise of the German people would be nothing like that. A social democracy was what they all wanted, along with support of the councils under Eisner. That he was Jewish never came up, at least not in this little circle. It made no difference to an idealist like Jurgen—she knew that. And for her, Herr Eisner had proven himself the day he'd orchestrated a revolution without a shot fired. That was no little feat.

She watched Christophe, wondering what he thought. He asked few questions, only nodded from time to time. Not knowing his thoughts, not even being able to guess at them, surprised her. Here before her was the first man she'd ever dreamed about. Childish hopes, but hopes nonetheless. And yet the Christophe she knew must have been an illusion of her own making. In reality, she'd never really known him. She'd been so young. She knew only what she'd imagined about him—dreams that had started when she was a child but had been rekindled when she'd become friends with his sister, Nitsa, just before she'd left Germany.

It was interesting to contrast him with Jurgen, who was so glib and self-assured, so unlike the peasant he said his father had been. Compared to Jurgen, Christophe was quiet, thoughtful. Careful.

What she didn't understand was the absolute absence in Christophe of the voice in his letters to Giselle. Those had been so forceful, so passionate about hating many of the same things Socialists railed against: big businesses like her father's, the helplessness of those who had only the sweat of their brows to offer as barter, the lack of compassion in the profiteering bourgeois class. Why was Christophe silent about all that when his letters had been so vocal? What had it all been for, then, inciting her sister to do what she did?

His lack of enthusiasm stirred more than just anger against him; it confused her. Perhaps, somehow, the last days of the war had changed him from the way he used to be when he wrote those letters. Perhaps the war had turned him so passive that he didn't even want to fight against what he once hated. But if that were true, it made what Giselle did even harder to bear.

Anyway, she could only hope he didn't want to jump into their cause. She certainly didn't want him around, a constant reminder of her parents. Her sister.

He spent the rest of the day with them, even sharing the evening meal. Food was still scarce—rumor had said the blockade would lift for things like food and necessities, although so far there was little evidence of that—but they had eggs and the inevitable turnips that had once been considered fodder only for animals. And bread, real bread, not the stuff of sawdust-laden flour the government had tried passing off, even here in Munich, not so long ago.

"Where are you living?" Leo asked when the last of the coffee had been consumed and it was time to say good night. "Can we take you somewhere?"

Christophe shook his head. "I'd planned to return home tomorrow, at least to resolve the business that brought me here." He glanced at Annaliese, then back at Leo. "I may return here to Munich, but to where . . . I don't yet know. I've been staying in the park, with other soldiers. We're used to living under the stars."

"Then come with us tonight. There is an extra room you can use."

Annaliese's gaze shot from Leo to Christophe, hoping he'd refuse. Perhaps that hope was all over her face, since he caught her glance, which curiously arrested his.

"That's very generous of you."

Leo patted Christophe's back as they made their way out to the truck, Ivo leading. "It's only fair. We'd like to have you stay and put you to work. You'll more than earn your keep."

When Ivo pulled up in front of the town house some min-utes later, Annaliese was the first to alight. She called a good-night over her shoulder, then hurried up to her flat. Without looking at either Christophe or Jurgen.

Instead of going to bed, she sat at her desk and tended to a handful of letters from a pile that, thankfully, only seemed to be growing. Her message might only be heard by working-class women, but each of them had been awarded the same vote every other woman of Germany had been given, regardless of class. That somehow made them equal—to each other and to men. Such importance wasn't lost on them, if these letters were any indication.

Sometime later she readied herself for bed, but sleep eluded her. She listened for noise from the rooms below, hearing nothing. After lying awake on her pillow for a while, she gave up any notion of rest and went to the window overlooking the street. She'd avoided thoughts of her parents all day, despite Christophe's presence. If it was true they were leaving—and really, why should she doubt it—it might also be true that this would be her last opportunity to see them, to speak to them. Perhaps forever.

Part of her wanted to return with Christophe, to cave in to his judgmental recommendation and at least say good-bye. But how could she? Everything she stood for today went against what they were, what they wanted her to be.

Could she just cast such a difference aside? And if she couldn't, why would her parents want to see her anyway? Wasn't her duty to be true to her beliefs as a woman, and wasn't that a greater duty than to honor the abandoned obligations she might have felt toward her parents? Even the Bible, she recalled, talked about putting aside childish things. Or something like that.

She was making her own way in life, had cut all ties for a reason. Once cut, those ties couldn't be mended.

Movement from the street below caught her eye. Someone had slipped out the door just below her window and stepped into the street to look at the house. His face was clear in the moonlight, staring up at the windows.

Christophe.

She was tempted to duck away but doubted he could see her from her darkened room anyway.

He was clearly studying the upper floors. Huey and Bertita had already been abed when she'd come upstairs, not even a peek from Bertita tonight.

Christophe disappeared, moving closer to the building and out of sight. Then he was back, and to her astonishment, a pebble hit her windowpane.

She leaned closer and knew he saw her because he held back what must have been another pebble in his palm.

She waved him away.

He shook his head, motioning for her to join him.

Annaliese stared at him. She could ignore him but guessed he might continue throwing stones at her window until she complied. She could open her window and demand he leave her alone, but the sound of voices might rouse Bertita. And yet to meet him . . .

Why couldn't he give up? accept that she wanted nothing to do with him or his mission to bring her home?

She waved for him to wait, then grabbed her jacket, slipped into her shoes, scrambled down the stairs, but stopped at the foot of the porch. "Go away, Christophe."

Instead, he joined her at the bottom of the stairs, so close the vapor from his warm breath touched her forehead. Even though she stood one step above, he was still taller. She pivoted away, intent on going back to her room.

"You can't avoid me forever, you know," he said. "Especially if I decide to become part of this organization."

On the second step she turned on him, nearly nose to nose when he leaned forward as if to follow. "And why would you want to join us, exactly? Do you believe any of what you said to Jurgen this afternoon? Do you believe any of what he believes, what the rest of us believe?"

"I wouldn't have said I did if I didn't."

"Then why did you act as if you hardly knew what we stood for? When you hate all the same things we hate?"

"Hate people like your father?"

"Yes!"

"Why should I hate him? It wasn't his decision to go to war, and in the beginning, he was hailed as a patriot, same as every soldier out there."

"What a liar you are, Christophe. Or do you just enjoy manipulating others around here, the way you're trying to manipulate me into going home?"

"You should go home for you own good, Annaliese. And for your parents."

How much more self-righteous could he be? Spouting the importance of family when he'd encouraged her sister to destroy their father's business. He might have had a change of heart from the hatred he'd expressed in those letters, but he was no stranger to broken family bonds. She knew how utterly he'd failed with honoring one of his own. "Why do you suppose your sister left home? Why was she so eager to leave, to make sure she was gone before you had the chance to come home?"

He was confused—she saw that instantly, even before his brows drew together.

Annaliese forged ahead. "She went off before you came home because she didn't want to face you. You with your high standards—she thinks perfection is attainable to you. Too bad she never felt she could live up to your expectation."

Anger joined the confusion on his face. "What are you talking about?"

How sweet it would be to plunge the knife of regret into his gut and give it a twist or two. To hear the truth about a sibling and have that truth let him down. "She was stealing, Christophe. From my father's factory, from empty homes, from strangers or neighbors. And selling what she could on the black market."

There, it was done. So quickly, too. She saw all the emotion she expected even as she came to the instantaneous, terrible realization that the knife didn't feel nearly as pleasurable as she thought it should. His eyes went from curious to astonished, skeptical to accepting. Moist.

She turned from him, ashamed she'd been so eager to hurt him, ashamed she'd succeeded. She went up one step, and he didn't follow. She stopped.

"I didn't blame her," Annaliese added over her shoulder, because as suddenly as the impulse had come upon her, she wanted to withdraw that knife, to erase the evidence she'd ever used it and banish the look in his eye. "She was left with too little; she sold her own goods first and not for luxury. She needed to eat. And she only stole from those who could afford it."

"But my parents—"

"Were too generous before they died. They helped so many others that they had too little left for themselves. Or Nitsa."

"But I sent money home, whenever I could."

Annaliese was fully regretful now; she wished she'd never told him. Nitsa wouldn't have wanted him to find out this way. "She suffered the same flaw your parents did. She was too generous with what little she had, and whatever was left to us was so expensive. It still is."

He rubbed his hands over his face but then looked at her again. "She left home because she thought I would judge her for that?"

"Wouldn't you?"

Christophe looked away so all she could see was his profile, one that seemed suddenly cut from stone. "Once, maybe. Not anymore."

"What changed?"

He faced her. "The same thing that changed you. And the rest of Germany."

She wished she could ask him how the war had changed him, how he could have written some of the things he did and speak today as if none of it mattered. She wished she could share her own memories, too, but so much stood in the way. Starting with Giselle.

She didn't want to look at him, but her eyes went to his anyway. "The last time I saw you, I was a child. I've grown up."

He took the three steps separating them. "No." He was so close, he nearly spoke into her ear. "It's more than that. I remember your smile. I remember you smiling at me. But now . . . it's as if you can't even bear my company. Why?"

If she told him, it would be like taking another knife to him, and she'd lost her taste for that. He didn't know he was the cause for what Giselle had done. Why tell him? It wouldn't change anything. "Perhaps it is the war," she said. "It's made me too serious. We're all that way."

He shook his head. "I don't believe you."

No one had ever called her a liar before, but until now she'd never deserved such an accusation. How could she tell him that since she was a child, he'd been her source of one disappointment after another? that he'd been the first to describe to her what love was about, and she'd wished that it had been her he'd talked about? that when he'd spent time with Giselle, it crushed Annaliese each and every time? And later, when she'd become close to Nitsa, who had spoken of him so fondly, it had resurrected that old infatuation in Annaliese, giving it a place in her maturing heart.

But worst of all, he didn't seem to have held on to anything he believed that had inspired Giselle. It took away whatever meaning she might have thought her actions had.

Annaliese took another step up, away from him, but he stayed her again, this time with a hand over the one she had placed on the banister.

"Come home with me tomorrow, Annaliese. Just see them."

"Why do you care so much, one way or the other? Wasn't my father one of the many who profited from the war, one of the many responsible for keeping you at the front for so long?"

"I don't want you to see them for their sakes. I want you to do it for yours."

She looked at him, wondering if her voice would work given the pounding of her heart. "The question remains. Why do you care?"

"It's the right thing for you to do."

She should have known. Other things might have changed, but he was still the righteous one.

"No, Christophe. Even if you're right, I won't do it."

Then she fled back to her room.

Christophe had little choice but to let her go. What else could he do? Follow her to her room? Drag her away with him tomorrow? Even if he wanted to, he doubted Jurgen and his squadron of bodyguards would allow such a thing.

And so Christophe descended the steps again, turning up the collar on his jacket. He should have let himself into Leo's flat, returning to that warm little room with its snug bed and plenty of covers. But he'd tried sleeping there earlier, and once again sleep had eluded him.

They'd come to him the moment his head hit the soft pillow. Those shadows, those faces. All the brighter, all the more clearly condemning in contrast to his comfort. Only now he knew they would be joined by a new face: his sister's.

She'd fled Germany, and that was his fault too.

An alcove out of the wind would suffice again tonight, and tomorrow he would decide what he would do next. Go home alone, or stay.

11

"So our new soldier has left already," Jurgen said to Annaliese when she swung through the kitchen door to join the others for breakfast. Bertita cooked for everyone who shared the multifamily living quarters but always used Leo's kitchen, which was the largest and the center of most activity.

If Jurgen's observation was supposed to surprise Annaliese, it didn't. From her window last night she'd watched Christophe walk down the street, then listened for his return throughout the hours that followed. She dozed fitfully, never far from awareness. Evidence of her poor night's sleep could be found in the puffy eyes she'd seen in her mirror this morning.

"I heard him leave during the night," Bertita said. "Do you think he will be back?"

Annaliese only shrugged. She didn't want to say she hoped not because she knew they considered it a feat indeed to have a former officer in their league. Most of those like him were loyal to the old government and the National Assembly. She accepted coffee from Bertita, along with a roll—dry, which meant butter was scarce again.

"You should have convinced him to stay." Bertita's tone was

level, cool. "He's your friend, isn't he? He's the kind of man we need. One with a gun, who can train others how to use them."

"I don't know that he'd be willing. He seemed less than certain about joining us. In any case, he's gone." She was eager to move on to another topic. "I'll be visiting the textile mill today to speak to women about their vote."

Leo pushed away from the table, taking his cup to the sink for Bertita to wash. "You're right about how we could use his help, Bertie, so let's hope he returns."

"Leave the dishes until later, will you, Bertita?" Jurgen asked. "I'd like a word with Annaliese before the day gets the best of us."

The room emptied in record time. Huey pushed open the door that swung between the kitchen and dining room—a door no doubt designed in the days of busy cooks needing easy access between the rooms—and Leo followed. Bertita left through the back door with a wicker laundry basket.

Annaliese sipped her coffee, but it was flavorless. Nothing penetrated her senses when Jurgen glowered at her, as he was doing now.

"Tell me about this friend of yours, this Christophe Brecht."

She tried a smile but was afraid he realized it was forced. "I think perhaps you know him as well as I do, after yesterday. We were never close friends."

"How can that be? He seemed intent on bringing you home with him."

Another sip. "And he left without me."

Jurgen leaned closer. "I heard him leave last night. And I heard your footsteps down the stairs shortly after."

She met his gaze. "Then you must have heard my footsteps going back up to my room shortly after that. Alone."

"I did. But why did you follow him out?"

"He threw a stone on my window ledge. I didn't want him to wake anyone, so I went to tell him to leave me alone."

"Why was he so eager to talk to you, and why are you just as eager to avoid him?"

"Because he wants me to see my parents before they leave Germany."

"And you don't want to?"

She shook her head.

"Why?"

Now was as good a time as any to tell him what would likely come out eventually, especially if Christophe did return as Jurgen must hope—if his interest in Christophe was any indication. "My father is a capitalist of the worst kind. I don't care if I ever see him again."

Jurgen smiled as he reached across the table to pat one of her hands. "Anya, Anya. You speak too passionately. He's your father."

She leaned away from him, taking her hand from his. "You of all people shouldn't want me to go, Jurgen. He profited from the war. He turned his metalworks factory into a munitions plant, and somehow, while the rest of us were starving, he still managed to receive shipments of metal."

"I don't doubt you. But he's still your father."

"You, too?"

"I want to be sure you know what is best for you, *mein Herz*."

"I think I'm capable of figuring that out for myself." She stared into her coffee cup instead of at him.

Jurgen took the spoon next to her cup and stirred his own with it. "So that is all that's between you and Christophe? He wanted you to settle things with your family?"

"Yes. Why?"

He smiled again and leaned closer, intimately so. "Let's just say I like to keep track of how many lions are in the den. If he returns, that is."

A week ago, if he'd used that tone of voice, summoned the smile he reserved only for women who interested him, Annaliese would have smiled back. Her heart would have fluttered. Instead, she looked away, pretending shyness even if she didn't feel such a thing at the moment.

"Anya," he said softly, "you've become very dear to me. You know that, don't you?"

"No less than you are to me." It was true, after all, even if in the past few days she'd thought less about being in his bed than how to understand—or explain—why she no longer dreamed about getting there.

"It's difficult for me," he whispered, "knowing you're upstairs every night, alone. I've often thought about coming to you."

He took one of her hands in his and she was glad because it steadied her. She hid her free hand in her lap.

She must say something, try telling him how confused she was. "I think—sometimes—that's what I want too. But I've never been with anyone before, and for me it seems to be an important step. More important than I once thought."

He laughed gently. "Are you worried that I will find you lacking? I expect your inexperience. Don't be afraid. It's all perfectly natural. What will happen is a beautiful thing, one I'd like to show you."

She didn't doubt that. And maybe he was right; whatever mysteries there were between a man and a woman should be beautiful. It was, after all, the most personal of things to share and would certainly make each vulnerable to the other.

"Come here," he said, standing and pulling her to her feet too. "Let me go through the day thinking of you. Tasting you."

Then his lips came down on hers. He tasted of the coffee they'd been drinking, only cooled.

"Until tonight," he said, pulling away.

And then he let her go.

Christophe neared the woman pulling in laundry, noticing her attention was clearly drawn to something inside the kitchen. He topped the last step behind her and followed her gaze with his own.

In time to see Annaliese in Jurgen's arms.

He must be twenty years her senior! Nearly as old as her father!

An immediate notion to barge in crossed his mind, past the woman watching from just outside the door in the chilly morning air. He would demand Jurgen leave Annaliese alone.

But then it all became clear; that embrace, that kiss—they were hardly one-sided. She'd welcomed him.

Christophe backed away, straight into a frigid sheet dangling on the line. Wordlessly, without apology, blindly, he took the opposite end of the material and together, as if by design, he and the woman stretched it taut; then with two steps he handed it to her to finish folding.

She thanked him, but he couldn't respond, not even a murmur. He left the porch and started walking, barely paying attention to his direction.

12

The women Annaliese met with that day were eager to talk to her. These were workingwomen, some of them supporting their families while their husbands—returned soldiers unable to find a job or others let go from factories still transitioning from war goods to civilian needs—looked for work. Others were unmarried women like Annaliese, drawn to the city from various agricultural villages, enjoying the independence their jobs provided. She knew if the war had afforded any favors, it was emancipation from the few roles previously available to women like her.

She welcomed the diversion, their enthusiasm, the questions and discussions about the privilege of voting for the first time in their lives. The world of politics had never been an option for them, and they were eager to hear her views on fairness and equality for everyone, about the People's Council who would speak for them so long as they were not dissolved should another party win the election. They were even eager to donate a few coins of their hard-earned wages in support of Eisner, because he'd been chosen by the council.

Working felt natural to her. It was not just a mindless way of escaping from more personal things on her mind. She contributed to the future of Germany by educating women who very much wanted to learn what she had to teach. And she added to the party coffers every time she spoke, no matter where she went.

But escape she must, not only from wondering if Christophe would return to work with their party, but from thoughts of Jurgen and what he expected of her when she saw him that night.

By the time Annaliese returned to the party office, it was late in the day. She'd extended her workday as long as she could, but with each footstep toward the butcher shop came thoughts of Jurgen, waiting.

It was times like this she missed Nitsa. Though Annaliese had known Nitsa all her life, they'd only become close friends shortly after Annaliese had caught her stealing money from the payroll office at the factory. She'd made Nitsa return it but had promised to give her something from her parents' home that would bring nearly as much on the black market as the puny sum Nitsa had managed to steal. Her parents had never missed the silver candlesticks they'd stored in the back pantry.

"Why would being alone with Jurgen be unpleasant now," Nitsa would ask Annaliese if she were here, *"when only a week ago you thought you wanted to be with him? to give yourself to him? What's changed?"*

Nothing, absolutely nothing.

The whole situation reminded Annaliese of a painting her father once owned, one Annaliese wanted to give to Nitsa to sell. But for some reason on the very day Annaliese had planned to remove it, her father had taken it from the closet where it had been stored. Everyone thought it had been the work of a minor artist from right here in Munich. While mildly respected, the painter's work had never garnered the attention he would have liked, not even upon his death. The artwork her father owned had been appealing enough, a nice use of color, which was why Annaliese thought it might sell on the black market. But when her father took it to an art critic who recognized it as the work of a famous Flemish artist, the price had leaped to the sky.

What had changed? The painting?

No, only its perceived value. Her father sold it immediately, pocketing a hefty profit.

She shook her head, refusing to compare her present dilemma to a capitalistic phenomenon. This was far more personal than that.

And yet what had caused the value of being with Jurgen to do just the opposite—to plummet? Had he changed? Had he done anything to make her see him differently? She'd known he had flaws since the day she met him. Like his pride. It had never bothered her much; she knew it took confidence and self-assurance to draw others to a vision.

But what he wanted to do involved her, and so personally . . . though it was almost as if he thought it had only to do with him.

And then there was Christophe.

His face often came to mind. Even if she'd been wrong about the letters he wrote to Giselle, even if they'd been written on the heels of battle fatigue or some kind of shell shock–induced hatred that had long since faded, he was still judgmental and rigid. Even if Giselle had been wrong to be inspired by what must have been a whim of passion in him, he was still responsible. He also thought her wrong to ignore her family.

His presence had brought with it a reminder of every rule

she'd been raised with, about virtue and fidelity and the bonds of matrimony every good girl ought to long for. Worse, he reminded her of all those childish dreams she once had about falling in love and then having a wedding, the kind of wedding her father could afford. Jurgen might compose unforgettable poetry about women and love, but not a single verse would he write about marriage; she knew that well enough.

Annaliese rounded the corner near the butcher shop and all thoughts abandoned her. There was a crowd outside the door, and from the clamor she knew it wasn't just a busy day of recruiting. Too much noise for that, and an undercurrent of tension in the shouts.

She hurried her steps and pushed through the crowd into a room full of chaos. Neither Jurgen nor Leo was in sight. The uneasiness was tangible. A crowd several layers deep huddled around what she knew must be someone sitting at the typewriter, perhaps one of their writers eager to get copy off to their press.

"What is it?" she asked Ivo, who towered above most others. "What's happened?"

He reached out to her, then pulled back, as if shy of his deformed hands. She caught him, though, because she'd once held his hand in a march and knew such contact didn't hurt him.

His palm closed around her hand. "One of the foremen at the tool works factory was thrown over a bridge. He hit his head on a piling and drowned. It happened after Jurgen's visit."

"Oh no!"

"The police are holding Jurgen for questioning."

"But he's a member of the council! He would never incite violence. How can they hold him against his will?"

"They say they're holding him for his own good," Ivo told her. "To protect him in case some of the bourgeois blame him for the death."

Jurgen couldn't go to jail, no matter why they said they were holding him. Not again, not after he'd spent so many months in the hands of the government. It had been a government under a different name when he'd been imprisoned the first time, but that would hardly matter. Not if he was to be deprived of his freedom.

And what would this do to the election? To have one of Eisner's most prominent supporters thrown in jail, no matter the reason, was surely a disaster.

"Where is Leo?"

"He's there, at the typewriter. Getting out a flyer defending Jurgen."

"Anya? Is that you?"

She pressed through the crowd and found Leo just pulling a page from the typewriter carriage.

He handed it to Ivo. "Get this to the printer right away. And you—" he looked at Annaliese—"you'll have to address the crowd outside the jail. I saw them; they've already formed."

Leo took her hand, pulling her along to the back of the room as he spoke. "We must make sure they know Jurgen is as grieved as the rest of us over what happened. And label those really at fault—the capitalists are the ones who continue to suck the blood and hope out of each one of us. That foreman who died knew nothing of freedom; he was hard-pressed by his capitalist bosses to force those under him to reach a certain quota. He was as much a victim as the rest of us. And now they want to make a victim of Jurgen."

He pushed open the door, and she followed him outside.

"Do you understand? It must be made clear that Jurgen in no way condones what happened, and the man who died must be made a victim, too. If the crowd can be made to see that he would have flourished with freedom and fairness, we might gain some new voices to join ours instead of losing any. Come with me."

The truck waited at the end of the block, and Leo coached her as he had when she first joined the party. Along the route to the municipal building, she heard each word, but his advice matched the assumptions she had already. A man had died today, a man whose identity she did not know, though he represented another loss of German life. She might not be able to put a face to the man who was lost, but she could define the grief and make sure Jurgen himself was absolved of any guilt.

There, in the street before the building where Jurgen was being held, was the crowd Leo had spoken about—and a speaker already on a platform above.

Her heart thudded as she heard accusations labeling the men who'd attacked the foreman a mob. And Jurgen as the one who'd inspired that mob.

The words might as well have been bullets aimed at him, but she could be his shield.

Annaliese fairly sailed from the back of the truck, Ivo scrambling after her with the sturdy wooden platform on which she could stand to grab the attention she needed.

"Don't add Jurgen to the wrong side!" she cried, and the crowd seemed startled to hear another voice from a nearby corner. The other speaker, a man she did not know, was startled too. His silence gave her time to cry out again. "The victims today are those trapped in a capitalist system that degraded the foreman to a slave driver. If he'd had a taste of the fairness

Jurgen offers through our council, nothing like this would have happened."

"Then why did it happen during one of his speeches?" the other speaker said. "Because he incited it!"

"No! We want peace. If you knew anything about Jurgen, you would know that. He spent a year in a prison just like this for protesting the war, for refusing to respect an antiquated monarch. Jurgen hates war! And violence! There would be no wars without the greed of others. Greed that made a foreman the victim of a senseless crime."

If not for the strength of her voice against his, Annaliese doubted she could have won the crowd over. But win them she did, offering volley after volley of discourse. These were Germans before her, war-weary, death-weary, just as she was. She knew that and reminded them Jurgen knew it too. This was an entirely new audience to her, one who hadn't come expecting to hear her message of peace and fairness and equality. Few were dressed as she was, in the worn clothes of the lower class; most of the clothing in this crowd represented the middle class. Seeing that made her all the more impassioned, because if she could win new voices to their way of thinking, then Jurgen's imprisonment would almost be worth it.

She saw them reluctantly come around to her, warm to her logic, her passion. This crowd, like so many before them, soon let her define the truth, because her vision of the world was simple and clear. A world in which the weak were cared for, the exploiters revealed for what they were. She longed with them for a better world.

One in which Jurgen would not—could not—be part of any violence.

Let the blame fall where it belonged: on the capitalist

system exploiting those who had no choice but to offer the strength of their backs, the dexterity of their hands, the test of their will in order to survive on what few scraps the bourgeoisie thrust their way. She was quick to reveal it was the system that failed, not the people—after all, who would knowingly set out to thwart another? It was a system that demanded greed, one that people could abandon in light of their love for others.

She had those present calling for Jurgen's release before she was finished with her speech.

Leo pulled her to the side, pointing to the municipal building, where armed police were emerging to disperse the crowd. She let him lead her back to the truck, and no sooner had he shut the back doors than Ivo sped away, beyond the reach of any officers.

"You did what you could," Leo said.

If only she knew it would be enough.

❧

Christophe closed the shop door against the wind, turning up the collar of his new coat. Perhaps he should have gone home, after all, if only to save the money this new coat had cost him.

Deciding to stay in Munich had been easier than he thought, considering how he'd felt that very morning on the back porch of the house where Annaliese lived. He could have convinced himself the last thing she needed—or wanted—was to have someone looking after her, especially someone sent by her parents. Somehow, though, that very thought had helped him decide. That, and what Nitsa had done against her family. He owed the Dürays that much, and it wasn't even a sacrifice of his time or energy.

Christophe had spent the afternoon scouting for someone to deliver a message to Annaliese's parents. Several hours before that had been spent choosing how he would word such a message. Their daughter was safe; she was busy; she was productive. She was working to improve the lives of common Germans. He left out any reference to Socialism or even politics in general, knowing he needed to keep the wording just vague enough if his note was to remain cheerful.

But there was no evading the one fact her parents most wanted to hear about. Annaliese would not come home, not even to say good-bye. He ended by saying he would continue to hope she would change her mind before they were scheduled to sail. If that happened, he would see her safely home. In the meantime, he planned to keep an eye on her and told them where they could contact him. At the home of Leo Beckenbauer.

He would go there, but not tonight. As determined as he was to watch over Annaliese, he wasn't quite sure he wanted to face her just yet—not while wondering if she spent all of her time in that little room upstairs or if she sometimes shared a room with Jurgen. By tomorrow Christophe would be adjusted to all that, he was sure.

Tonight he would return to the park, enjoy the warmth of his new coat. He would stare at the stars for as long as he could, demand himself to keep awake. Sleep so rarely brought him any rest, he doubted tonight would be any different.

13

Annaliese scrambled to the bottom staircase of the municipal building, which Jurgen was just descending. Free after more than twenty-four hours of being held "for his own protection."

She fell into his arms, not even caring that others were around to see him kiss her. She'd once vowed if she ever did carry through with sharing his bed, no one but the two of them would realize such a thing had occurred. She didn't want others watching, measuring the length of such a personal relationship. But she was so relieved to see him, she didn't care who saw them. "Leo has arranged a celebration at the beer hall," she said breathlessly. "Everyone is eager to see you."

"I suppose I could use a clean shirt first," he said.

She smiled, taking his hand and leading him to the back of the truck. "There's one on the bench."

Leo held it out for him when they joined him. Before Jurgen had even unbuttoned the shirt he wore, Annaliese averted her eyes. But he reached across the aisle and caressed her cheek as if to tell her there was nothing he wouldn't share with her.

She offered a smile, then looked away again.

The music in the beer hall was so loud, it greeted them

before they'd even stepped inside. Upon Jurgen's entry, cheers drowned every other noise.

Beer was thrust at all of them, and Annaliese raised a glass mug along with the others, saluting Jurgen.

More supporters than ever clamored nearby, and countless new faces welcomed them. Annaliese recognized some she'd seen at rallies supporting the SPD, the more centrist social democratic party theirs had broken off from some time ago, before Annaliese had ever come to Munich. Having them here was something she was sure neither Jurgen nor Leo missed.

Annaliese drank beer while the tension from previous days slowly dissipated. This day was a triumph. The near-nonstop street speeches in support of Jurgen could end. She could go back to speaking about workers' unity and encouraging support for Eisner in the election. And Leo could go back to writing pamphlets instead of battling behind the scenes for Jurgen's freedom.

More than once, Jurgen caught her eye over his beer. He even whispered in her ear, but it was too noisy to hear what he'd said. She couldn't help meeting his gaze, knowing from his smile the meaning behind whatever words he'd spoken.

Annaliese let her mug be refilled. Now, right now, was the time to celebrate Jurgen's triumphant return. She would worry later about whatever was to happen once they reached home.

The crowd provided a lure for both of them. Surrounded by those of like mind, they took turns speaking to the entire hall. In between speeches they drank more beer and sang songs, and after a while a sense of pleasant security settled on Annaliese. She had a place here. Those around her had nearly as much faith in her as they had in Jurgen, if she could judge by the hurrahs that greeted her speech. Her place among them had been secured by no less than Jurgen himself, and for that she was grateful.

Others took their places on the tabletop, presiding over the crowd, echoing sentiments she and Jurgen had inspired, all in support of Eisner and the People's Council. She accepted yet another drink Jurgen pushed her way, toasted with the traditional *"Prost!"* and drained the contents. Annaliese wasn't accustomed to taking more than a few sips of beer, but today was different. The atmosphere was holidaylike, even though Christmas was more than a week away and the election a couple of weeks after that.

And she needed whatever fortification the drink could bring. Hadn't Jurgen said wine would enhance what took place between them? Beer would provide the same help tonight. She hastily finished the entire mug and let it be refilled again.

Before long, sleepiness shrouded the edges of her vision. She considered taking a short nap even amid the noise of the still-crowded and jubilant beer hall. What would it matter, anyway? Ivo and Huey were nearby. She picked up her mug to finish the last of her third beer—or was it her fourth?—before she would push it away to rest her head on the table.

But the glass was taken from her hand before it reached her lips.

"I think you've probably had enough."

The voice belonged to Christophe Brecht.

She looked at Jurgen instead of turning to Christophe—Jurgen, who was far deeper in his own cups and just now sharing an animated recitation of one of his poems. Undoubtedly neither he nor Leo had seen Christophe, or they would have invited him into their circle.

"Go away," she said over her shoulder.

"Come outside with me, Annaliese. Get some fresh air."

He'd already dispelled the deliciously sleepy feeling she'd enjoyed only moments ago. And the beer hall air *was* heavy with smoke and malt.

"I do want some fresh air," she said, standing. "But alone."

Her head spun and she wondered if she'd gotten up too quickly. She had no idea what time it was, but for her the day was over. She wanted only to go home. With or without Jurgen.

"Ivo, will you see me home, please?"

She touched the side of the table to steady it; somehow it had moved, despite having so many people sitting around it. Squinting, she peered through the smoke and spotted the front door, but there were hundreds of people in the way. She never should have stood; she might have easily fallen asleep right in her seat and been happy enough.

But she was up now and wanted only one thing. Her bed. Alone.

She felt the large shadow behind her as she made her way through the throng. Ivo steadied her once when someone stepped unexpectedly in her path, but she never took her focus from her destination. How foolish she'd been to have more than one mug of beer. It made her vulnerable even to someone stumbling around her.

Or perhaps she had stumbled into him.

Outside, the crisp air pierced her lungs. She'd forgotten her coat. But to swim back through that sea of people was unthinkable and so she didn't even turn around. She stepped toward the street.

"Here, put this on," said a voice behind her, with some exasperation.

The wrong voice. Not Ivo, but Christophe.

"Where is Ivo?"

"It doesn't matter, Annaliese. I'm taking you home."

Then he draped a coat—hers—on her shoulders and she put her arms into the sleeves, letting him tie it closed with the belt.

"Does Jurgen know?"

All she heard was a grunt in response. He looped her arm through his and started walking, and for a moment it was all she could do to keep up.

"Slow down or let me go!"

He slowed.

She took another breath of the night air, and after a wave of nausea passed, she tugged on his arm. He didn't let go.

"You didn't answer my question," she said. "Does Jurgen know I left with you?"

"I don't know. Ivo saw us leave; he'll probably tell him."

She looked behind them, toward the front of the beer hall that seemed far away already. A few people lingered outside, but the air was too cold for more than the thinnest crowd beyond the warmth of the hall.

"I told you to go away."

"And so I did. Along with you."

"That wasn't . . ." She didn't finish. It was no use. Although he'd slowed his pace, he had her arm twisted around his so she couldn't escape.

"You shouldn't drink alcohol," he said. "At least not so much. You're too small to drink."

"I'm not too young. For anything."

"I didn't say you were too young. I said you were too small. Your body. It's too small to hold much beer. And you are too young, too, or else you're just foolish. You don't have any sense left in you right now."

"Yes I have!" She would have been proud of the firmness behind her statement, but a hiccup compromised her.

"Really? Then how is it that you left with me, when I heard you clearly say you wanted me to go away? If you hadn't drunk so much, you would have known it was I behind you, not Ivo. You're just lucky it was me and not some thug from in there."

"I wasn't with any thugs. I was with friends."

He didn't dispute that, and she considered the argument won. But after another block of walking, she stopped. "Why didn't you let Ivo take me home? He has the truck. He would have come back for the others, and I would be home now. I'm tired. And cold."

"Keep walking," he said.

"I'm not foolish."

"It's foolish to drink so much that you lose awareness of your surroundings. Any number of things could happen to you, the way you are right now."

She laughed. If only he knew! Tonight was supposed to have been the night she gave herself to Jurgen, and being tipsy wouldn't have made one bit of difference to him. It would have been easier to get it over with. Decision made before any hesitation could arise.

"He's not going to be happy."

"Who's not?"

"Oh, no one you need to know about."

"Jurgen?"

She stopped short but he didn't let her linger, tugging her forward again.

"How did you know I was talking about Jurgen?"

"He's old enough to be your father. What do you see in such an old man?"

"He's . . . he's . . . experienced."

He snorted. "I've no doubt of that."

"*He* wants me, you know."

"I've no doubt of that, either."

"You do?" She felt a smile on her face, although she had no idea why it was there. She needed to sit down. "He's going to make it right. Make right what my father and those like him made wrong."

"How is he going to do that?"

"He's going to . . . to . . . give the workers a voice. And make people share. He's noble, you know, even though he grew up a peasant. He's a very wonderful man."

"Of course he is."

"I'm tired, Christophe. I want to sit."

"It's too cold. Come on."

"No. I believe I'll sit."

And so she did, right there on the pavement in front of Westermann's Department Store, where they handed out soup on Tuesdays and Fridays. The store was closed, and not even the soup alcove was open tonight, so there was no one on the street to get in the way of her rest.

"Annaliese . . ."

She looked up at him, but his head was spinning. Or was that her head spinning? She would rest, if only for a few minutes. That was all she needed.

❦

"Annaliese," Christophe repeated.

He stared at her, befuddled and amazed. She was sleeping! Right there on the cement.

"Of all the idiotic . . ."

Maybe this was what people of passion did: they gave everything to whatever was in front of them. And for tonight, for Annaliese, that had been beer. He wanted to feel more irritated than amused and thought if he sounded exasperated, his emotions would follow suit. So far, he was simply glad to have returned to her side in time to protect her from her own unwise choice.

He bent over her, slipping his hands beneath her arms and heaving her up over his shoulder like a sandbag. He'd carried his share of those in the last four years. He'd carried more than a few fellow soldiers this way too, some wounded, others in their cups every bit as deep as Annaliese.

He'd just never carried a woman before.

If her parents could see her now, they'd have every right to demand she come home. In fact, if he were any kind of friend, he wouldn't stop before taking her to a train heading in the direction of her parents' village this very night. They'd want her, even as drunk as she was.

But her Munich flat was closer than the train station, and as much as he'd like to make the decision for her, he knew it wasn't his place to do so. Once there, he took the porch steps two at a time, let himself in, and then climbed the inside flight of stairs to what he guessed was the door to her flat.

The door opposite hers opened, but only a sliver. Christophe ignored it, even if he would have welcomed some help. But he wouldn't ask.

There was no need to say a word before Bertita, obviously having heard him shuffling up the stairs with Annaliese, came bustling out of her flat.

"What's happened to her!"

"Nothing serious. Too much beer to celebrate Jurgen's release."

Annaliese's flat was a one-room apartment. Tidy, sparse. The bed was off to the side, neatly set with covers and pillows. He let Annaliese's head gently meet one of the pillows.

Leaning above her, Christophe loosened the belt on her coat even as Bertita stood at the foot of the bed to remove Annaliese's shoes.

"No woman should let herself get in such a state," Bertita muttered.

"It's little wonder her mother is worried about her."

"So you know her family?" Bertita asked.

"We grew up together."

"Are either of you talking to me?"

He looked at Annaliese; her eyes were open, though rimmed with red.

"I didn't think you'd wake up until morning," he said.

"Where am I? . . . How did I get home?"

"On my shoulder."

She scanned the room, but it was as if she didn't even see Bertita. "Is . . . Jurgen here?"

Impatience filled Christophe and he might have turned away, but something stopped him. Something in the tone of her voice. Fear?

"No, he's not here. Why?"

She rolled over, away from him, one shoe still on. She mumbled something he couldn't decipher, so he put a hand to her shoulder, pulling her back to face him.

"What did you say?"

But she was either already sleeping or purposefully ignoring him. Christophe turned to Bertita. "Does Jurgen spend time up here . . . with her?"

Bertita shook her head. "I saw the same kiss you saw yesterday, but it's the first one as far as I know. She's never had anyone up here, and she's abed early every night."

Annaliese let out a laugh and made an attempt to raise one of her hands. Evidently it felt too heavy because it flopped down beside her. "You're funny, Christophe. You know what would happen if Jurgen came up here, don't you? As loyal as Bertita is to the party, I think she believes it wouldn't be right." Annaliese rolled over again. "And it wouldn't. Even I know that."

Christophe caught her shoulder, and she faced him again. "What do you mean?"

Her smile was lopsided. "My mother wouldn't like it either." Then her smile broadened, the first one she'd ever aimed his way, at least since he'd known her here in Munich. "And neither would you, would you, Christophe?"

He wondered how she knew. It was true: the thought of them together made him sick. Only he hadn't realized it until just now.

Christophe backed away from the bed, undeniably relieved by what he'd learned. All evening he'd watched them exchange glances and smiles, whispers and drinks. It spoke of an intimacy well established. He'd thought . . .

He was half-tempted to fasten closed her coat again, lace up her shoes, and take her to the station as he'd envisioned only minutes ago. If she'd taken all that beer tonight because she'd *expected* Jurgen, it meant only one thing. She wasn't sure she wanted him up here at all.

He shook her shoulder. "Annaliese, wake up. I need to talk to you."

She didn't stir.

Sleeping so peacefully, she seemed more like the portrait in her parents' parlor. Young. Vulnerable. Beautiful.

"Annaliese, what have you gotten yourself into?"

He looked around the room. There were only two doors—the one from the hall and another open door leading to a toilet. Going to the window, he peered down at the street. No one was out at this hour. No sign of Jurgen or any other member of this makeshift family of revolutionaries.

He considered asking Bertita to stay with Annaliese, but he feared she might refuse.

So he pulled down the shade, stopped to throw a cover over Annaliese, then went into the hallway. Bertita followed.

"I'm going to stay right here for the night, Bertita. To make sure she gets the rest she needs."

"I'll hear the door if anyone opens it," Bertita said. Then she looked embarrassed, as if he hadn't already noticed that she left her own door open so she could hear everything. "The walls are thin. Like paper."

"It's here or the park for me. It might as well be here."

Then he slid to the floor and leaned against the jamb, adjusting his brand-new coat. Bertita went into her own flat, shutting the door this time.

Christophe tried finding some sleep for himself.

Voices invaded his rest, but they were still outside. The downstairs door opened moments later, and there at the bottom of the steps stood Jurgen, steady enough but grabbing the handrail as if to come up the stairs. He stopped when he caught sight of Christophe.

"Ivo said you took her from the hall."

He shook his head. "I followed her. She fell asleep on the street, and I brought her here."

Jurgen eyed him. "Then what are you doing here now?"

"I had no place else to go." He didn't care if it sounded pathetic; it was partially true anyway. There was no place else he needed to go.

Jurgen climbed the remaining stairs, far steadier than Christophe would have suspected possible judging by the amount of beer he'd seen the man consume.

"Thank you for taking care of her, then," Jurgen said. "When did you return to Munich?"

Christophe stood. Was the man planning to go into Annaliese's room anyway? past him? "I never left. I saw the flyer about welcoming you back at the beer hall. I was surprised to hear you'd been in prison."

"Unfairly, of course. Another reason we must fix Germany, to prevent this sort of thing from happening."

Christophe nodded. "About that," he said, "about fixing Germany. I've decided to work with you, if you still have a place for me."

Whatever suspicion, whatever hesitation Jurgen's face had hinted at before suddenly disappeared. He slapped Christophe on the shoulder and took one of his hands in his own. "That's fine! Good news! Come downstairs; let's have a toast."

He followed Jurgen down the stairs—gratefully away from Annaliese's door—then inside Jurgen's flat. Christophe wondered how the other man could hold any more liquor without having it get the best of him, but he offered Christophe wine with a steady hand.

"I thought you came from the hinterland, Christophe."

"Not very remote. A short train ride from Munich."

"Ah. That explains your coat."

Christophe looked down at it, made of the finest wool. Soft.

Expensive, at least in comparison to anything he'd seen Jurgen or Leo wearing. He could tell Jurgen what a bargain he'd gotten, since so few people had money for such things these days, they were nearly giving them away. But somehow he thought it wouldn't make any difference.

Jurgen's distaste had been clear. "I came from north of Dachau myself, out with the farmers and peasants."

"There is agriculture everywhere around Munich. Even where I am from." Christophe didn't mention that the town where he had grown up—with Annaliese—was better known for its lakes and resorts that attracted the wealthy of Munich than for the farmland that separated the two spots.

"Right so! Eisner envisions a Peasants' Council. Did you know that?"

"Yes, so I've read."

"Kurt Eisner—you know the name, of course? Our recently named prime minister of Bavaria?" He gulped his wine and sighed. "That should have been me, you know. He was nominated by a Workers' and Soldiers' Council, and they'd have nominated me if they'd only known me. But I was too freshly out of prison. I hadn't my chance yet." He looked at Christophe. "Now I do, though. Even tonight, more men were with me. Did you see all of them? Some even from the SPD."

Christophe nodded, although he had no idea which of the numerous faces he'd seen that night might have been won over from the other, softer Socialist camp.

"We want many of the same things, only I'd be the better voice in Berlin."

"Why isn't your name on the ballot for the election, then?"

"And split the vote between me and Eisner? I don't think so. It's too soon, anyway. Our message is just beginning to take hold. Change—peaceful change—takes time. The people might not be ready to vote for our ideals yet. They have to know more first."

Christophe nodded.

"We need more voices behind us," Jurgen went on. "Soldiers, workers, and peasants, too. You can help with the soldiers as well as the peasants, by virtue of being from outside of Munich—if you trade away that coat, of course, for one that will better match those who need our message. How does that sound to you?"

Christophe held up his glass but set it aside without drinking from it. "I would be happy to discuss it in the morning, when our heads are clear."

Jurgen finished what was in his glass. "You're right." Then he laughed and looked at the ceiling—perhaps thinking about who was above that ceiling. "Though it's a shame to sleep alone, isn't it? Ah, well. Good night, then, Christophe. I would offer you the empty room, but you hardly used it the last time you were here. Did the bed not make you comfortable? Surely it's better than sleeping on the stairs."

He wondered if that was a subtle hint to stay away from Annaliese's door. "The bed was fine."

"Then it is yours again, if you like. I will see you in the morning?"

He nodded. Tonight, at least, he would accept the comfort of that bed. Blast the nightmares; he wouldn't sleep anyway. He'd be listening for footsteps—up or down the stairs to where Annaliese lay.

14

During the next few days, Christophe never saw Annaliese alone. At first he was convinced it was her doing. If she remembered anything about the other night, perhaps she was embarrassed.

He could understand that, although he was no less embarrassed himself. Hadn't she teased him about knowing he wouldn't like the idea of her with Jurgen?

Not that he would admit such a thing, least of all to her. He'd been embarrassed more than once by women. First there had been Giselle, whom he'd hoped one day would receive his attention, though she never did, at least as anything more than a friend. Then there had been a German woman working in France; she'd flirted all right, smiling his way as if she'd welcome his attention. But he'd been slow about investigating those smiles, and then his unit had been called away. By the time he'd been able to get back to her, she'd already married another soldier.

Then there had been a woman named Julitte, a Frenchwoman who seemed to have a faith stronger than that of any other woman he'd known. Stronger even than Giselle's. He'd wanted to spend time with her, too, but once again he'd been refused. When it came to women, not a single memory gave him much confidence.

And now Annaliese. She'd known, somehow even before he'd acknowledged it himself, that he didn't like the idea of her with Jurgen. How did women know men better than they knew themselves? Her teasing had served the purpose well enough. He wasn't going to make a fool of himself over a woman again.

He didn't have much chance of that, anyway. Jurgen and Leo kept him busy—and removed any possibility of time alone with Annaliese. They were her best bodyguards.

If only he could be assured they prevented themselves from being alone with her too—at least Jurgen.

Christophe was assigned to train the men who'd sworn loyalty to the USPD and specifically to Jurgen. Each day he rose early, before anyone else, grabbed a dry roll from the cupboard, then made his way to the warehouse where most of the men bunked. He would have taken up a cot in the warehouse with the men if he'd been ordered to, but he knew if he did, he would never see Annaliese. As it was, he saw her only in the evenings and on the rare occasion she rose early enough to spot him leaving for the day.

Nearly a week into the training program, on the day before Christmas, Leo caught the door before it had even closed behind Christophe. Leo held up a roll of his own as if in a toast; then side by side they walked to the warehouse.

"I want to see how the men are coming along," Leo said. "What do you think of them?"

"I think they're young, mostly foolish, and itching for a fight they thought would wait for them. In their minds, the war ended too soon, before they were old enough to fight.

But—" he eyed Leo, who still looked ahead—"I think they're loyal and willing to follow you or Jurgen or Eisner."

"Can they fight? Will they, if it comes to that?"

Christophe lifted a shoulder. "I've seen older men better trained than these turn tail and run. But the majority will fight if they're threatened. Maybe the younger ones, like these, all the more. That's what you've told me to do with them—teach them to defend themselves and others. And that's what they'll do."

He didn't voice his greatest fear, that someday their band of men—presently numbering a few dozen—might have to use the training Christophe supplied. It was no secret everyone wanted control of the scattered army, and it was anyone's guess what would happen if such a power were used badly. Only one people lived in Germany these days: Germans. Could Christophe watch one shoot down another, even in defense? Could he be responsible, because of his training, for yet more killing?

At the warehouse threshold, Christophe noted as he did every day the signs someone had painted espousing their political messages: *Universal Brotherhood. All People are Equal. Take Care of Your Brother. End Exploitation. Down with Greed.*

"Hey, Brecht," one of the men called as they filed into line. It was one of the things Christophe had accustomed himself to, no longer being addressed by rank. Such titles as Hauptmann or Major did not lend themselves to equality, so rank had been outlawed.

This man was called Popoff because on the day of his arrival he'd popped off in anger every time someone mispronounced his name. *Ottokar* came more easily to the lips than *Odovacar*; even Christophe had made the mistake once. He'd been Popoff ever since.

"How many men do you think it would take for another revolution?"

"No need for a revolution when we have a vote coming up," Christophe reminded Popoff, irritated as much by being waylaid before entering the warehouse as by Popoff's eager tone. The closer the election came, the more whispers spread about a counterrevolution if the election didn't go the way they hoped. And with so many weapons sprinkled throughout the city, sometimes Christophe wondered if one election would be enough—no matter who won.

He'd seen the look in Popoff's eye before, at the front when an untried soldier wanted to lead a skirmish over no-man's-land to raid an Allied trench. End the war quicker, they'd said. More likely to end their own life quicker.

Still, it looked like Popoff needed more persuasion.

"Jurgen brings in new numbers all the time. Every march he leads shows growth. Let the election do its job."

Christophe led the way to the far side of the warehouse, where they'd erected a long tunnel lined with bricks and mattresses; at the very end, a target was propped against a thick block wall.

He ordered the men to line up, beginning as he always did before this portion of their training. He inspected their guns. Christophe was aware that Leo watched but was glad he didn't interfere. As much as Leo knew about politics, Christophe had the feeling the man knew nothing about weaponry.

The men were aware of their guest, though. Anyone who knew Jurgen knew Leo.

"Why does the assembly continue to meet?" one of the men called to Leo after his gun passed Christophe's inspection.

He held it up. "We should storm them and force them to disband."

"Which is what the election will do if Eisner wins," Christophe said before Leo could respond. "So we don't need to storm into another revolution, do we?"

"But what if the vote doesn't go the way we expect? Then what?"

"A state, a country—" Leo's voice was as patient as a parent with a child—"can be taken over with a small number of men simply because the majority of people either don't care enough or aren't keen enough to think it matters who sits in office. Unless a gun points directly at them, the masses will allow almost anything to happen. Even a German education can't teach them enough to want to make decisions for themselves on the running of society." He smiled. "But if the election goes as we hope, there won't be a need for any more guns."

Christophe wished Leo hadn't answered or at least hadn't answered in the way that made Popoff's eyes maintain that gleam. Half the men in front of them were as young as Popoff and almost all of them too eager to learn how to fight rather than defend.

He prayed they'd learn sooner than later that a vote was better than bullets—and added a prayer that if the vote didn't go their way, it wouldn't come to bullets after all.

❧

Annaliese helped Bertita in the kitchen, not because she was expected to but because she wanted to. Although Bertita hadn't said a word about the night Christophe had brought Annaliese home, Annaliese remembered it all. The disapproval on

Bertita's face, the admission that she'd seen the kiss Annaliese had shared with Jurgen. And so had Christophe.

But because there was nothing Annaliese could do to change what Bertita had seen or what Annaliese had done, she chose to ignore it. She counted herself lucky that Bertita was as good at ignoring everything she knew as Annaliese could have hoped.

Tonight she would forget all of that and help Bertita in the kitchen. It was Christmas Eve, but there would be no special feast, no tree draped with fruit and candles. No carols sung, no Christmas story read. No gifts. No prayers.

How many years had it been since she had marzipan or *Lebkuchen*, anyway? Four, at least. . . . Her heart twisted with longing for a past that could never be again, a past that she shouldn't want to see again anyway.

Ritual. Tradition. Habit. Waste. That's all any of it ever was.

But some habits used to be nice, even if none of them meant anything anymore.

So she helped Bertita by stirring the same stew they'd had yesterday. She would dole it out into the same dishes they always used, no special plates for members of this "family."

"Ah! I'm hungry tonight," Jurgen said as he entered the kitchen from the dining room. "Don't let any of us go to bed with empty stomachs tonight, Bertita, or we'll be visited by demons in our dreams."

Then he laughed over the silly folk tale that gave everyone an excuse to overeat, at least on this particular day.

He came up close behind Annaliese, placing his hands on her shoulders and gently rubbing. Instead of relaxing her, the contact made her stiffen. Things had been different between them lately. Having Christophe in the fold created a new balance.

Almost as if Jurgen had been watching them, trying to decide whether or not he was in competition for Annaliese's affection.

He might have sensed her tension, for he started to pull his fingers from her neck and shoulders. But when Leo opened the door from the back porch, with Christophe just behind him, Jurgen's hands remained where they were.

"Sit down, sit down," Bertita said. "While it's hot. It'll taste better that way." She often complained how impossible it was to make a tasty meal with such a scarcity of food.

Annaliese let Bertita take the spoon from her, allowing the woman to portion the meal evenly into bowls and set them in places around the table. Annaliese took a seat at Jurgen's right side, watching Bertita fill the last two bowls and set them on a tray to take upstairs to Huey. She'd insisted he stay in bed with a cold they all hoped was nothing more than that. Not the influenza that ravaged so many families these days.

"Tales of Christophe's training are spreading, Jurgen," Leo said as he patted Christophe on the back. "More men are coming every day because they know they'll learn how to handle themselves with a gun."

"Defend themselves," Christophe said.

Jurgen smiled. "Good, that's very good, Christophe. I knew we'd benefit from your help."

Annaliese eyed Christophe across the table. He was already looking at her and smiled when he caught her eye. She turned away; ever since that night at the beer hall, she'd barely been able to look at him. He might be smiling now, but she knew he thought she was foolish. Her only comfort was in knowing she would never, ever, allow herself to be so vulnerable as to make a fool of herself in front of him again. At least not with the help of beer, which she could easily avoid.

The meal went quickly, a meal that might have lasted longer had there been enough to offer seconds.

"Tonight is Christmas Eve," Christophe said.

He'd spoken to no one in particular. Annaliese didn't have to see anyone else's face to know they all stared at him at the same time.

"I will be going to midnight services, to welcome in Christmas. Would anyone care to join me?"

Annaliese was almost tempted to say yes, if only because she'd missed some of the traditions her family held. And just now such an answer would save some of the awkwardness that Christophe was either too slow or too uncaring to recognize.

Even though she wouldn't go, she knew someone had to say something. It might as well be her; she'd thought about the subject, after all. "None of us will go with you. The church is like capitalism of the worst kind. It claims to have the power to sell a happy eternity. People allow themselves to be fooled by talk of souls and heaven. Fairy stories for puppets and puppeteers."

Christophe smiled. "I just wanted to extend the invitation. So it won't be said I'm stingy in my faith."

Leo, beside him, patted his back again and laughed. "No converts yet, my boy. Everything Annaliese said is true. Besides that, what priest hasn't dipped his hand into the coffer when necessary? What organization asking for money can really be trusted, especially one claiming to control eternity? It's just one more hierarchy where those in the right position exploit those of lesser means—and lesser intellect."

Christophe shrugged. "So you say. I don't think the church is always right—the church told us to go off and fight, and they were wrong, weren't they? So maybe some churches are guilty of what you accuse, too, and maybe I'm a fool. But man getting something wrong isn't God's fault. We all need to worship something. Even you. Politics is your god, Leo. And you, Jurgen?" Christophe let his gaze briefly touch Annaliese, and she was afraid he might say her name—not that she was Jurgen's god, but that women were. And he might be right. "I think you and Annaliese share the same god. The crowd. It entices you, so you think you receive something from it. Do you want to know what my God does for me?"

No one spoke, even though Annaliese would like to know the answer. Certainly God had never done anything for her.

"He taught me that everything around me doesn't make sense unless there is a God who wanted all of us here to begin with. Out of love."

"A loving God has let this world get into the shape it is?" Jurgen nearly spat the words. "This I cannot understand. What kind of cruel god would let his creation get into such a state as the world has been in the last four years?"

"I've done a lot of thinking about that," Christophe said. "About why He didn't stop the war. I couldn't understand why He didn't."

"And you didn't come round to our way of thinking?" Leo's question echoed Annaliese's thought.

"I wanted God to stop it. Certainly He could have. But the war was all tied in with our own doing, not His. If He were to stop something as big as a war, then what's to stop Him from interfering when each of us do anything wrong, even on a smaller scale? That made as little sense to me as Him stopping the war. That was supposed to be a gift, that ability to choose. He won't take back the gift just because we make a bad choice. Doesn't having to allow the little mistakes mean His having to allow the big ones, too?"

Leo's arms were folded across his chest. "Wait until the election; then you'll see how fairness will take care of the things religion has failed to do."

Christophe stood. "We'll see, won't we? All I ask is that you think about God if He ever comes to mind. Maybe it's Him nudging you. Consider that if God had created a world without war, without pain, then none of us might *ever* think of Him. Those with the most talent, like you, Leo, and you and you." He eyed Jurgen and then Annaliese, where his gaze remained. "Everyone with the most ability to work hard and make a comfortable living—those people God gave the most gifts to—probably wouldn't ever think about Him, not even to thank Him. Who needs God when things are going well?"

Christophe grabbed his coat from the back of his chair—a coat of plain wool, having traded his finer one at the charity line— then placed the cap on his head and left the kitchen through the same door he'd entered, without a word of farewell. Not even a "Merry Christmas," though he knew the phrase would mean nothing to any of them.

It was too early to go to midnight services, but he needed to leave this house. He wished Annaliese would come with him for the evening. He had a number of things he wanted to ask her if he could find her alone.

Did she really believe what Jurgen and Leo did? disbelieve as they did too? For a moment he imagined her as impassioned about God as she was about Socialism, and he wanted to smile but didn't let himself.

Her doubts befuddled him. Certainly there was a God . . . because if there wasn't, all those faces haunting him would haunt him forever. God was the only One who hadn't abandoned him, in spite of all Christophe had done.

He walked aimlessly, his shoulders hunched against the cold. At least he could trust that Annaliese would steer clear of the beer halls tonight. He'd seen the care with which she'd walked the day after her last visit and had hoped her headache had been severe and lasting enough to establish a permanent aversion to such places. Leo had said the others would be going there, but he'd overheard her tell him she never wanted to see the inside of a beer hall again, no matter how big the crowds.

Christophe would check back before long to make sure they really did leave her behind. He hadn't missed Jurgen's territorial attention toward her, like tonight, when he'd come in to find Jurgen's hands on her. Sometimes Christophe was sure Annaliese must be interested in the man after all, despite having said Jurgen's being in her room would have been wrong.

But there were times Christophe caught her staring his way that proved she wasn't as oblivious to him as she wanted him and others to think. He couldn't ignore that she felt something for him, and he meant to find out what—even if it was mostly the dislike he also saw in her eyes when she knew he was looking her way.

Somehow he would find a few minutes alone with her. He knew he would have to take matters into his own hands again, and as he walked through the freezing streets, he collected a few pebbles for his pocket.

Leo and Jurgen would be out late tonight; of that Christophe was sure. The beer halls never seemed to empty on holidays. Jurgen undoubtedly wouldn't be able to resist a ready-made crowd.

Leaving Annaliese alone.

15

Annaliese looked at the closed door, wondering where Christophe had gone on such a cold night. She glanced at the cuckoo clock that hung on the kitchen wall. Even if he went to midnight services, that was still hours from now. Where would he go until then?

Jurgen leaned close. "Anya, come along to the beer hall. There's bound to be a crowd. A friendly one, especially tonight."

She shook her head. "I don't like beer."

Both he and Leo laughed.

"What kind of German are you," Leo asked, "not liking beer?"

She smiled. "A tired one. I have some letters to answer from women asking good questions about the election." Standing, she pushed back her chair. "So I'll spend the night here, I think, and go to bed early."

"We plan to march in the afternoon," Leo reminded her. "There will be more people than ever."

She lifted one brow. "Headache or not?"

"Headache or not."

They both stood and she watched them put on their coats,

much the same as Christophe had a while ago. Somehow, though, she wasn't sorry to see them leave. At least not as sorry as she was when Christophe left for the service without her.

She went to her room planning to do what she said—spend the evening at her desk, then go to sleep. Far different from the way she'd spent last Christmas Eve. As tense and worried as her family had been over the scarcity of food and the changing opinions of the war, Giselle had been with them. And underneath all the worries, they'd been happy enough.

Annaliese ought to find something to be happy about again. Perhaps Jurgen should talk about starting other holidays. Surely they would celebrate if the workers of the world everywhere were united, allowed to live a life of dignity rather than scrimping for the food they ate and the clothes they wore. Freedom from tyranny would be a day to commemorate.

But not Christmas; this was one holiday bound for extinction if the party found its majority.

Christophe might simply have gone up to Annaliese's flat, tapped on the door, and asked to speak to her.

But if he did, Bertita would surely hear. So Christophe stepped below Annaliese's window and withdrew a few pebbles.

It took only a moment for her window to open. She leaned down with arms crossed against the cold.

"You'll break the window if you're not careful!"

He ignored her angry tone. "Come down and talk to me."

"No. It's late."

"Then I'm coming to your room, and Bertita will hear it all."

"No!"

She slammed the window and he thought Bertita might hear them after all.

He saw no movement from the upper story, no light in the other window. Waiting, he tossed other little stones into the air, catching them one by one. He would toss more at her window if need be.

But there she was. Fully dressed, including her coat, hat, and gloves. "What is so important that we have to freeze ourselves at this hour instead of talking during the day in the party office?"

"I wanted to speak to you alone. Here, come this way."

To his relief, she followed.

"I want to know something, Annaliese. I want to know if you believe everything the party stands for."

She stopped, facing him with wide eyes. "You dragged me out on this freezing night to ask me that? Isn't that something you should talk to Leo or Jurgen about?"

He shook his head. "I know they believe in the party. I want to know if *you* do."

"Of course I do."

"Why?"

"Because what they want is best for everyone, on the whole. To take care of the poor, to give those of lesser means a voice. Fairness for everyone."

"Even the rich?"

"Wealth is a trap. It makes people treat others poorly."

She shivered and he took her arm to lead them forward again; he had an idea where to take her, but it was a good distance away.

"Why do you dislike me, Annaliese?" The question was

there between them almost before he knew it. And yet, once said, he wasn't sorry, not even if he was about to make a fool of himself. "You didn't used to, you know. I remember. When you used to follow Giselle and me around, you were never short a smile for either one of us. What happened?"

She pulled away and stiffened so visibly he thought if he touched her, she would topple back to the pavement, balance lost in her brittleness.

"Don't talk to me about Giselle." She started walking again.

"I'm sorry if it's painful for you. I don't even know how she died, except that they said it was an accident."

He stopped talking when he saw the growing horror on her face. She stared at him with tears pooling in her eyes. Eyes so like Giselle's and yet so different. Wider, more green than blue. A color he'd never seen before.

"How can you speak of her so casually? When *you* are responsible for what she did? for her death?"

The words made no sense, but even so, they sliced him like a knife, hot where he was cold, igniting pain where he'd felt nothing only a moment ago. So deep inside his heart, he feared he'd never dislodge it, never be free of it.

"What are you talking about? I haven't been in contact with Giselle for three years."

"No." Annaliese shook her head. "That's not true. I know it isn't."

He started walking again, faster now, away from her. "I had nothing to do with her death." He threw the words over his shoulder at her because she didn't keep up with his pace. Other deaths, yes. Twenty-three to count with certainty, enough for their faces to haunt him each time he closed his eyes.

"But she died trying to please you."

Annaliese had sprinted to catch up, and her face was close to his, the eyes that had seemed so lovely only a moment ago now accusing and ugly.

"Don't put another death on my head!"

He kept up his pace, not caring if she followed or not. He'd been a fool to want to talk to her alone, a fool to chase after her because of her parents. A fool to start caring.

But she did follow; he heard the patter of her footsteps. When she caught up to him, she grabbed his arm as if she were itching for the fight he was only too eager to give. "Didn't you wonder what became of her? And yet it took you weeks to return after the last bullet at the front was finally shot."

He grabbed her arms then, not caring that she winced from the grip or that she leaned away when he pressed his face close or that for the barest moment she was afraid of him. "I had nothing to do with her death! Not hers."

And then, because she still looked afraid, Christophe was as disgusted with himself as he was with her unfounded accusation. He thrust her away and she stumbled back but did not fall. He wondered if he would even have helped her if she had. He didn't stop long enough to contemplate it; he walked away.

"Tell me the truth, then," she called after him. "Prove it to me."

That made him stop. He faced her, seeing her shiver. Whether it was from the cold or leftover fear of him, he didn't know.

"Come with me."

He led her down the final two blocks he'd meant to take her all the time, to a quiet café where he could eat as he looked at the faces of others who understood. He'd come here during the middle of more than one sleepless night, because the door was never closed to soldiers. Even those like him, no longer wearing a uniform. A man didn't have to wear a uniform to be recognized as a soldier these days; almost everyone his age had served one way or another.

The dining room was three stairs down from the street, rarely busy because so few people had money to spend on café fare, and their menu was limited anyway because of the shortages. Though it was late, the café was well lit and a few people sat in various spots around the room.

"*Ach!* Christophe! Merry Christmas!"

Hearing the familiar voice was the balm he needed just then, this woman who'd lost her only son in the war and was now "Mama" to all the soldiers who came through her restaurant door. She was small, softly rounded, with graying hair and a smile that never stopped at her lips but always reached her eyes, too.

Christophe let Mama hug him the way she always did. With his arm still around her, hoping the tension between him and Annaliese didn't show, he introduced her.

"Come in, both of you; come away from the doorway," Mama said. "I'm glad you're here, Christophe!" She pulled something from her pocket—something that looked like a picture, but he saw that it was a postcard. "You speak English; can you help me to know what this says?"

He took the card from her, welcoming the diversion from the tension he'd carried in with Annaliese. It was a picture of a ship in a harbor—a passenger liner, not the sort of ship the German fleet had produced lately. Christophe flipped it over to look at the writing. "This is in German—"

"Just the name of the ship, please. On the front."

"Great Northern Pacific Steamship Company, Great Northern, between San Francisco and Portland, Oregon . . ." He had no idea if his pronunciation was accurate, but the words were clear enough. "It says it's entering a bridge—the Golden Gate Bridge at San Francisco."

She accepted it back, laying it to her heart. "*Ach*, thank you, Christophe! From my nephew. He says he may join the Americans. Who knows! He may be with them now that they're here, over along the river." Then she tried pronouncing *San Francisco*, but Christophe didn't know if her version was any closer to correct than his. She leaned toward Annaliese and winked. "It's late to be out even on a holiday, but if Christophe is your friend, you've nothing to worry about, *Fräulein*. He's the kind of friend we all need, *ja*? Did you know he speaks English so well?"

Annaliese had the decency to shake her head but stay quiet, for which Christophe was grateful.

He took Annaliese to his favorite table, in a darkened corner where he could see the door but could not easily be seen by anyone else. Then he ordered coffee for both of them.

The forced intermission to their argument had lent them both a renewed calm.

"Now tell me, Annaliese. How could I have had anything to do with Giselle's death when I haven't seen her for years?"

Instead of mirroring his confusion, her face went hard. "I saw the letters, Christophe. From you, telling her how you hated the war, hated that the soldiers were being pushed to fight even when they had nothing left in them. That you would do anything to stop it, and the Russians had a sound idea in shooting every last officer and simply going home." Her eyes narrowed. "That if she had half the courage she possessed in her letters, she would sabotage every munitions plant in Germany to help end the war. Starting with our father's."

"I never wrote such things! Ask someone to destroy a munitions factory? How would that have made a difference, except to hurt the men I fought with?"

For a moment one of her brows dipped, but then she shook her head. "No. I saw the letters. They weren't signed, but they were in an envelope with your name on it. I knew you loved her—you started loving her when we were all still children. I *remember*—"

"Why would I want men to shoot officers? I was a Major; they would have started with me."

Her brows lifted in surprise, but before she could speak, Mama brought their coffee. Two steaming cups, delivered with a smile that might have erased the tension between them if either he or Annaliese had let it. But he didn't, and he could tell she didn't either.

When Mama left their table, Christophe leaned closer and kept his voice low. "I was interested in your sister for a time, years ago. Right up until a month before I left for training in the army, I held a special place for her. Until she told me she loved me only as a friend and didn't want me to go away thinking the wrong way about her."

"But—but I saw all those letters!"

"I wrote three letters, telling her how I was doing. She'd written to me first, and I was obligated to return the favor."

"No, no, no! I saw dozens of them. Dozens!"

"Not from me."

Now she slumped in her chair, rubbing away tears that spilled over her lids but thankfully were not replaced by more. She was shaking her head, mumbling something about the letters and envelopes clearly marked with his name. Then she stopped and looked squarely at him. "Did you really not have a romance with Giselle?"

He shook his head. "Why would I lie? She wasn't interested in me. She said I was too much like a brother to her."

Annaliese charged from her chair. Christophe started after her, but she was at the pay counter, then turning back before he was much more than a step away from their table. She had a pencil in her hand and a blank receipt paper.

"Write something here. Write anything."

"Annaliese—"

"Just do it."

And so he did. He wrote, *For God so loved the world, that he gave his only begotten Son, that whosoever believeth in him should not perish, but have everlasting life.*

She snatched it from him before he'd dotted the last *i*.

Annaliese stared at the handwriting, at the tallness of the capital letters, the lack of flourish in the curve on each *g*. This writing was sizable and bold, letters slightly too close but legible all the same.

And entirely unlike the smaller, somewhat smoother and more pleasing script she remembered all too well from the letters she'd secretly snatched from her sister's room.

The words couldn't have been written by the same hand, unless he was practiced in disguising such details and had reason to suspect what she was trying to find out.

Yet the envelopes had said his name so clearly: Christophe Brecht. Of course, those had been neatly printed rather than written in script, and smudged, stamped, even a bit tattered. She'd assumed what handwriting she'd been able to see had been different only because he'd wanted to have the address written larger for ease of the delivery system.

Was it possible the envelopes had been written by Christophe . . . but the letters written by someone else? "I don't understand. She received dozens of letters, and I thought they were all from you."

"I wrote her about my training and about approval of my commission to Hauptmann and then one last time when I was reassigned from behind the front to the battle lines. She wrote to me, too, and told me how things were at home, how everyone was making do. Three times."

Annaliese put her face in her hands, if only to hold back a scream of purest frustration. All this time, she'd been jealous of her sister over nothing. Over a romance that had never been.

She pulled her hands away from her eyes and stared at Christophe. She'd also hated him for something he'd never done.

"I'm sorry."

"Don't apologize," he said. "Just tell me what this is all about."

How could she tell him what little she knew without revealing her own silly infatuation with him? It was all too embarrassing. And tragic. Giselle was still dead, and there was no way to find out the truth now.

"My sister was corresponding with someone—another soldier I thought was you. I don't know how or why it happened. I saw the letters myself, and the few with envelopes were addressed to her from you."

"Not more than three, then—envelopes, I mean. But the letters you saw weren't the friendly sort I wrote? More . . . romantic?"

Annaliese nodded. "The envelopes had Brecht on the return—and your regiment."

He leaned closer. "I didn't write them, Annaliese."

She tilted her head, studying him and for the first time in a very long time feeling happy. She wanted to trust him about this. "I believe you."

"I know one way we might clear this up," he said. "We could go home. Ask your parents if they know anything about it."

"They don't; I'm sure of that. My sister never showed a single letter to my parents and never spoke of you—or this other man, I mean. I always assumed it was because of what he said in his letters: that you—or he—hated those who kept the supply of guns going. That's why I thought you wanted to join the party, because of what those letters said about my father's business. That if my father and those like him hadn't thought money more important than stopping the war, we might have been done with it a long time ago. But you seemed so different from what was in those letters; I wondered what changed you."

"I joined the party to talk to you about coming home."

"That's all?"

"That's all."

"Then you don't believe any of it? any of what the party stands for?"

He sipped his coffee. "Some. There is a verse in the Bible that tells us to walk in justice, mercy, and humility. Fairness sounds like justice to me, but it's fairness and equality in practice that baffle me. I believe we're all equal in value. I understand that much. But we aren't born equal in a lot of ways: in talent or looks or strength or energy or even in less obvious ways, things I can't put to words."

"Yes, that's exactly why we need to be more noble-minded. If we're all treated equally, it'll be easier to think of each other as equal in value, too."

He nodded. "Yes, that's where mercy and humility make up the difference. Mercy to take care of those who can't take care of themselves, humility to carry through with what mercy calls us to do: giving our time and fruit of our work to others who can't take care of themselves."

"That's right; so you *do* believe . . ."

Now he shook his head. "I've worked with too many men to believe any of that could work. Even if we have equal opportunities, there won't be equal results because none of us has an equal amount of the other things I talked about—energy, talent, effort. It's like other things in the Bible: it shows the way we're supposed to be, but it records a lot of evidence that we can't do it, at least not without God helping us do it. And if the party won't let God help, I don't see how the ideals will ever be put into practice. If the army taught me anything, it was how men behave."

"I'm not sure you should compare civilian life to army life, especially in the last few years."

"Men are men, civilian or soldier. For every talented man who doesn't mind those with less talent, who is even willing to take care of them, there is another who either resents those with less talent or will take advantage of them. And what about those who'll take advantage of things on the other end? those who can work but won't, not if someone else who is stronger can do it more easily for them?" He shook his head. "Men just aren't good at being perfect examples of fairness. Not without God, and even then, men get in the way. It's the way we are. Even when we want to be good, we aren't. Not always."

"But if everyone were part of the same system, even the reluctant ones, eventually we'd all see the wisdom that can only come with fairness. We could all be more consistent if everyone has the same thing in mind every day. No one would be allowed to take advantage of anyone else; every single person would be valued."

"You have more faith in man's goodness than I do, then."

"How can that be, when you're the one who's always done the right thing? Even now, you want to take me home because you think it's right."

"If you want everyone to be valued, then why won't you see your parents? value them enough to see them before they leave?"

She looked away. "That's different."

He laughed. "So it's all right to impose fairness on someone else, just not on yourself? My guess is your parents don't think it's fair that you won't even talk to them."

She looked down at the table between them, eyes on her coffee cup instead of him. She would have liked to put her palms over her ears or just leave, but something made her stay. Made her listen.

"I imagine they're home tonight," he went on. "Alone. Probably thinking of last year or other happier years, when you and Giselle were with them."

But that was enough. She would listen no more. She raised her gaze to meet his. "Stop, Christophe. You don't even know how Giselle died."

"Then tell me. Did she . . . did she kill herself?"

"She might as well have. She wanted to destroy my father's factory but got caught in her own sabotage. The last letter that man sent to her said if she wanted to prove she loved him, she would do something to show she supported him—not only be waiting for him when he left his ranks, but do something to show people like our father how wrong they were to keep supplying the war, to keep it going. So she did. She started a fire in the factory, only it exploded before she had the chance to get out."

When he reached across the table to take her hand in his, she didn't draw away. Instead, she stared at the difference in their hands, feeling his strength and the comfort he offered.

Something stirred in her heart, something too willing to take up residence when it came to Christophe. An old, familiar infatuation, the same thing that made her want to be with him and run shyly away whenever he smiled at her.

"Come with me, Annaliese."

She looked from their hands to his eyes. "Home? I don't think I'm ready for that."

"Then come with me to church tonight. For old times' sake. I know that's how you used to spend every Christmas."

She looked at him, knowing she shouldn't go—shouldn't even want to. Tradition was one thing, but Leo had convinced her of the dangers of an organized church. She should let Christophe go on his way, and she would find her own way home.

But she was caught by his hopeful smile and the eagerness in his eyes. If God struck her down for the hypocrisy of stepping inside a place of worship with a heart like hers, so be it.

16

Annaliese had been to St. Luke's only once, on the twentieth anniversary of its completion. Her mother had asked her and Giselle to accompany her to services that day, just three years ago. So much had changed since then. Her father had stopped attending services first, just as the food shortages worsened. Her mother had told them all that they needed to pray more, but he'd refused. And the prayers Annaliese prayed had gone unanswered.

The tall dome, the brown brick, the colorful stained glass of St. Luke's all remained the same. For a moment she stared at the ornate threshold and imagined her mother nearby, both their arms looped with Giselle's. The three of them together, worshiping a God who loved them.

So long ago.

She followed Christophe inside, wishing he would take her arm. Funny how quickly she'd abandoned her distrust of him. She'd never been able to connect him to the hatred those letters had shown, not even when she'd read them. She thought the war might have changed him, but after seeing him here in Munich, she knew it hadn't. Not really. He was the same Christophe he'd always been.

She glanced at his profile once they took their seats, side by side at the back of the sanctuary, back where those dressed like they were dared to sit. She should have resented the class difference, seeing those more regally dressed taking up the pews in the front the way her family once had.

But instead she thought about Christophe, wondering what he'd been thinking when she'd accused him of having something to do with Giselle's death. Another death, he'd said. Accompanied by desperation, desperate unhappiness. It hadn't been about Giselle at all, but about the idea of being responsible for her death.

Annaliese would ask him about that . . . maybe.

No sooner had the service begun than everything came back to her, the songs she knew so well, the tone of the sermon as it echoed from the dome. She nearly succumbed to the inevitable feeling that came with being part of the crowd instead of the one addressing it, that unity she should have felt by virtue of being here, listening to a man talking about the love of God, the gift of Christmas, the forgiveness one and all could receive.

It was a tempting message, but her heart would soon cool once the memory of a few well-spoken words faded. She knew that.

After the last hymn had been sung, Christophe led her from the church in no particular hurry. Outside, the air felt colder than ever.

Christophe put her arm through his. "See those stars up there, Annaliese?"

She spared only a quick glance. The air might have felt cold a moment ago, but the chill dissipated with his familiar touch, as if her arm belonged where he'd put it. Wrapped around his. She didn't want the evening to end. She looked again at the stars above them. The night was clear, the stars bright, with just a sliver of the moon lighting the way.

"See how some of them are brighter than others?"

She nodded.

"We don't have to look any farther than right up there to see we weren't all created the same. It's not fair, maybe, but it's true. And apart from God, I don't see how the party is going to make all of us equal in each other's eyes. Bright or dull, there's a difference. It's not going to be an easy task to keep the dull ones from wanting what the brightest earn, or the brightest from ordering around the dullest."

She had his gaze now, and her heart thudded in her chest the way it used to do when she was younger and shy. Looking away, she forced her feet to take careful steps and her mind to stay on the subject. "A society is only as good as its care for the least of those within that society. Maybe people will surprise you, Christophe, the bright and the dull. Maybe once we all have a voice, those sinners you're so worried about will see a better way—the fairer way."

His eyes were still on her. So close an added warmth came from him. For a moment she would have liked to lean closer, to have him kiss her in the way she used to dream about.

But instead she increased their pace, making her mind behave, reminding herself she already had one man wanting more from her than she should be willing to give. Besides, this man at her side didn't hold any of the beliefs she had, and she none of his.

More importantly, he didn't believe in the most basic goodness of man if he didn't think fairness attainable.

So she walked silently at his side, wondering why he thought so little of the men God claimed to love.

Christophe opened the door to the house they shared, letting Annaliese go inside first, sorry the evening was over. He watched her walk all the way up the stairs. Something was different, and it had changed the moment she learned he hadn't written those letters.

Still, smiles didn't always mean what he thought them to mean.

So he let her go up to her room without another word. He opened the door to the flat he shared with Leo and Jurgen— to see Jurgen bent over the table, a glass of wine next to him, papers in front of him.

Now here was a man who knew how to pique the interest of a woman. Christophe had seen it happen.

Jurgen lifted his glass when Christophe approached. "Welcome home."

Christophe nodded and shook off his coat, eager for his own room.

"She went with you? to your church?"

Christophe had been so close to the door to his room that Jurgen had said the words to his back. He stopped. "Yes, she did."

"You'd do well to leave her alone, Christophe. She's young and easily misled. Church will only confuse her, when she left all of that behind."

He faced Jurgen. "I think she has a strong enough mind to decide for herself."

Jurgen stood, taking his wineglass and approaching Christophe. "I wonder if you know that Annaliese and I . . . have a rather close bond? Both politically and personally?"

"Yes, I've seen your interest in her."

"And hers in me?"

Christophe regarded the other man. If he admitted he'd noted Annaliese's interest in him, it would be as much as admitting Jurgen had sole rights to her affection. On the platform the two of them had *something* special between them, but Christophe wasn't at all sure the connection extended beyond political ties. He'd stopped believing that the night he'd taken Annaliese from the beer hall. Even if her fear had been slight, it had been there all the same. Christophe was sure of it.

"I've known her a long time," Christophe said carefully. "I can see why you might seem a hero to her."

A quick, almost-unnoticeable twitch appeared in the corner of Jurgen's mouth. "And why is that?"

"Because you're the opposite of what her father is. And right now at least, she wants nothing to do with him."

Jurgen smiled, so if there was any hint of annoyance around his mouth, it was banished. "Let me assure you, what Annaliese feels for me has nothing to do with her father."

Christophe shrugged again, then turned back to his room. "As you say."

"Just one moment, Christophe. I know it's late. I wanted to ask you something about the men you're training. They're young, but Leo says they're loyal. Do you think so too?"

A chill—leftover from the outside air?—skidded along Christophe's shoulders. He was used to training men and had rarely doubted their commitment to the army when fighting in France. But this was different. All Jurgen and Leo wanted from those who'd pledged their guns was to defend them in the dangerous streets of the city. What was there to worry about? Defense came naturally; all Christophe did was train them in the best way to do that.

"None have given me any reason to doubt them."

Jurgen was silent then. With one last glance behind him, Christophe opened the door to his room. Even if he didn't doubt the men—or at least their abilities to defend themselves—it looked as though Jurgen wasn't so easily convinced.

17

Annaliese held the collar of her coat closed against the cold January air, but she barely felt the wind. How could she, leading a group of women to the polling booth? Thoughts of voting spread warmth through her veins.

She'd invited women all over Munich to meet her on the street corner this morning, to join together as they dropped their ballots into the boxes. She'd heard them before seeing them, laughter and chatter from around the corner, cheers when some caught sight of her as if she alone had arranged for them to have a vote.

She'd laughed, then with a song of unity led the way.

Christophe stood on the street just outside one of the polling centers, rifle in hand. Not that he—or any of his men—intended to use a weapon. It was enough of a reminder that peace would be kept, at any price. Especially in this neighborhood, where Leo and Jurgen knew their vote was strongest.

He watched Annaliese lead the women to the municipal

building, singing and smiling all the way. Her smile brought one to him, but she never looked his way.

He'd already cast his own vote. Annaliese and Jurgen and everyone around them had said a vote for anyone but Eisner was a vote for the old regime. No more government of lies, as some of the signs read. But while Christophe certainly wanted change, he hadn't been convinced the new Socialist government was the best choice.

A decision he would keep to himself if he could.

Like many other soldiers, Christophe patrolled the streets and was relieved at the end of the day when he'd never had to issue a single bullet from his gun.

Annaliese spent the day on her own, visiting with women's groups, celebrating their vote . . . because surely that *had* been a triumph.

But what was already being said about the election results made her anything except celebratory now.

It was past midnight, but she couldn't go home . . . not yet. The party office was unlit and morosely quiet. Upon entering, she realized it wasn't empty, though. She hadn't been the only one drawn back to the center of their work. She heard low voices from the shadows in the corner.

For the moment, all she could do was stumble to a chair and slip out of her coat, all the strength in her limbs gone. Perhaps she should have gone back to her flat, after all, but she was too tired to make the six-block walk. She'd expected to be alone, to adjust to the election results in privacy, where she could let her tears flow without check.

She just needed time to rest; then she would be off. She didn't even need to speak to anyone . . . or see the loss reflected on another's face. Somehow, at least for now, she knew company wouldn't help.

How could she have been so fooled? How could all of them have been so wrong? Jurgen? Eisner? Leo?

The crowds had done it; they'd convinced her, convinced all of them that their support would flow into the ballot boxes.

But it hadn't.

Pitiful—that's what it was. The majority of Bavarian votes had been won by the bourgeoisie. Her father's capitalist party. They had voted Eisner out, and even though a respectable number of votes had been cast in favor of the softer form of Socialism, it was the same form of Socialism that had sold them out four years earlier by approving the war. How had *they* won more votes than Eisner?

With the capitalists in power there would be no atonement from people like her father now. Had everything Eisner stood for, everything she and Jurgen had worked for, been for nothing? Hopes of spending the rest of her life in a future full of solutions were already evaporating.

Eyes adjusted to the dimness, she became aware of those around Leo's desk—Jurgen, Huey, Ivo, Leo himself. They were whispering as if at a funeral.

She looked around for Christophe, but he was nowhere to be found. Did he even know? Had he heard how absolutely they'd lost?

"They didn't see it," she said, and from the corner of her eye she saw Jurgen, at least, look her way.

"Who?"

"Them." She pointed with her nose out the door, toward

the street. "That even the bread we provided was evidence of how it could work."

"They'll see," Jurgen said, his tone an odd mix of gentleness and steel.

"What's to become of the councils?" she called to Leo.

"They'll go on as before. They were elected by consensus; nothing in this election can say otherwise."

"But without the support of the assembly . . ."

Leo exchanged a glance with Jurgen that seemed to say more than words.

"Are you planning something?" she asked, first sitting up straighter and then, because they looked so very serious, standing and joining them at the table where they sat. "What were you whispering about just now?"

Jurgen took one of her hands, stroking the top of it. "It's been a long day, *mein Herz*. Why don't you let Ivo take you home? We'll fill you in on whatever decisions are made."

"What kind of decisions are you considering?"

He stood and put his arm around her as he led her to where she'd discarded her coat. He picked it up, inviting her to put it on. "Not to worry. We still have the same hopes. The election has done nothing to our resolve. The people will be heard."

"I think I'd like to stay—"

But Jurgen was already shaking his head. "You're tired, Anya. And discouraged. Let us mull over the options. Ivo?"

He was there in a moment, leading the way out the door to the truck.

Instead of getting in the back, she took the seat beside him in the front. "What are they talking about, Ivo? Do you know?"

He shrugged. "Only what you would expect. Surprised at the numbers."

"It means we need to work harder to spread our message," she said. "We can hold more rallies . . ."

"But there won't be another election for some time now." He looked at the street instead of her. "And they say the councils are being dissolved in the rest of Germany."

"The important thing is to make sure the councils *here* stay in place."

Ivo nodded, then sighed. "Maybe the Communists were right about boycotting the election. It was too soon. They want the councils too, you know."

She nodded, although the very word—*Communism*—struck fear in her. Munich might not have easy access to the news from around the world, but everyone knew what started in Russia in 1917. A bloodbath, and in the name of some of the same things she believed in. But no one wanted that here, not in Germany.

18

Christophe had left open the door to the front hall so he wouldn't miss the sound of someone coming in. The lightness of the step told him it was Annaliese. Exactly whom he'd been waiting for.

He reached the threshold of his doorway just as she put a hand on the rail and a foot on the first step up to her room.

"Have you heard?" she asked.

She looked so forlorn that he wished he could change the truth, make it somehow different in spite of the way he'd voted. Assure her all the work she'd done in the past few months hadn't been for nothing. His vote wouldn't have helped anyway, and for that he was grateful. It absolved him of any guilt over the disappointment on her face now.

He nodded. "Just some early results. Enough to know how it was heading."

She sank onto the stair instead of going up. "How could we have been so wrong? All of us?" She glanced at him when he stood in front of her, and for a moment he thought a flicker of annoyance outweighed her sadness. "I shouldn't include you, I suppose. Your heart was never really with us, was it? You probably didn't even vote with us."

He took a seat beside her. "Your vision is good. To take care of everyone, stop the exploitation. I believed in that. And the councils are a good idea too, at least so the National Assembly doesn't have all the power in one place. And Eisner . . . he's a good man."

"But you didn't vote with us, did you?"

He shook his head; no sense denying it.

She only looked away. "I've heard the free corps are disbanding the councils in other places around Germany. By force."

He'd heard that too. One of the reasons the men had to know how to defend themselves. Supporters of the councils would be fair game if the free corps came here to Munich.

"What will you do now, Annaliese? Now that the election is over, I mean?"

She rested her forehead in her palms, closing her eyes against tears. "I . . . I should say I have more work ahead of me. The election should teach me that much, shouldn't it?"

Christophe put an arm around her shoulders. He hadn't let himself near her in the three weeks since Christmas. Not that avoiding her had been difficult, since she seemed to be doing the same. It was as if that night, those moments when he'd sensed sincerity behind her smile—the same smile he remembered from long ago—had been the beginning and the end of anything growing between them.

They'd been right to be cautious, he'd decided. Everything around them reminded him how little they had in common.

But seeing her now made all those cautions disappear.

"I'm sorry, Annaliese."

Annaliese sagged against him, her head on his chest. A few tears seeped past her closed lids, and she raised a hand to wipe them away. She shouldn't let herself take any comfort from him. She should rail against him for not voting with her, call him a traitor to the party. Tell Jurgen to send him away, tell Leo not to let him use the extra room.

But then he'd never claimed to be loyal to the party, had he? He'd allowed his name on the roster that day but had been honest enough as to why: he'd been tracking her down for her parents. He'd taken a job and he did it well, but even that had been done for reasons she'd never been entirely certain about.

"What will you do now, Christophe?"

"I'll continue what I've been doing. The men still need training, so I'll stay as long as I'm welcome—and as long as defense is the goal. If that changes, I'll try finding a job, earning a living."

"Back in Braedon or here in Munich?"

"Braedon, I suppose."

So he would leave Munich, just that easily? Maybe she'd been wrong to think he might care for her, in spite of how badly she'd treated him when she thought him responsible for what Giselle had done. Had she been wrong to think he'd taken that job to train Jurgen's men because of her? Her parents had sent him to find her, but he hadn't needed to stay nearby once she refused to see them. Yet he had stayed, and she'd been silly enough to let herself think it was because he had come to care for her. Somehow she'd hoped whatever differences they'd had would fade. Once the election was won and he saw how successful their plans for the future were, he might have come around to her way of thinking. . . .

"I have a house waiting for me back home. So do you."

She stiffened, leaning away from him now, closer to the wall. "My sister died because she hated the way the war changed my father. Everything I believe in now is rooted in trying to make up for that. Do you think I would just toss it all away without another thought? run home to Braedon, even if my parents aren't there?"

"Hasn't the war ruined enough lives without letting it destroy the rest of your life, too?"

"How can you say that? My life isn't ruined by my work. It's better for it. All we have is what we do here and now, Christophe, and I'm doing my best to make the future better."

"Life is important; I know that. What we do here matters. But this life isn't all there is."

She shrugged, unwilling to argue about his faith.

"Is politics really so important to you?" he asked. "Or are you going to spend the rest of your life trying to make up for what others think your father did wrong?"

She stood, away from his words. She didn't need to listen to his arguments. Not now. Not ever.

But Christophe stood too, and he didn't stop talking. "You may not want to hear this, but God can't help but love you. Not for what you're trying to do, not for what you're trying to fix. Just you. And He loves your father, too."

A corner of her mouth twisted downward. "You stand here more passionate about God loving my family than about anything we might agree to believe in for the future—the here-and-now future, the future of Germany."

"Because the future—any future, here on earth or in heaven—is only as important as the people who are in it. Your family wants you in theirs. It's why I've stayed here in Munich so long, Annaliese: because your parents are so concerned for you, I knew they would want me to be sure you're safe. Don't you see? They care for you as much as any parents care for their child."

Her pulse had picked up speed with their argument but now it seemed to stop altogether. What had he said? He'd stayed in Munich, stayed to watch over her . . . because of her parents? Only because of that?

She shouldn't be surprised. His vote had proved how little he cared for her or her politics. Perhaps no matter how long she waited, their differences would never fade.

"I hope they compensated you for your time, then." The words sounded distant, so cold and formal it didn't sound like her voice. "After all, if they know how to do anything, it's how to get the best price for someone's time."

Christophe's brows met, then rose, obvious confusion all over his handsome face. "You're angry? How can you be angry that your parents cared enough to want to know you're safe? They're worried."

"Then why don't you run home and tell them all about how I'm doing? And don't come back!"

She would have turned from him, run for the safety and privacy of her own room, but Christophe stood in the way. He caught her wrist and kept her in place. She tried pulling away, but he held her firm, shaking his head and holding up his free hand like a policeman stopping traffic.

"Wait. Just wait. You can't run off without explaining to me what's upset you so much. Are you angry with me . . . or your parents? Or—" his brows dipped further—"because of the way I voted?"

She almost laughed; the idea that he might have cared for her was so absurd now. Except when his grip around her wrist loosened and the hand he'd held up fell gently to the side of her face, to caress her cheek in a way she'd only dreamed of him doing.

Yes, she'd dreamed of him holding her, kissing her, in spite of her cautions, in spite of his lack of interest in her . . . but it was all so hopeless now. Nothing was real about him, nothing genuinely his idea. He was nothing more than a messenger of her parents'.

"Don't let me trouble you any further," she said, then drew away from his hold and ran up the stairs to the privacy she'd longed for since the first awful rumors had reached her of the election results.

Christophe heard the door to Annaliese's flat close with a thud. What had he said that was so wrong? He shouldn't have admitted how he'd voted. But she hadn't been surprised; he was sure of that. She'd already guessed as much.

She'd only become angry when he told her how much her parents wanted her safe, proving they loved her. How was that worthy of anger?

He started to take another step up, demand she explain to him exactly what had annoyed her. If it was his vote, he could explain why he couldn't have voted for her party. Not when everything they talked about looked only to the future, to an illusion built on the belief that men could be better than they were . . . but without God's help. He'd voted for the party he thought looked at the present, without forgetting the past or ignoring the limits of every man and woman around them.

He leaned on the hallway wall, staring at her closed door. Did they agree on *anything*? He'd tried being reasonable about convincing her to see her parents. He'd tried patience. He'd tried taking her to church because he knew faith was important to Annaliese's mother, at least, and might have been to Annaliese herself once. But so far, he certainly hadn't succeeded in uncovering anything they shared.

He couldn't charm her into agreeing with the things he believed the way Jurgen did. But did she really agree with Jurgen on so many things, or had she been persuaded by him so Giselle's death might mean something?

If that was so, Annaliese was forgetting something else Giselle had once believed, at least when Christophe knew her. She'd believed in God.

And so had Annaliese, once. He wasn't foolish enough to believe he could persuade her to change her focus from politics to God. But God could. If she could ever find the passion for God that she had for Socialism, she would be unstoppable. What a force she would be then, one no one could resist— least of all Christophe himself.

He should go up there, ask to speak to her. But what would he say? He wanted to see her drawn back to God, not push her farther away.

Christophe turned to Jurgen's flat. He needed to find his Bible. Prayer always came easier when he opened that book, and asking God to touch Annaliese's heart was the only thing Christophe knew that might work.

19

Annaliese left through the front door, without visiting in the kitchen. It was early, just after sunrise, but she had too much on her mind to waste time sleeping. One night of defeat had been enough; the only way she would be able to prove the last few months had been worthwhile was to keep fighting. She would prove to herself—and Christophe—that her work made a difference.

She didn't bother to find Jurgen. He had his own challenges, and she wouldn't divert his attention. Once he was ready to receive her help—and she had no doubt he would seek it—she intended having something to offer. He'd said there would be a time for a Women's Council, and she knew such a thing wouldn't happen spontaneously. It needed a foundation, direction. Inspiration.

The party office was quiet. She'd half feared Jurgen would still be there, planning how best to protect the People's Council. The council would certainly lose a measure of its power once the results of the election took hold, even if they followed Leo's suggestion and refused to disband.

Which was why the rally for popular support must continue, and that was exactly what Annaliese intended. Let her efforts match the ones they put forth to reach the men of Munich. She still had a voice and could certainly reach more women than she had in the few short months she'd been working for the party.

She found her way to the typewriter; her job started here. She would stir the hearts of women until they were a voice no one could ignore.

Christophe left as usual in the morning, shortly after dawn. He stopped in the kitchen and went out through the back door, heading to the warehouse.

The loss of the election might have changed the role Eisner played in Germany's future, but if the councils insisted on remaining in place, they would need protection. And that protection was still the job of every man Christophe trained.

The warehouse, however, was oddly quiet when he entered. Most of the men were still on their cots amid a distinct odor of stale beer—and worse.

If Christophe had carried a whistle, he would have used it.

"Get up!" he yelled. "This is not a holiday."

Popoff was nearest the door, and he lurched to attention like many of the young soldiers Christophe had worked with in the army. But when he stood, he clutched his head as if afraid without holding it together, it would explode.

"It's over," Popoff said, half his face covered with his arms. "We lost."

"So you think the streets will be quiet from now on?" Christophe said, keeping his voice loud enough to rouse the rest of those still grumbling from their bunks. "Haven't you heard the council is still in place? Now get up! All of you!"

Ivo, who Christophe knew rarely stayed in the warehouse since his family lived not far, approached him, fully dressed and armed.

"I wasn't sure you would be here, or I would have gotten them up myself."

"Do you know where the others are? Leo and Jurgen? They weren't at the flat at all last night."

"They went to meet with a man named Leviné."

The name meant nothing to Christophe, though he suspected by the look on Ivo's face that it should ignite some kind of reaction.

"He's on the council with Jurgen." Ivo had lowered his voice considerably, lending secrecy to whatever he had to say, tinged with a bit of tension. "He's from Berlin—from the Communists. Leviné has wanted to grow the Communist party right here in Munich ever since he came."

Christophe had no trouble keeping his gaze steady on the other man. He wasn't sure what to think just yet, though a warning did flare in his gut.

But his outward calm only seemed to increase Ivo's agitation. "Haven't you heard what the Reds are doing in Russia?" Ivo glanced over his shoulder because a few of the men, assembling, stopped what they were doing as if to listen in. "It's another French revolution! They might not be using the guillotine, but they're still killing people."

"That doesn't mean it'll happen here. Especially with the numbers from this election. If there isn't enough interest in leftist Socialism, then there won't be enough in Communism."

"I don't think you understand, Christophe." Ivo held up

his gun. "It's the ones with the weapons who win, not the ones with the numbers."

"Are they talking about another revolution? Is Jurgen?"

Ivo nodded.

Another revolution . . . and with these men, right here.

"How soon?"

Ivo shrugged. "They're waiting for news from other parts of Europe. Hungary, for one. The Communists are talking about revolution there, too."

Christophe wished he hadn't come to the warehouse, wished he'd stayed behind and seen Annaliese. If there was ever a time to whisk her away—even against her will—that time might be now.

He knew one thing: if Jurgen threw his support to the Communists, there would no longer be a place for Christophe here. He wouldn't train men to kill others; he'd done more than enough of that in the last four years.

Christophe eyed the men nearby, all of whom seemed to be moving in slow motion. He barked at them to prepare for training even as silent doubts flared.

He turned back to Ivo. "What about you? Do you want to be a Communist?"

Ivo looked down, perhaps seeing, at least peripherally, his marred hands, hands Christophe knew Ivo himself found ugly because he often tried hiding them. He was still strong, though. And he could still fire a gun. Barely.

"I don't know. Leo says the Communists want to take care of everyone, even people like me. I don't want to be taken care of like a boy, having a government or a monarch or a general telling me what to do. But . . ."

Christophe wanted to snatch the gun from Ivo's hand if he

was considering using it for the same cause that stirred up all the violence he'd heard about in Russia. "Someone else taking care of us comes with rules. Less freedom. Isn't freedom what we fought for?"

"But what choice will I have?"

"Do you think they'll really take care of you, Ivo? or just control you?"

"I know I don't want to watch people go hungry anymore. Do you? It's time to start again, spread things evenly."

That could have been a line from one of the speeches Annaliese gave. Such lofty ideas, this notion of sharing and fairness. Christophe was willing to do just that, and he was sure God would want that too. There was nothing more satisfying than helping someone who needed it. But he just wasn't sure everyone could always be as helpful as Ivo might hope. Christophe had always imagined God letting people take turns at generosity, inspiring each within their own means. How could men, by themselves, keep their generosity going for very long if they were told by men how to share and then forced by men to do it? If sharing didn't come out of the heart, there was bound to be trouble.

Christophe's own gun was slung over his shoulder; he knew he would have to follow through with the day's training. The men were finally assembling, waiting for him. But what was he training them for? Perhaps not to defend the council against Berlin's army that wanted to do away with them, but maybe soon to fight for a new idea. Socialism to its extreme: Communism.

Christophe shifted his gun to one hand, preparing to meet the men for drills.

But Ivo took a step closer. "You'd best talk to her," he whispered.

"Talk to . . . Annaliese?"

Ivo nodded. "She shouldn't stay here. Not now."

"Why do you say that?"

"Because they won't have use for her anymore. The Communists have no concern for elections, and Jurgen only wanted her this long to bring in the women's vote."

"But she believes the way they do—"

Ivo was already shaking his head. "Are you as naive as she is? They've never invited her into their inner circle. They've never asked her what her opinion is on anything. They tell her there will be a Women's Council alongside the workers and the soldiers and the peasants, but they don't have any plans to put one in place. She has no voice because they don't listen to her. That will likely get worse, not better. I know you want to take her, so I tell you it's a good idea."

Christophe watched Ivo leave, convinced the man was right . . . but entirely uncertain how to carry out such advice.

20

Annaliese was nearly ready. After a week of planning, writing, and visiting with some of the women she'd met at rallies or in the factories, she had honed what she wanted to say and was ready to print the first of her pamphlets. She rubbed the back of her neck, feeling a headache coming on. She hadn't slept much in the last few days, but the extra work had been worth it.

Looking down at the pages in her hands, she couldn't help feeling a hint of pride. In front of her were words aimed directly at the women of Munich, appealing to their natural sense of nurture, inspiring a willingness to do what was best for all, even if it meant sacrificing old ideas.

She also aimed to protect the ideals Eisner had stood for—without mentioning his name. She emphasized the hope for a Women's Council, one that would take into consideration things like new educational routes and the protection of women, new opportunities for work with a goal to be paid more fairly, and the creation of opportunities in a political world never accessible before.

Annaliese left the party office—a place that had been nearly empty during the recent days she'd spent there, even opting to sleep there on occasion. Jurgen and Leo had gone to Berlin, although neither had invited her along or even said good-bye. She assumed they went in support of the People's Council here in Munich—and councils elsewhere—to make sure no soldiers were sent to disband them now that popular support for Eisner, so connected to such councils, fell short in the election.

Without Jurgen and Leo home, she preferred avoiding the house altogether. Huey had gone with Jurgen and Leo, leaving only Bertita . . . and Christophe. Annaliese wanted nothing to do with him, knowing he thought so little of the work she'd done. Seeing him only reminded her how senseless her stubborn infatuation with him was.

She should have left the party office earlier in the day but had wanted to go through the text of the pamphlet one more time before taking it to the printer at the warehouse. It was late afternoon already, and the streets were full. She avoided lingering or even looking around very much, even when shouts or the screech of wheels on the brick pavement drew attention.

Confirmation was everywhere that even with the election behind them, Munich still wasn't working. Trash filled alleyways; people with dour faces stared at her while waiting in line for food or for jobs. She refused to allow the slightest eye contact. Yesterday a fight had broken out in front of the party office between two people who'd simply passed each other on the sidewalk. She'd watched, but from well inside, afraid they would crash through the windows.

All of it made her nearly want to leave the city, but only in moments of cowardice. She couldn't give up now. She wouldn't.

Annaliese kept her pace brisk and reached the warehouse

quickly for such a long walk. It was a place she'd rarely visited since joining the party. There had never been a reason to go there, and Jurgen had been careful to steer her away since it was reserved for men. But the printing press was here, the press he used freely to produce flyers that filled the palms of Bavarians, even if they did sometimes litter the streets of Munich.

Spoiled air and male voices greeted her—not a single sound aimed at her, though, for which she was grateful. She knew only that the press was tucked away in a corner somewhere, a place Leo had said was out of the way. It was too large to take up space in the party office, so she imagined it would be easy to find.

"Annaliese!"

Christophe's voice made her heart jump to her throat. She stopped, seeing him trot over to her.

"What are you doing here?"

Thankfully, he'd asked the question with what sounded like interest rather than scolding, even if he would likely agree with Jurgen that this was no place for her. "I'm here to use the printer. Do you know where it is?"

He nodded and directed her attention to a corner at the far end of the warehouse. "But no one is here to run it, and I don't think there is any paper. What do you want printed?"

She held up the small stack of papers she had painstakingly typed and retyped, until she thought it her best effort of expression. "I want a pamphlet made of this, for the women of Munich."

His brows rose and he reached for it. "May I see it?"

She hesitated but quickly realized how silly it would be to keep something to herself that she hoped to spread everywhere. She handed it to him.

"'Women of Munich . . . ,'" he read her title aloud, then looked at her with a smile. "So this is how you've spent your time lately. I wondered."

She reached for the papers again. "I know you don't believe the things I do, Christophe, but—"

He pulled the pages closer, still reading, but spared her a glance. "I don't believe some of the things Jurgen believes, but maybe I do believe some of the things you've written about here. Encouraging women to be involved in voting and society is something we agree on. Maybe there is more."

"This is something I need to do, Christophe."

He nodded, then looked over his shoulder as if to see if anyone had noticed them talking. For the first time since entering, Annaliese took a sweeping glance of the warehouse. *Dirty* was the only word to describe it, but she'd guessed that from the stale smell upon entering, a smell that even now compounded her headache from overworking and too little sleep. There were a couple dozen men around, all armed, many of whom stared in her direction. She suddenly realized how grateful she was not to have had to come here before.

Perhaps Christophe guessed at her discomfort, because when she let her gaze return to him, she saw him studying her. "If you leave this with me," he said, "I'll make sure it gets printed."

She wanted to smile but under so many eyes couldn't make the effort. She knew she would have to trust him, finding to her surprise that she did. Entirely. "Thank you." Then she turned back to the door.

"Will you be at the house for supper?" he asked.

"No." She was meeting with a widow friend who might be able to help her with funds, perhaps enough to cover the paper upon which she hoped to print her pamphlets. But Christophe didn't need to know that. Trusting him was one thing; spending time with him and encouraging feelings her heart would be safer to ignore were other matters altogether.

Christophe watched her go, wishing she were happier about his help. If she'd only let him, they might find something they could work on together. But he could start with completing the task she'd allowed him to do.

"Ivo!"

He wasn't sure where the man was, but Ivo would know where to find the printer—who hadn't been seen since the election, when Jurgen's press became little more than a dust collector.

There were few places not clearly seen in the openness of the warehouse, and Christophe spotted Ivo near the firing tunnel. Something Ivo kept in good repair, replacing mattresses and sandbags whenever necessary.

"Annaliese wants this printed," Christophe said. "Do you know where the man is, the one who worked Jurgen's printing press?"

Ivo nodded, but with a frown. "I saw him this morning. He stopped in to check on the press, then said he was going to purchase paper."

"Good! He'll have supplies for this, then."

Ivo was shaking his head now. "He received something from Jurgen last night. A flyer."

"Did you see it? What does it say?"

"I haven't read it, but I talked to Popoff—he brought it

from Jurgen and gave it right to the printer. Popoff said Jurgen has been with Leviné this whole time, ever since the election. I think they're expecting Jurgen to switch to Leviné's side on the council."

"What's the hurry?"

"Waiting for Eisner to resign is long enough, out of respect for him."

"So it's happened, then? Jurgen has joined the Communists?"

Ivo lifted his shoulders. "I don't know. I only know the paper that's bought today will go for Jurgen's flyer—not whatever Annaliese brought you."

Christophe's gaze wandered to the door, where Annaliese had disappeared. If she knew Jurgen was fraternizing with Communists, would she remain loyal to him? Would it even make a difference?

Well past dark, Annaliese trudged up the steps to the town house, counting each one beneath her tired feet. She couldn't remember ever being so exhausted, and the cot in the back of the party office offered little comfort, which was why she'd left it. She longed for a real bed, with plenty of covers against the late-winter air. Such a bed was only fifteen stairs away.

Halfway up, she heard a door opening. Not Bertita's, which was likely to happen at any time of day or night, but Jurgen's. She turned, half-expecting to see him there despite the near-midnight hour. Finally, back from Berlin.

But it was Christophe, and her weary heart made an unruly attempt to dance despite her fatigue.

"You're working harder without Jurgen here than you did when he and Leo gave the orders."

She stopped on the steps, grateful for the rest. "Did you give my content to the printer?"

He nodded. "But he has another job keeping him busy for a couple of days. He said he would get to it as soon as he could."

"What other job?"

"Something from Jurgen."

She waited for her heart to do something at the prospect of Jurgen's return. Nothing. "Is he back?"

"Not yet, but from the printing order, I assume it'll be soon."

"Why? What does it say?"

"Much of what he's said before. About fairness. But . . ."

She wished she weren't so eager to hear what Christophe had to say. She was tired; she should go to bed and tell him she would speak to him in the morning. But the look on his face, so somber, held a warning she couldn't ignore.

He folded his arms on his chest. "The flyers aren't supposed to be distributed to the public until after Eisner's official resignation."

She was confused. "So why couldn't the printer do my pamphlet first?"

"Because Jurgen wanted some of the flyers sent to a few people in the labor unions. It's his way of seeing what kind of support he'll have . . . for a different approach at change."

"Such as?"

"He's talking about public ownership, Annaliese. Starting with the factories. Not with a hope of doing away with private property *someday*, when everyone accepts the idea of fair sharing. It looks like he wants it now."

She sank to the stair beneath her, following the downward movement of her heart. "You're talking about a takeover, aren't you? a revolution—a Communist one?"

More than anything, she wanted Christophe to deny it, to assure her Jurgen hadn't left his ideals of society gradually accepting an equally shared partnership. That was the only way toward a better society, when people chose it at the ballot box. With a bit of hope, that could happen. Someday. Hadn't Jurgen himself said so?

To demand private property become public . . . that was something else altogether. Had he entirely abandoned the value of elections?

"Are you certain? certain he's talking about switching to such measures?"

Christophe didn't answer for what seemed like forever. He approached her, going to the bottom stair but stopping there so their eyes were level. "Do you know a man by the name of Leviné?"

The name was answer enough. Annaliese dropped her gaze, away from Christophe's sympathetic stare. She nodded slowly. Then she pulled herself to a stand and counted the rest of the steps to her room. Why hadn't she seen it? Leviné was from Berlin, where Jurgen was now.

Maybe that was the very reason Jurgen had gone there. To associate with those who'd sent Leviné to Munich.

Communists.

21

Annaliese sneezed yet again, wiped at her nose, then pushed another pamphlet into an envelope. For the past week, she'd worked mostly from here in her room, ignoring the weight to her spirit that had nothing to do with the sniffles filling her head. She couldn't stop asking herself the same question she'd been asking since talking to Christophe that night on the steps. Would everything she was doing be for nothing? She was willing to work, to wait for the next election, but knew she couldn't push the Socialist cause by herself. If Jurgen had gone farther than that, if he'd grown impatient for the fruits of Socialism to spread—if he'd given it up for Communism— then she was alone. Not even Christophe would help her. He served God, and she knew there was little room for Him in Socialism, and none at all in Communism.

It was midafternoon, and on her desk was a stack of letters she'd hoped to distribute today . . . if she could summon the energy. Her head throbbed not just with pressure building toward another sneeze but with questions. Would women really listen to her and to her alone? Were they ready to put the past behind them, now that so many of them had a taste of working outside the home? Or would everything go back to the way it was before the war, when women were bound to the home, without a choice? If there was a God—One as loving as Christophe wanted her to believe—surely He didn't mean to give women other gifts beside childbearing and expect them not to be used? Women could be a formidable force for the good of society if they were given the independence to do so.

Such thoughts made her wonder about her own choices. Here she was, living in a flat that wasn't her own. Dependent on the charity of men. How was that taking care of herself? While she'd been working for the cause of Socialism, responsible for bringing in a hefty portion of donations, she'd felt useful. But now . . . how could she stay here, with Jurgen, if he'd abandoned what she thought he'd believed?

Another sneeze, another tight swallow. Her throat felt as if a knife were lodged inside.

"Annaliese, are you there?"

Jurgen's voice! She knew he would return sooner or later, but now that the moment was here, she found herself unprepared after all.

Annaliese crumpled yet another handkerchief, glancing at the messy room. She'd taken two naps today and hadn't bothered to set the covers right. Ever since the thickness in her head had loosened to a steady leak through her eyes and nose, she'd gone through one handkerchief after another. She feared she looked even worse than she felt.

"Yes, I'm here. Just a moment."

She rose from her chair, smoothed a stray strand of hair behind one ear, slipped her shoes on, and tucked her blouse into her skirt before opening the door.

Jurgen stood smiling like an eager suitor. He half-reached

for an embrace before leaning back, his brows fallen and his smile gone. "You're sick?"

Holding a handkerchief to her nose, she nodded, only slightly offended by the aversion on his face. Perhaps it was her imagination, but he seemed to step back, farther away from her. "Yes, a little."

"I've heard nothing but how hard you've been working for the people's cause. Christophe told me at the warehouse that you haven't left your room in days."

"That's true." She sniffed. "I've been busy. But I'm glad you're back."

His smile returned with full charm. "Are you, Anya?"

"There are rumors going around that when Eisner resigns in a couple of days, you'll announce your support for Leviné."

He tsked. "And here I thought for a moment you missed *me*, not my politics."

"Is it true?"

He shook his head. "None of this should worry you, Anya, especially when you need rest. Nothing has changed. I still want what is best for everyone." He held out a piece of paper she hadn't noticed in his hand. "Maybe this will make you feel better."

"What is it?" She reached for it eagerly, wondering if it would confirm or deny the things Christophe had warned her about. "News of some kind?"

He shook his head. "No. I wrote it for you while I was away." He looked around, past her, perhaps seeing the rumpled bed, the used handkerchiefs. "I was going to read it to you, to prove you're never far from my thoughts . . . but I'll wait until you're feeling better."

Then he turned on his heel, whispered good-afternoon over his shoulder, and took the stairs down to his own flat.

Annaliese closed the door, reading the words on the page over the handkerchief at her nose. She saw instantly it was a poem and that the title was nothing other than her name—or the shortened version of it. *Anya.*

She read it through once, then again, barely believing he could have been thinking of her when he wrote the words. Of springtime and hope and beauty, of energy and the inexplicable power of love—irresistible and mysterious, impossible to deny.

Not a hint of Communism.

It was simply a poem, words Jurgen had conjured for her. Words, both spoken and written, were his greatest gift. And here were some meant only for her. Beautiful words.

She wiped away the moisture from her eyes, suddenly unsure if it was the words on the page or the sickness in her head that dampened her handkerchief this time.

She set the poem on her desk along with the letters. Surely someone who wrote such words couldn't join a group as violent as the Communists she feared. Part of her wanted to follow him down the stairs, to make sure nothing had changed, the way he said.

But she stayed in her room, knowing that he didn't want to be around her while she felt so ill. It was just as well—she needed more rest.

So she went back to bed, more eager than ever to be healthy again. She needed to know where her future efforts would be best spent.

Annaliese shaded her eyes from the sun shining directly on her face. She'd forgotten to close the window coverings the night before. Forgotten to change from her skirt and blouse and into her nightdress. The sun almost made it look like spring outside, but that was still weeks away. The chill in her room reminded her that even such bright rays as these did little to cut winter's touch.

She turned at the sound of a gentle tap at her door. Maybe it was Jurgen, to see how she was feeling this morning. "Yes?"

"Are you still sleeping?"

Christophe's voice made her heart react in its usual, fluttery way, even though she wished otherwise. "I'm awake."

She rose too quickly and her head throbbed. Slipping a shawl around her shoulders to cover at least some of the wrinkles in her blouse, Annaliese opened the door. There stood Christophe, snug in a sweater of his own, holding out a steaming mug and a plate of toasted bread.

"You weren't at breakfast this morning, and Bertita told me you weren't at dinner, either. I wasn't here. Are you sick or just back to work?"

Seeing Christophe so neat and fresh, smiling so warmly, made her aware of her own unkemptness. Smoothing down what was sure to be a nest of hair atop her head, she reached out to take the hot mug. It was just what her throat, dry and sore, needed. Through the one nostril that still worked, she smelled a hint of honey.

"Oh! This is wonderful. I'm not sure about the toast, though."

"Dunk it."

She smiled. Soggy bread didn't appeal to her, but it was probably the only way she would be able to swallow anything of substance.

Annaliese turned away from him then, savoring a sip of the hot tea, and to her surprise heard him follow her inside. Christophe was at her bed, holding up the blankets.

"Get under the covers," he said. "Here, give me that until you're settled." He took the tea and toast and put it on the table beside her bed.

She should most definitely send him away, but surely not even her mother would object. He was only doing what she would have done had she been there: tucking her in.

After covering her, he took another pillow from the chair by the window, something she'd wanted earlier but hadn't been willing to leave the warmth and comfort of her bed to retrieve. Placing it behind her back, he pulled the covers up to her chin, then reached for the tea.

"Where did you find honey?" she asked.

"From Mama, at the restaurant. And the tea flakes, too. She said it would be good for any mood, from an ailment to overwork."

Annaliese smiled, letting the hot steam break through the swollen interior of her nose. "Thank you, Christophe."

"What else do you need? company? or just a book? maybe paper to write on?"

He went to the desk and there, on top of the letters she'd been answering yesterday, was the poem Jurgen had written for her. She said nothing, watching Christophe as his gaze was caught.

He didn't even attempt to hide that he read something so personal. Christophe picked it up with one hand while with his other he turned the chair toward the bed and took a seat.

"Annaliese," he said softly when he finished reading, "do you want me to leave?"

"I . . . I suppose sleep is the only thing I need right now."

"No, Annaliese." He wasn't accepting her stall. "I mean do you want me to leave Munich? leave you alone? with him?"

The weight on her chest, in her head, in her nose . . . in her heart . . . felt too much to bear just then. Why was he asking her this? Because of the poem? Or did he want to leave, be done with the assignment he'd been hired by her parents to do?

"He said nothing has changed, that he still wants what's best for everyone," Annaliese said. "He knew about all the work I've been doing lately. The same sort of work we've always done."

"I wouldn't expect him to say anything yet. I asked him about it too—bluntly, the only way I know how."

"What did he say?"

"Nothing. Nothing at all."

She wanted to feel relieved, wanted to believe Jurgen was still the same man he'd been before the loss of the election. "Then nothing has changed."

Christophe shrugged, then made his way to the door.

"Are they paying you to stay here, watching me?" She'd called the words after him in spite of herself. She shouldn't want to draw out this visit, but these past days of work and sickness had left her lonesome.

"Your parents? They offered to do that, yes, but—"

"Then consider yourself free of whatever obligation you felt. I'll send them a letter if you like, telling them you were every bit the watchdog they meant you to be, in case you're worried they won't pay you for the time you've been here already. I'll tell them your services are not required."

Was that the hint of a frown? She'd hurt his feelings! Part of her was pleased, but she reminded herself he would count himself less than a gentleman if she believed him only motivated by monetary decisions. Even if he was.

"I like the idea of your sending them a letter," he said. "It's a start, anyway."

She shrugged.

"If you can't blame me anymore, you blame *them* for Giselle's death, don't you?"

She didn't answer, didn't look at him. He didn't know, he couldn't know, how accurate his guess was.

"You lost your sister, but they lost a daughter. Have you forgotten that? Do you really think their greed is bigger than their love for you or Giselle? If you do, you don't know them at all. You don't know me, either. What if I told you I'd be happy to deliver the letter, but that I would return here the same day? that I'm here watching over you because it's exactly where I want to be, whether or not your parents had a say in it? that even now, with your red nose and crumpled dress, I might not want to leave your side?"

The knife in her throat jabbed her as she swallowed, but she suddenly wondered if she might be hallucinating. Maybe she was more sick than she realized. Did hallucinations come with the sniffles? Perhaps she did have the influenza.

He appeared to be waiting for her to reply, but she didn't know what to say, at least not without making herself vulnerable to what she hoped he had meant.

He returned to her bedside, leaning over her. "Whether it's true or not, Annaliese, I'm convinced you need me. If only to remind you of your parents' love. And God's."

She released the breath she'd held. God again. . . . Christophe always spoke on behalf of God or her parents, never for himself.

"Don't feel obligated," she whispered, then took another sip of the soothing tea to mend her sore throat.

He stood straighter, turning away but going only as far as the chair by her desk. "I don't. Somehow you make everything I say or do sound different from what I mean it to be. So I suggest you not talk. I won't either. Let me just sit here with you. I'll wait until you're finished with the tea and I'll return the cup to Bertita. I'll bring more if you like. But don't speak. All right?"

She started to tell him to go, claim she didn't need a nurse-maid, but held back. It hurt to talk, anyway.

And the undeniable truth was, she didn't want him to leave. Not Munich. Not this room. Not her.

Christophe sat as promised, without saying a word, offering his company until she'd finished the tea and toast. In peaceful silence.

22

February 21, 1919

Annaliese tucked a handkerchief into the pocket of her jacket but doubted she would need it. She felt much better today—and just in time. She needed to go out on this day especially, as a show of support for Eisner and regret that his role in Bavarian politics would be more limited than it was before.

The flat was empty when she went downstairs. She knew Christophe had left already; he had tapped on her door with tea and toast again, telling her he would be at the warehouse if she didn't need anything else.

Leo and Jurgen would join the council members today, though she had hoped they would wait for her. But even they were gone.

So she hurried out, making her way along the Promenadenplatz, tripping on one of the streetcar rails. She headed toward the Bavarian Chamber; the public gallery was probably already full, but that didn't matter. She wanted to greet Herr Eisner on his way in so he would know he would be missed.

Even now, she could barely believe he had so soundly lost the election. More incredible still was that the council—the council their November revolution had created—would meet in one wing of this building while in another wing, the eight ministers of the Provincial Assembly would gather to hear Eisner's resignation.

Surely Eisner still had plans, particularly for the council of which Jurgen was a member. She took comfort in that; somehow they would remain united in their support for the people. Jurgen wouldn't abandon Eisner, no matter what Christophe thought. How could he, after working so hard for him?

A loud bang in the distance startled her, like a clanging of two metal cans or the backfire of an engine. Then another pop and another. She'd never heard such banging before, sounds close in succession, and she quickened her step.

A boy ran past her, nearly knocking her from her feet. She would have turned and cautioned him to slow down, or at least mind his manners, but he was gone so quickly, she knew he would pay no heed. He was just a boy, after all.

She walked no farther than a dozen steps before hearing shouts from around the corner, voices bouncing off the tarnished brick-and-mortar buildings. Hope sprang up. Perhaps it was a rally. A protest against Eisner's resignation. But wouldn't she have known about such a thing? She rushed toward the sounds.

Instead of the earnest clamor of a rally, chaos greeted her. Men shouted, people ran—both men and women, young and old. A few onlookers stood frozen in their step, while some pointed down the avenue.

"Shot him!"

"He fell there—he's there!"

"A man yelled, 'Down with the revolution!' and shot him, just so."

"And see the blood! Look, you can see it through the crowd."

Annaliese followed their directions, and horror sprouted through her confusion. People clustered around a body splayed out on the street. Outside the crowd, others ran one way or the other, to or fro, as if no one knew which way to go.

Annaliese darted forward, then stopped, sickened at the sight between those swarming around the fallen man. So much blood, and the body only partially visible. But the name rang around her, repeated from every side as if it ricocheted from one set of lips to another.

Eisner, she heard through one ear.

Eisner, in the other.

The name resounded in her head, whether or not those around her still said it aloud. Already, police whistles burst through the sounds. New shouts, demands for order and authority overrode those of fear and chaos. The fringes of the crowd dissipated, and she heard the news spread along the street until the same sound came from everywhere.

"Eisner! Shot dead."

"Right on the street!"

Annaliese stepped backward, away from the police who were already making arrests. Some cried out that they were only witnesses but were carried off in a police cart anyway, while Eisner's body was left on the street. That no one bothered to tend him confirmed the truth. He really must be dead.

Fear and confusion filled Annaliese. She tore her gaze from what she could see of Eisner's body, looking at those around her instead. In their fear-sparked excitement, none of them understood the loss—not even her. What would it mean to the councils? to Jurgen? How could anyone on this street know what would happen if Eisner was really gone?

News of the shooting outpaced her as she headed back

toward the Assembly Building. Every step she took echoed the shock. Eisner—dead! The path she followed was the same one he would have taken to the Assembly Building for his resignation. The image of his body dizzied her, but no other picture could squeeze in to take its place.

Guards surrounded the Assembly Building already—guards who wouldn't let her in.

"I need to go in!" she protested. "I work with Jurgen, and he is there with the council. I need to speak to him."

The guard only shook his head, ignoring her as more people approached from behind. He told them all to go away.

But she didn't. She would wait. All day, if necessary.

"Annaliese!"

She didn't know when her name had become entwined with the growing noise around her. The crowd had thickened, all wanting access to the same building as she. What did everyone want but the same thing? Assurance that inside this building someone was still in power, still there to set limits. If any authority was to be found, it would be found right here, inside this place of power.

She turned, but Christophe was already upon her, his eyes full of worry, his grip on her arms frantic.

"I called and called to you through the crowd. Couldn't you hear me? Are you all right?"

"Yes . . . yes. It's Eisner—"

He was already nodding, pulling her close even though people in front of the Assembly Building thronged the steps, uncertain about where to go instead.

"Come back to the flat," Christophe said, "away from here. Out of the streets altogether."

"But . . . Jurgen is inside. He might not know."

"He must, by now. The whole city is crying the news. Look, they're not letting anyone inside, anyway."

She glanced back to the door of the Assembly Building, where guards pushed people away. But some had slipped inside anyway, she'd seen it happen herself. With Christophe at her side, perhaps she might succeed.

"We should go inside—or at least try!"

But he shook his head and started to lead her away. She could barely follow. Her limbs moved as if filled with lead, while her head was so light, it seemed filled with air. She leaned on Christophe, thinking he was surely right, she should go with him away from the chaos.

Even as she did, someone rushed past, a man as broad-shouldered as Christophe, cloaked and indomitable, despite an apron flowing out from beneath his coat. One arm was stiff, as if he concealed something underneath. Judging by his face alone, he was set on some grim mission.

Annaliese stopped, watching the man force his way inside, past guards who had enough to deal with from those in the crowd more stoppable. "Wait," she said to Christophe. "Did you see him? that man?"

Christophe shook his head. "No. Come away from here with me. Come now."

"But that man! Did you see his cloak? The way he held his arm, his hand in one pocket. As if he had a gun."

"Half the city is armed, and you shouldn't be out. Come now."

"No! Let's go after him—to see what he's doing."

Christophe's gaze followed hers, between the door she pointed to and the guards closer to them. "I doubt we can get in."

"Tell them you're one of Jurgen's bodyguards. It's true enough."

She pulled his hand, grateful when he followed. But the crush of the crowd was great, and they made slow progress through a knot of others being pushed away from the door, more forcefully than ever.

"We're with Jurgen! On the council," she called to the guards over the noise around them.

"Step back! No one is allowed inside."

"But I saw a man get past you—with a gun!" Only after the words left her lips did Annaliese regret them for fear of panicking the crowd. Like a shudder, the words rang out from one end to the other. *A gun! A gun!* As if some of them weren't carrying a weapon of their own or didn't see armed men every day of the week.

"What did you say?" At last a guard turned to Annaliese, the one nearby. "What man?"

Annaliese couldn't see through the doors, though they were open. There were too many people in the way.

"Where is the council meeting?" she called. "Are there guards there, too?"

The sentry was still too intent on holding people back, including Annaliese and Christophe. "Step back!"

From behind them whistles blew and soldiers arrived, cutting through the crowd with their shouts and commands. Some obeyed orders to disperse, but instead of following those who went away, Annaliese stumbled toward an officer.

"I saw a man go inside—I think he had a gun."

"Go home, *Fräulein*," he shouted above the cries around them, then directed his gaze to Christophe. "Take her home. Do you want to be trampled?"

"He's right, Annaliese. There's nothing we can do."

"But—"

Christophe was already tugging at Annaliese, and she knew she had no choice. What could she do? Christophe was right . . . and yet, to leave . . .

Another commotion sounded from inside the doors, shouts raised to new heights, a swarm of people no longer intent on getting in, but the opposite. People rammed the door from within, pushing at anyone in their way.

"Shots!"

Annaliese saw an opportunity to run through the crowd, in the space left open behind those fleeing the building. But Christophe held firm, throwing an arm around her shoulders, hovering over her as any of the bodyguards might have done in a crowd mixed with supporters and protesters. He gave her no choice.

Only when they were blocks from the Prannerstrasse did he loosen his hold, settling only for her arm looped inside his. Still, he said nothing, just led her on the shortest route back to the house they shared.

She wanted to fight him, to cry out that he should have let her go. But outside the crowd—which had offered protection of its own kind—the fear started to take hold, and she was grateful they were away. Along every street people ran amid cries of news or alarm, accompanied by the screech of automobile tires or the zoom of an engine going too fast.

Not until Christophe hurried her up the porch and got her inside the flat did he speak. "Isn't it time, Annaliese? to leave Munich?"

Heart still racing, knowing he might be right, she still shook her head. Never mind that it was only Jurgen's inconsistent attention that sometimes made her feel wanted. Leo no longer talked of a Women's Council, not since the party had gained so few seats in the assembly. No matter how hard she worked to start one anyway, support for the councils themselves was in question. Never mind that under the whispers of everyone connected to Leo and Jurgen, she'd heard the word *Communism* too often to ignore. In truth, none of that mattered.

Hadn't Christophe himself said her parents were leaving for America? Perhaps they were already gone; he'd told her they were sailing this month. Surely they'd sold everything, including that mansion she detested.

Annaliese couldn't leave Munich.

Munich *was* home. She had no place else to go.

23

The horror of the day was slow to fade, particularly when neither Leo nor Jurgen returned. Even Huey didn't come home, convincing Annaliese that Eisner's death had ignited more than just a few hours of panic and confusion on streets that were always too close to desperation anyway.

That night she didn't have to open her window to hear the noise from two blocks over, of shop windows being smashed, guns firing, men shouting or—more than once—women screaming.

By morning Annaliese was eager for news of any kind.

"I'll go over to the warehouse with you," she said to Christophe at the breakfast table, which they shared only with Bertita. "That must be where Leo took Jurgen."

Christophe's stare lasted just long enough to emphasize his words. "You're not going anywhere, not until we know it's safe."

She started to open her mouth to protest, but he was already shaking his head.

"Nowhere, Annaliese." His glance landed briefly on Bertita. "Neither of you. I'm staying here too."

"That's exactly what Huey told me to do, and I have no

intention of doing otherwise." Bertita looked at Annaliese. "We stay here. Right here."

The day dragged on, made worse by Christophe's pacing. He held his rifle across his chest, standing guard like the most loyal defender. But it made talking to him senseless. All she saw was his gun.

By the next day, she wanted a glimpse of the city, to see if the chaos had settled, if anything had changed. She longed for normalcy, for fresh air. But Christophe kept a watchful eye on the front door, night and day, leaving open the door of the flat he used, beyond which no one could come or go. After a couple of attempts to leave on her own, Annaliese not only gave up trying, she gave up speaking to him altogether. She stayed resolutely in her room, asking Bertita to bring her meals so she wouldn't have to look at Christophe, the warden of her prison.

Although the street below Annaliese's window usually remained empty, eerily so, occasionally someone would run by, or a march would pass that was blatantly absent any women or children. Once she saw a band of men being arrested for no apparent reason.

She guessed most women hid in their homes . . . or were hidden against their will, like her.

By the third day of being closed up in her flat, she had no intention of letting her imprisonment continue. At the very least, she wanted to see if a newspaper could be found. Even if it was full of half-truths, intentional lies, or mistaken errors, it would be more news than she'd had lately. The least she could do was go on a surveillance run. She wanted to know who killed Eisner and why.

She decided to leave and return before first light; Christophe would never know. She would tell him after she returned, with a newspaper in hand if she was lucky. Surely she could find something, and if not, at least she would see for herself if the streets were as dangerous as Christophe claimed.

Annaliese crept down the stairs, stopping abruptly when the stair beneath her feet creaked. It was still dark, but moonlight shone through the transom above the door. Slowly, slowly, she moved on, taking one step, then another until she was nearly at the bottom.

The door to Jurgen's flat was open as it had been the night before and the night before that. From inside the room, she heard Christophe breathing. Deep, steady. Another pair of careful strides and Annaliese was at the landing. Nearly free.

The breathing changed then, drawing her vision inside the room. There he was, not in the bedroom he could have called his own, or any of the other two he could have taken over since Leo and Jurgen had disappeared. Christophe lay on the couch, fully dressed, without a blanket, his head on a pillow so small it didn't seem to offer any comfort at all. Boots still on.

His breathing was erratic now, as if something far heavier than his own folded arms burdened his chest. *Leave, just leave.* She should go outside before he woke, or she would never have her taste of freedom, of air, of counterfeit peace in a street now quiet.

Yet she couldn't go. She stood rooted at the threshold, watching him sleep, hearing his breathing become yet more strained.

Until he popped right up as if afire, eyes wide, a low cry escaping his lips. He stared straight ahead, directly at her. And yet he didn't see her; whatever he saw, it couldn't be her. Not with such a look in his eye.

Sweat glistened on his brow, despite the chill in the nighttime air and his lack of any blanket.

"Christophe?"

She took a step closer and he moved again, jumping from the couch, his gaze bouncing around the room as if he'd forgotten where he was or even who she was.

Then his rigid shoulders went limp; his legs—so strong—seemed unable to hold him. He fell back to the couch, rubbing at his face. From there, he looked up at her at last, and she knew he saw her.

"What—what are you doing, Annaliese? What time is it? Why do you have on your coat?"

"I was going for a walk."

He looked at the window. "In the dark?"

"You won't let me go during the day, so I thought . . ."

His lips went tight, but not as tight as they'd been a moment ago in sleep. "It isn't safe yet."

She was only a pace away from him, and when he stood, passing between her and the window, his shadow darkened the room altogether for a moment. He went to the door where she'd stood, as if looking to see if she was alone.

"Has Huey returned yet? Bertita said she had a note from him."

That was news to Annaliese. "No."

"Go back upstairs. When the sun comes up, you can sit on the porch in the back if you need fresh air. It's too cold now, too dark."

She had no intention of settling for such a short leash, but she wasn't going to argue that yet. "You were having a dream. Do you want to . . . talk about it?"

"No. What I want is for you to go back to bed." He looked beyond her, to the table next to the couch, the one that had a clock on it. "It's four in morning. Neither one of us should be awake."

"Do you have dreams like that very often?"

"Who said I was having a dream?"

"Of course you were dreaming."

He put a hand to her elbow. "Wait until sunrise; then we'll go out. The streets are quietest then."

"They're quiet now."

"But not safe. Go upstairs."

"Christophe. If you claim to have the right to keep me here, even if you think it's for my own good, then I claim the right to ask you about that dream. For *your* own good."

"It might be a fair exchange, if I believed the subject really was for my own good. But I don't. So good night."

She remembered something he'd said once. . . . "It had to do with those deaths, didn't it?"

He stopped, not looking at her, profile frozen. "What deaths?"

"The ones you think you're responsible for. When we talked about Giselle, you said you didn't want me to add another death."

He let go of her elbow, crossing his arms again, now leaning against the doorframe instead of staring at her through it. "All right, then. If you're so curious, I'll tell you. But you won't like hearing about it any more than I'll like talking about it." Christophe hesitated then and took another wipe at his brow. He paced away, went to the window, turning his back to her. "It was a dream about the trenches. Battles and guns and ugly things like that."

"Maybe you shouldn't worry about what I want to hear. Talk about it anyway."

He was silent so long, she thought he wouldn't speak. Then, "In France . . . most of the time out there—at the front—men shot at anything that moved. It was usually dark or dusty or foggy. Most of the men didn't know if they hit anything or not, but I suppose they must have hit something or so many men wouldn't have died."

He pivoted again, this time staring at her. There was something new on his face now, not reluctance to talk but anger. "It wasn't so unclear from where I sat. For the last six months of the war I was in a sniper's nest. They didn't care about my commission or my rank; they put me where they needed me most. Out there, in a place where I could see exactly what I hit. Men, with real faces—just like mine, just like my trenchmates. Faces like my brother's. Young men who had families waiting for them, mothers who loved them. A wife, a girl. A child. Men who never went home because their bodies were left to rot right where I felled them. Eaten by rats or bugs or the sun. Do you want to hear more? about the smell when the wind was just right? or perhaps about those who moved after I thought I'd killed them, so I had to hit them again just to keep them from their misery? Men, real men, put out of misery like animals . . . not like men God loves."

Then he sank to the chair behind him in much the same way he'd fallen to the couch just moments ago, head down, arms cradling his forehead. She moved closer but he held up a hand.

"Go away; just go away. . . . Dreaming about it is hard enough. I don't have to talk about it too. Just go."

"No, I won't go. I won't go away any more than you've gone away when I told you to leave me here in Munich."

Then she was on her knees next to him, her own arms taking the place of his, to take the weight of his head and shoulders against her, to feel the sweat and the tears on his face, to see her own tears mingle with his as they fell. He spoke again, about the faces, about those who saw him but too late, when they were already in his sights, when they knew they were about to be shot and there wasn't a thing they could do but take his bullet. Young faces—men who, like him, had probably never been loved by a woman, never knew how big the world was, never saw anything beyond their own village or town or city, except that stinking, rotten, rat-filled trench and sandbags and mud and sores and boredom and fear.

Then, as if realizing he'd spoken thoughts he had never shared before, he leaned back and searched her face, perhaps expecting to see the horror of his words reflected on her face.

Annaliese didn't move, still holding both his hands now that he'd broken from her embrace.

"I think," he said softly, "that you've probably heard enough, at least from someone who is supposed to be protecting you. You probably think I'm the one needing protection, from my own dreams."

She shook her head. If he thought she believed him weak because of what he'd said, just the opposite was true. "You survived all that. How could I not trust you to keep me—or anyone—safe?"

He lifted a hand to her hair, stroking it once. "Thank you, Annaliese."

She should leave; she knew she should. She should go back up to her room, not give him any more trouble. She knew—had known all along—that he wanted her to stay inside because it was for her own good. And that was true. If she were honest, she would tell him she was grateful he hadn't deserted her the way the others had, that if he weren't here in this house, she would have nightmares of her own. And she'd seen only one dead man, not the scores that he had.

Instead of going or voicing her thoughts, she remembered her childhood dreams where she'd been bold enough to do what her heart wanted her to. In those old dreams, she'd caught his eye and not run away. And now, she did just that. She let her eyes linger on his, knowing her face was more illumined than his, with moonlight through the window behind him. She let her gaze slip to his mouth, imagining what it would be like in just a moment, if he let her kiss him. What it would feel like if he would welcome her.

But instead of waiting until her lips found his, he leaned forward, closing the gap between them, pressing his lips to hers before she had the chance to claim his.

She smiled when they broke apart, and so did he. For a moment he looked as shy as she felt, and she was a child again, wanting to run away. But he looked at her with such welcome in his eyes. Those nightmares from a moment ago might never have happened, the light in his eyes was so inviting.

"That's one way to banish nightmares," she whispered.

He nodded but then pulled away. "You should go upstairs, Annaliese," he said. "I'll take you outside in the morning if you still want to go. All right?"

She stood, feeling awkward and wondering if the kiss had meant anything at all to him. She had only Jurgen's to compare it to, and his hadn't meant anything more than pleasure. If that was all this had been to Christophe, then she wished they hadn't kissed at all.

24

Christophe did not go back to sleep. Instead, he turned the chair to the window, where he could see a slice of the sky. Those were the same stars he'd watched when he was out there, in France. They'd looked down on him and the fighting and killing back then, too. Just as they looked down on him now, indifferently, when inside him a battle was raging almost as fierce as he'd fought on any field.

He hadn't wanted to send her away; he'd wanted to keep her right here at his side, close by. Kiss her again, talk again. Somehow having told her a little of what haunted him hadn't sent her running off, hadn't made her think less of him. He knew God had forgiven him for what he'd done out there, but he wasn't sure anyone on earth could. Especially someone like Annaliese, who'd said often enough that the war had been a weapon against everyone, not just Germany against the Allies, but capitalists against those used as soldiers on both sides.

But he knew if she'd stayed, he'd have been tempted to do more kissing than talking. Was he no better than Jurgen, who did the same thing?

After a while, he went into the kitchen and heated water for coffee. The sun would be up soon, and he hoped Annaliese would return before long, though part of him still feared it might be too soon to let her venture outside, even with him beside her. There might not be chaos in the streets right now, but how easily could it resurface?

Waiting for the coffee, he looked at the door that would swing into the kitchen at any moment, imagining how it would be when she joined him. He would battle not to kiss her again, but he knew they must talk about it. He had to know if his attention meant more to her than whatever considerations Jurgen had sent her way.

Taking a seat at the table, he accidentally jostled one leg, tipping the saltshaker that Bertita kept in the center. It spilled a white circle of granules and for a moment he was taken back to France again. Not to the memories that tormented him in the dark—the ones of his dream—but to another memory he'd nearly forgotten. Suddenly the salt was dried dirt, so often caked along the pillbox walls of the trench. Back then he'd used the tip of his bayonet to draw a line, but now he used his finger. The length of the line always varied, but it was his place on that life line that mattered more. In the trenches, he'd most often imagined his spot toward the end. Now he hoped it was the opposite, with years spread out before him.

"You're not superstitious about spilled salt, are you?"

He looked up, glad to see the smile on Annaliese's face. "No, it's something I used to do." He rose and poured a cup of coffee for each of them. "You did the same thing my trench-mates used to do when they saw me staring that way. Do you see the line I've drawn?"

She nodded, taking a seat opposite him at the table.

"I used to draw in dirt. It's a life line. In the trenches, I wasn't the only one wondering how much time I had left. Drawings like this one started more than a few conversations about what was at the end of the line."

If she guessed why he'd taken the opportunity to bring up God again, it wasn't clear on her face. She looked from the line to him, her face placid. She took a sip of her coffee, and he wondered if her silence meant God was the last thing she wanted to talk about.

So he waited. Finally she met his gaze and he knew she would speak after all.

"Why do you still want God to be part of your life, Christophe, when you've lost more than I have? Your parents, your brother. Everything you suffered in France. And yet you still want to go to church; you still think He loves you. Even after all the things the war made you do."

"God never stopped loving me, even when I was in those sniper nests. I can say I was just following orders, that I was trying to save my own life, and my trenchmates behind me. That I wasn't killing because I liked it or even because I wanted to kill someone. War makes sin a complicated business, but if it's a sin—what I did—then God loves me enough to forgive me."

She looked away again, and he knew his words hadn't made an impression—not a good one, anyway.

He tried again. "God doesn't love me—or you, or anyone—for what we are, what we do or don't do. He loves you, He loves me, because He can't help it. He's love inside and out, in every part of Him. That's why I still want to think about Him, why I still want to go to church. And why I still want to celebrate His birthday."

"But He hasn't given you peace, at least not when you're sleeping."

"That's because this isn't heaven. I don't expect things here to be perfect."

"So you don't think this world, right now, right here, can ever be a better place, where the rich take care of the poor, where everything is fair? That heaven is the only place for things like fairness?"

He shrugged. "All I know is that a hundred years ago or so, France tried having the workers rule everything and it didn't end well. Men haven't changed since then. We're not getting more noble; we're still the same. Why should this generation think we could do a better job at fairness?"

"We could try."

He nodded. "And we should. All of us. Individually, to the best of our ability. I want that too, Annaliese, but I want it to be my choice. I don't want a ruler of any kind—a peasant or a prince, a Kaiser or a prime minister or even a council—to force me into a definition of fairness. If it's my choice, my sweat, my money, I know I can be more generous because then I'll have the satisfaction of doing it myself instead of being told like a child to share."

"But people don't want your money—they don't want charity at all. They want fairness."

If there had been no awkwardness when she'd first entered the kitchen, it was fully between them now. There was nothing else to do but face it.

"I'm sorry—I didn't want to argue. I wanted to talk about last night."

She was already shaking her head, and he knew it was too late—their differences were right there between them again—but he continued anyway.

"I wanted to tell you—" he leaned closer, lowering his voice in case Bertita came through the doorway—"that I've never recovered so quickly from one of those dreams, and I have you to thank."

"I would do anything to help you, Christophe . . . but I don't think I can. Not enough that it would matter." She suddenly stood, half a cup of coffee still left at her place. "I intend to go out today. But you don't have to accompany me, not if you don't want to."

He stood too, knowing her sudden coldness was as much because of God as because of him. She was fighting them both. "I said I would take you. They're marching in the streets for Eisner's funeral today. It should be safe enough; Huey's note to Bertita said they know who shot him. It wasn't about the party or against the councils. Eisner was shot because he was Jewish. By someone half-Jewish, wanting to prove he could shoot another Jew. As insane as that sounds, that's what happened."

She clutched the back of her chair. "But that's . . . Oh, Christophe, that can't be true. It makes no sense."

"Not to us, but evidently to the shooter."

"I'll get my coat."

"Wait . . . it's too early. Sit. Finish your coffee."

But she just shook her head and fled from the room.

Still running like a child, even after last night had been a dream come true. At least it had been for her.

Annaliese rushed back to the room she'd been calling a prison; suddenly it was a sanctuary. How much clearer could it be? If Christophe didn't look down on her views of God, then it was clear yet again he did that very thing when it came to her politics.

Her politics. *Her* politics? Whatever politics she'd taken on since coming to Munich had been to make up for the wrongs of her father, to take a stand so opposite his that it would ease her conscience and give Giselle's death meaning. Annaliese had put aside her old faith and taken on a new one—in Socialism.

Jurgen's faith had once made sense to her, faith in this world and its future. If everyone shared his vision, the world was bound to become a better place. Men, being more good than selfish, would be inspired by their own goodness, and once fairness was within reach, it would stay in their grasp.

Annaliese still wanted to believe that.

But the world had become so awful a place that a man felt driven to prove himself by killing someone just for being Jewish. That was faith of a different sort altogether—an evil kind. It made her want to renounce *all* faith, to stomp out everything from politics to God, banish faith from every part of society. She grabbed her coat but stopped. Christophe had said it was too early to leave, and he was no doubt right if there was to be a funeral procession. She sat; she would resume her isolation. And later, she would accept Christophe's company the same way she always had. The way she had before last night, before his kiss had changed everything.

The air was cold but clean, refreshing after the last few days inside. Annaliese set a quick pace away from the house, and Christophe walked beside her without a word.

It wasn't long before she found a crowd to lead the way to the funeral procession. Thousands filled the streets, not just workers and soldiers who'd followed Eisner, but farmers and mountaineers, too, men and women dressed in their country attire alongside those from the city.

Annaliese followed as mourners passed the spot of that awful day. In her mind she heard the shots again, knowing now what they were. A man shooting Eisner; a sailor with a gun wounding the assassin.

For another kind of faith, one man had killed another.

A bloodstain was still visible beneath a picture of Eisner, a photograph held up by bayonets. She was glad then that Christophe had taken her arm. She needed his strength.

Though she looked at the faces around them, she saw no one she knew among so many mourners. Not Leo nor Jurgen nor any of their bodyguards. Perhaps Christophe knew where they were, but she didn't ask. She let him lead her away, not caring where they went, whether it was with purpose or not, as long as it wasn't back to her flat. She wasn't ready to return yet.

Before long they were at the restaurant, where Mama showed them to a table.

"He couldn't change things fast enough," Annaliese said after Mama left soup on the table for them. The small, half-filled bowls seemed ample evidence of why Eisner hadn't drawn sufficient votes. The blockade was still in place, preventing most imports. He couldn't get the people and the factory owners to cooperate, couldn't get their society working again, couldn't even hope to make an impact on a peace settlement that might be bearable by Germany. There wasn't enough, not of anything, but especially of what they needed most: jobs and food. "If he'd had more time before the election, more time to fix things, the voters would have kept him in place. And maybe this wouldn't have happened. Maybe he would still be alive."

Christophe put his hand over one of hers and quietly prayed, not only in gratitude for the soup but also for their safety and for the future of Germany. Annaliese bowed her head but said nothing.

She hadn't planned to ask but found herself speaking anyway. She asked Christophe if he'd seen the others.

"I saw Ivo," Christophe said. "He told me Jurgen will return to the council tomorrow. Leo hid him away, but they both know the only power left in Munich right now is still with the council. The Provincial Assembly scattered during all of the chaos. Someone did burst into the gallery, just like you feared. He started shooting, killed one deputy and wounded another. He surrendered himself."

Her pulse pounded. So . . . there was better reason than she knew for Leo to spirit Jurgen away and into hiding. He hadn't abandoned her, after all.

"They're calling for a general strike in support of the councils everywhere in Germany because they're afraid the councils will be abolished otherwise. It's still chaos, Annaliese. And for some people, Eisner's death is an opportunity, not a tragedy."

Anger pierced through her thoughts. "You mean for Jurgen, don't you?"

"Isn't it obvious? He was waiting for Eisner to resign before formally supporting the Communists. Ivo told me half the council is Communist already. Is that what you want for Germany? To see every last capitalist thrown to the wolves?"

She shook her head. "I don't . . . I don't want any killing. It's not supposed to be this way."

"But it is."

"What is *your* answer to all of this? To leave? To give up on Germany?"

"I know the answer isn't in a group—Socialism or Communism—if it rejects God. Do you really believe there is no God, or have you put Him out of your life because the party said so?"

"I only believe what makes sense to me. And it made sense to me that the church might be part of the problem."

"Some people in the church, maybe. Not God."

"I don't know!" She knew only that she wanted this conversation to end. But how could she say she didn't know? How could she not know what she believed when she'd spent the last few months lecturing on the street to help others define what they should believe?

"If you don't know, Annaliese, then why do you argue with everything I say?" He shoved back his chair, exasperated. "I want the same thing you do. I want the future to be better. But I don't hold the past against the wealthy or the factory owners. Those are the ones risking their ideas and their money, maybe because they think their ideas might be popular or help someone or provide jobs or make society better. But according to you or to Jurgen, they do everything for money. There has to be a reward for all the risk, doesn't there?"

"But they let greed take them too far! They take advantage of the ones who don't have the same opportunities. It's like they're stealing—stealing years of life from those who have no choices. At least Nitsa was honest in her stealing, more honest than my father ever was."

Instead of matching the anger behind her tone, Annaliese saw the light of confusion behind Christophe's gaze, settling in faint humor. The look made Annaliese reconsider her own words, and she might have seen the humor in calling Nitsa an honest thief if her mood had let her. But it didn't.

They finished their soup in silence.

"I don't think anyone has the answer for Germany right now," Christophe said at last, when neither made any effort to leave the restaurant. "Even if Eisner was on the right track, everybody is too angry. And people like Jurgen aren't helping that."

"Jurgen . . . and me?"

He neither confirmed nor denied it, and she knew he thought she'd had a part in the chaos too. Maybe she had, by reminding those who had too little of how unfair life was, that the factory owners and those with wealth had taken advantage of them not only in their work but by sending them to the fields of France to be slaughtered. It was easy enough to define what made people angry, easy to nurture that anger with a speech.

"What would you have had us talk about instead of demanding change? Don't you think greed is a sin? Or should I just remind people how God loves them in their poverty? The churches do that, and it hasn't helped."

"Turning our backs on God isn't the answer—He's the *only* answer. Because greed *is* a sin, and if people believed that, they might change." Then he was quiet, because Mama came and took their empty bowls away. Annaliese saw him attempt a smile at Mama, but Mama didn't look at either one of them. Perhaps she didn't like fighting of any kind, not even this kind.

Christophe folded his hands on the table between them and she knew he wasn't finished yet. "They're killing people in Bremen, in Wilhelmshaven and Cuxhaven, and there will be more death in Berlin. How long before it comes here to Munich? The best choice is to leave, at least for now."

"No one is stopping you. Not me, anyway." She held his

gaze in a pause and her pulse sped. Anger and fear pushed her to say the opposite of what she felt inside. "One kiss shouldn't keep you here. Go."

He stared at her, silent, for what seemed a very long moment, and she wondered what he was thinking.

"Is it too soon to go back to the house?" he asked at last.

So he wouldn't tell her what he thought—not that she couldn't guess. He wanted to leave Munich. Christophe certainly had less to turn his back on than she did; it wasn't as if he'd come to Munich because he wanted to. "I'm ready."

The air outside felt all the colder in comparison to Annaliese's warmed cheeks. She thrust her hands in her pockets, her heart so heavy she could barely breathe.

It wasn't long before they rounded the corner of the block to their home, and Annaliese's heart raced anew at a familiar sight. A truck was parked in front of the house—that same old, pockmarked ambulance.

Only now its sides were draped in flags. Red.

25

Christophe saw the truck, and while the sight had made Annaliese speed up, his pace slowed.

She flew up the porch stairs, and Christophe followed. The inside door, the one he'd left open for the last few days in order to better guard the front door, was open again. As soon as Annaliese crossed the threshold, the tall, blond outline belonging to Jurgen met her. He pulled her into an embrace, kissing her soundly. On lips that in this very room, only hours ago, had been pressed to Christophe's.

She pulled away and slid a glance back toward Christophe, as if embarrassed, but he saw something else that he didn't want to see. She was glad to see Jurgen, glad that he was back.

"Christophe told me someone stormed the assembly!" She was looking at Jurgen again now. "It was so awful that day. I tried to get in to see you, but we were sent away. Why didn't you tell me where you were?"

Leo stepped closer, a smile on his face. "We've been at work, night and day. It's done, Anya. We claimed Bavaria as a republic of councils—and even if the government refuses to honor us, it's only a matter of time now."

Jurgen nodded. "The assembly that was just voted in is

powerless. I wouldn't have hoped for a crazy assassin to show up at their first meeting and start shooting, but it made all of the power fall into our hands. The shooter thought the assembly had hired someone to kill Eisner! One assembly-man is dead, another wounded; one is still in hiding. Two fled Munich altogether, so far as we've heard. Our council is every-thing now—at least for the moment. It's time, Anya. Now is the time to make sure the people everywhere are heard."

"We saw the flags," Christophe said, stepping farther into the room. "Have you joined Leviné, then?"

"Yes! With Berlin's full support, too. They have communi-cations from workers nearly all over the world."

Christophe glanced at Annaliese to see if the words had any impact, but she wasn't looking his way. Jurgen used to echo Eisner by saying, "Berlin isn't Germany." He'd supported Eisner in refusing Berlin's edicts more than once on behalf of Bavaria.

Evidently none of that mattered under Leviné.

"We're uniting everywhere!" Jurgen continued. "Do you know, if everything goes the way we expect, there will never be another war? You among all of us here should welcome that, Christophe. What will we have to fight over if we get rid of things like boundaries and nationalism and militarism and capitalism? Oceans may separate us, but people everywhere will join together. It's only the beginning, but it's begun!"

"Unity will certainly be different from the last four years," Christophe said, low, his eyes still on Annaliese's profile. He wondered if she could believe such things, like international unity preventing future wars. Jurgen was certainly convinced, with all of his passion and confidence. As if by his faith alone, all of what he promised *could* happen. As if people who not more than five months ago had been sticking one another with bayonets, pitching mustard gas at one another, crushing each other with tanks and artillery, and dropping bombs and bullets from airplanes could somehow be made to get along. Forgive, forget. Unite.

He wanted to hope Jurgen was right; the last thing Christophe wanted was another war. Even Leo looked gleeful.

Instead, Christophe's thoughts were just the opposite. *Foolish, all of them.*

He knew he had to walk from the room . . . before he voiced such words.

Annaliese watched Christophe leave, refusing to give in to a wish to leave with him. Why should she feel so alone without him in the room when she didn't agree with any of the things he believed in?

Jurgen was like a man on fire, full of hopes and dreams and with the energy to push it all forward. He'd been that way ever since she'd first met him—but then he'd been pushing for an election.

Something Communists, if she wasn't mistaken, had little use for.

Jurgen squeezed her hand, pulling her to the table where he'd strewn stacks of papers. He was searching for something just now among the flyers awash with red. He drew several from the pile.

"Here, look at this—from Berlin. We're going to call for a national strike, beginning in just a couple of days. And here— flyers in support of the people from Hungary. And here, from

England. And this—all the way from America! It's the people's turn. Now is the time as never before. Now that the war has proven what murderers capitalists are!"

She looked at the piles of literature, almost afraid to touch any. "I don't know, Jurgen. . . . I've heard awful stories about what Communists are doing in Russia. It frightens me."

He took her by the arms and laughed. "Of course some things must be destroyed in order to create! But once the old ways are gone, everyone will see this is the better way."

He sank to the chair next to the table with a sigh of what sounded like pure satisfaction. As he pulled Annaliese to his lap, holding her close almost like a child, she saw the red rimming his eyes, the shadow of fatigue drawn on his skin.

He held her gaze. "We'll teach you everything you need to know. But first, you must do your part and forget the rumors you've heard. We can't teach you something if your fears get in the way."

If there was any good to be learned from Communism, she trusted Jurgen and Leo would find it. But even now, she didn't want to hear what they had to say. She needed time to think, away from him, away from his assurance and hopefulness, away from all of Jurgen's persuasive sympathies that matched so many of her own.

"No, first you need rest," she told him. "And probably something to eat, although we don't have much. Bertita hasn't been able to go to the market, and from what I saw at Eisner's procession, most of the shops are closed anyway."

"Coffee would be enough. But not yet. Stay. Stay right here." He settled her head on his shoulder. "I've missed you yet again, Anya."

She knew he undoubtedly expected a reciprocal comment,

but she could not bring herself to issue one. In truth, she hadn't missed him, and beyond thinking he'd abandoned her, she hadn't thought of him very much at all.

"I'll get your coffee." She stood and passed a frowning Leo on her way to the kitchen.

A moment later Jurgen came through the kitchen door. Alone.

"I'll have the coffee here. Will you join me?"

Nodding, she poured two cups. It was reheated from that morning and no doubt as tasteless as it was then, but it was better to employ her hands at her own coffee cup than sitting there not knowing what to say or do.

Taking the seat opposite her, he entwined his fingers with hers. "The months ahead will be glorious for the people. You may not be speaking on the street for a while—it's too risky just yet—but soon, when the bourgeoisie accept the truth of their place, it'll be safe again, and we'll have need of your voice. Until then, I'll be heard at the council, where the real power is. If you were there, in the gallery, waiting for me, cheering each word, agreeing with each decision I make for the people, I would know real happiness."

She slid her hand away from his, back to the side of her cup. Why did he assume she would automatically agree and work toward something so different from what they'd worked for together? "I liked working for an *election*, the very first one where women had a voice. I still like the idea of voting, even if the majority wasn't with us this time."

"The election failed us because we didn't have the time to prove that the fairest way of life is best for all. And I agree a vote might be best, but we have to take advantage of the circumstances we have now—it's a rare opportunity. We mustn't let things settle down again unless it's into a *new* way of life, one that makes all of us equal. I need you, Anya. By my side." He reached for her hand again, kissing it.

"For how long, Jurgen? How long will you want me if I stop asking you to wait?"

He smiled. "I'll want you for as long as we both find all the happiness we can have together. I can make you happy."

She pulled back, folding her arms, feeling the chair press into her. "I know that you want to. I know you want to make others happy. Ever since I came to Munich, you've been kind and generous to me. You gave me a place where I felt needed, a roof and food and safety. And I know you have noble ideas. A Robin Hood of Germany. There is so much I admire about you—"

He held up a palm and she stopped, although she wasn't at all certain about what she would have said next. It was easy enough to count the virtues he possessed that had benefited her, but was she ready to refuse following this new direction he was taking? Just like that?

"You can stop, Anya. I know the kindest method to disappoint someone. It's just as you're doing. By serving sugar first. I've always said you have special intuition when it comes to dealing with people. And you're so young."

He'd known better than her where she'd wanted this conversation to go. "I'm sorry, Jurgen. Your ideas are too high a reach for me—at least with some of the boundaries you want to be rid of. Like . . . marriage, for one. If I ever fall in love, I'll need security behind love, some promise we'll remain together even when either one of us might think the happiness could taper off."

"*If* you fall in love?" he asked. "I thought that was what

took this conversation here, because you already are. With Christophe."

She grabbed her coffee cup, shook her head, took a sip. It was bitter. "Why do you say that? It started with talking about politics, not love."

"I saw the way you looked at Christophe when you came in. When I kissed you, you didn't look at me afterward. You looked at him."

"There is nothing personal between Christophe and me."

Jurgen stood and rounded the table, pulling her to her feet and into a gentle embrace. "Then if there is still hope for me, I'll tell you he isn't right for you. You already know that, though. He doesn't believe any of the things you've learned since you came to Munich."

She wondered if he felt her stiffen. "Don't you think I brought any beliefs with me?"

"Whatever you believed before, you wanted to forget. I know this because you never spoke of your home, your family, the way you used to live. You only spoke of now, of my beliefs, what Leo and I taught you. It's understandable. It's natural to imitate; man is made to imitate. I don't think our crowds would have been nearly so pleasant if this weren't true."

He drew her closer so that her head rested on his chest. But it wasn't of her doing; he let his hand remain in her hair as if he knew she might pull away.

She wanted to do that very thing—pull away—and more, to deny every word he'd said. But she was motionless, only her pulse racing. She couldn't refute a single word. Not really. He was only voicing the things Christophe had made her suspect.

"I wouldn't like to see you take on Christophe's beliefs," Jurgen told her, and his voice seemed all around her. It emanated from his mouth and from within him, her ear pressed so close to his chest. "When he looks at the future, happiness can only be found in heaven instead of right here on earth. He is too glum. You would be glum, too, with him. But we have hope now, hope for a better Munich, a better world. With me you would be more hopeful, happier."

She drew away at last, turning back to the table but not sitting down. Annaliese didn't want to hear any more of what Jurgen had to say; she wanted to start over. Not as an imitator. She wanted her own thoughts, her own beliefs, her own future.

And clearly, she couldn't do that here. Not with Jurgen, who went from a socialistic appeal for justice to a communistic demand, then assumed she would go along.

Perhaps she couldn't even remain at Christophe's side, seeing his disappointment every time something came up to reveal just how far she was from believing in God the way he did. She needed to be away from both of them, where she could think.

Home was the first place that came to mind. But to go there . . . No, that would be going backward, not forward.

Then . . . where?

26

"You don't know where she is?"

"That's correct. I do not know."

Christophe eyed Jurgen, not believing him. It was Jurgen who kept as close an eye on Annaliese as Christophe himself, whenever he was under this roof.

"She went out? When the city is still in a state of emergency, and nearly anyone could be arrested by a police force who isn't even sure who governs them?"

For someone who earlier that same day had welcomed himself back into Annaliese's arms, Jurgen looked surprisingly unconcerned about her safety. "I didn't send her away. She went by her own design. I suspect it'll be some time before she returns, though."

Christophe had started to turn away, to leave through the door he'd just entered by, but stopped. "What do you mean, some time?"

"Because she took her little bag, the same one she arrived with, and left."

Christophe lurched forward, hands that wanted to throttle the other man now shaking in restraint. "And you let her go without knowing anything more?"

229

Jurgen pushed aside the papers in front of him and stood. "She didn't give me the chance, didn't say good-bye. Bertita saw her walking away toting the bag, or even I wouldn't have known." He looked Christophe over as if mirroring the judgment he saw aimed his way. "You think me cold for not worrying over her; I can see that. It only proves I know her better than you. I've seen her take care of herself in a crowd, seen her confidence and know how independent she is. She doesn't need you. Or me, for that matter. Let her go, and if she comes back to either one of us, it'll be all the sweeter."

Christophe didn't stay to argue. He turned to the door, hurrying down the steps and out to the streets. To find her.

The church spire shot straight up, drawing the eye heavenward. Annaliese stood across the street from St. Luke's, where she'd been for the past half hour, pacing and shifting her bag from one hand to the other, wondering if she should go inside. There was no reason to enter; there was no service today, no one inside at all as far as she could see.

Except . . . maybe . . . God.

Another cold wind whipped at her, stinging her cheeks, forcing tears from her eyes. At least it would be warmer in there than it was out here.

She glanced around again at the empty street. Nothing kept her away from the church except her own fears.

But why should God want any part of her? She'd been shaking her fist at Him since the day Giselle died. She'd grieved the parents He gave her. She'd denied His existence to anyone who asked ever since she came to Munich. Everything in her political choices refused to acknowledge the existence of God at all.

Despite all that, her feet had brought her here. Not by her design, yet here she was. Drawn as though God Himself *did* want to see her, to hear her speak to Him.

Christophe had once said if God came to mind, maybe it was His nudging. Maybe He'd nudged her all the way here.

She crossed the street and walked up the wide cement stairs. The door was open and she went inside, into the dim light. She took two steps past the narthex, where the sound of her footsteps reverberated within the cavernous sanctuary, echoing from the dome. She tiptoed after that, only as close to the altar as one of the side chairs at the back. Not far from where she'd sat the night Christophe had brought her here.

She stared ahead, seeing only what she expected. The columns, the mystery and majesty of the dome, so perfectly set, so huge yet so securely towering above her head. Beautiful, a work of worship in itself. Yet empty. Had she really expected God to be here, to tap her on the shoulder?

"If You're the reason I'm here," she whispered, closing her eyes even to the artistry of the man-made church, "then tell me. Tell me what to believe. I don't want to believe things because of other people. I want to discover on my own what's real. Faith in You or faith in this world . . . I don't . . . know. . . ."

Then she sat, silently. She didn't know how to pray, so she let her mind say what it would to the God who'd inspired this building. Giselle came to mind, and Annaliese told the God of the universe that He shouldn't have let her sister die.

She thought of her father. A father who had let Giselle die. He'd said as much when he came back that day, when he'd sobbed in her mother's arms. Annaliese had heard every word, though neither of her parents knew that. He'd said he saw Giselle running from the factory. She'd spotted him and run back, away from him, too close to the fire she'd set. It was his fault Giselle had been so close to the explosion that followed, because he'd frightened her simply by discovering her.

While her mother had turned to God for comfort, her father had resolutely refused to acknowledge God could benefit either one of them. His failure to save Giselle hadn't softened him toward God. Just the opposite.

Maybe that was part of the reason it had been so easy to leave God behind, to adopt the politics of man that excluded any hint of a God concerned about governments and people. It had been so easy to leave God out, especially when others showed her how. She thought of Jurgen and Leo and Ivo, of how God had been absent to her since knowing them, silenced by their influence and by her anger toward her father for Giselle's death.

Why had God surrounded her with so many people who didn't acknowledge Him if He wanted her to know Him? Even her mother hadn't spoken of Him with any regularity, though Annaliese had often seen her reading the Bible. Only Christophe . . .

Then, knowing it probably wasn't her place to scold God, she thought of what she and Giselle had believed growing up, because of their mother. That God was always there, always with them. She wondered if Giselle remembered that after she'd been surprised into running back toward the factory, when she knew it was going to take her life. When she knew she would see God face-to-face.

Annaliese sat with her memories of people she knew, of things she'd done, trying to see God in any of it the way she'd seen Him bring her here tonight. Because here she was, complaining to the very God who'd given her life. In a building that had inspired enough love in someone to make it lovely.

Christophe came to mind more often than anyone else. Christophe, who'd broken her heart so many years ago. She was afraid he was doing it again. It was Christophe who'd said he didn't want to be stingy in his faith. Maybe it was God who'd put Christophe here in Munich, not because of her mother at all. If not for him, would Annaliese be here, seeking God's guidance on what to believe?

Surely He wanted the things she did: an end to poverty, help for the needy. If His plan to help people was to be carried out *through* people, then history had shown often enough they would have to be forced. Hadn't it?

She settled back in her chair. Christophe believed it was up to the individual to make the world a better place, not the government. But individuals had let people down. And yet what government had proven up to the challenge of stomping out unfairness?

Christophe was undoubtedly right about one thing. Neither a government nor the people could make the sacrifices necessary to meet the needs of the poor—not without God's help.

A God that Communists—and most Socialists she knew—refused to acknowledge existed.

⟡

Christophe turned yet another corner, noticing his own shadow defined by the moonlight on the cold pavement beneath his feet. He couldn't wander the streets much longer; it was senseless. And yet where else could he search? He'd been to every corner she'd called hers, back in the days she'd used those corners for her lectures. He'd been to the old party office, the warehouse where some of the men still loyal to Jurgen—no matter the party—housed themselves. He'd even gone to the last place she'd been before joining Jurgen, the hotel where she'd known the widow. Not even Frau Haussman was to be found there, and no Annaliese.

He would return to Mama's restaurant, where he'd already been several times to see if Annaliese had turned up. He would tell Mama to watch out for her, to keep her there until he came for her. It was late, past midnight, and he was tired from the weight of his boots and the weight of his spirit.

Where could she be? And why hadn't she told him she was leaving or where he might find her?

Perhaps he shouldn't try to find her; perhaps he should let her go. Maybe that was what she wanted.

Yet he couldn't give up so easily. In the last few steps toward Mama's, one passage from the Bible came back to him again, a passage that described the nature of love.

Beareth all things, it said, *believeth all things, hopeth all things, endureth all things.*

He wouldn't give up, not even if that was what she wanted him to do.

Part Two

FEBRUARY 1919

27

Annaliese stared out the window. The sight had nearly blinded her when she'd first turned her gaze to it that morning. Bright sun reflected on a ground quilted with the white of a late February snowfall. Even a lake in the distance was cast in pearl, shadowed by a cluster of pine trees whose branches served as platters for snow. Slopes swelled the landscape, picturesque and so reminiscent of the little village where she'd grown up.

She'd sledded down just such foothills, so happily free of every worry, not even feeling the cold. Trudging uphill through the snow with a heavy sled behind her hadn't been difficult. Not with neighbors like Christophe, who had more than once pulled not only his own sled but the one Annaliese had shared with Giselle.

She was well south of that little town now, closer to the mountains, away from everything she knew. Away from the city, too—from its strife, from the dangerous tension between the workers and those of the bourgeoisie and upper classes. The bourgeoisie like Annaliese used to be, and like the widow Meika Haussmann, who had taken Annaliese in.

". . . so I ran away," Annaliese finished, bringing Meika up to the day before, when Annaliese had returned to the hotel where she'd begun her trip to Munich and found the note Meika had left at the desk, directing Annaliese here to Meika's country estate should she ever want to leave Munich.

"And you didn't tell either one of them where you were going? neither Jurgen nor Christophe?"

Annaliese shook her head, then looked away, letting her eyes rest instead on the white dog on Meika's lap. "I suppose I should have—at least Christophe." She thought of how he'd watched over her during those days between Eisner's shooting and his funeral. For her own good, he'd insisted, and she knew he'd been convinced of that. "Christophe is prone to worry."

Meika stroked her pet's long fur. "Why didn't you tell him, then?"

Annaliese returned to the chair in the cozy sitting room where they'd shared small biscuits and coffee that wasn't much better than what Bertita had served. Evidently coffee was the taste of fairness, since even the wealthy could not bring in what the blockade did not allow. Meika's dog, a little white Maltese named Schatzi, wiggled a welcome for Annaliese, as if to say he was glad she'd decided to come nearer.

"When he kissed me that night," Annaliese said, "I wanted so much for Christophe to tell me nothing else mattered except how he felt about me—despite our differences. And yet last night, when I was thinking how afraid I was that he would only break my heart the way he did when we were children, I realized how wrong I was. It sounds romantic, doesn't it, to have someone say you're more important than everything else? But what would that really mean? That the very things I admire about him—his faith, even his politics—aren't important?"

"Are you so different? your politics? your faith?"

"I thought we were. I know he thinks we are." She remembered the look on Christophe's face when she'd accepted Jurgen's kiss. She knew he'd felt betrayed. "He felt obligated to watch out for me because of my parents. But I'm sure they've sailed by now, so Christophe is free of whatever obligation he felt."

"I don't think that obligation extended to kissing you," Meika said softly.

"No. . . . But I couldn't see him. What he believes really is more important than whatever he feels for me." Annaliese settled her coffee again. "That's why I was so happy to accept your invitation, to think on neutral territory. All I have to do is figure out what *I* believe, and if any of it is compatible with what either he or Jurgen believes, I'll go back."

"You're welcome to stay as long as you like, of course. Only don't keep them waiting too long. They say women are fickle, but with men . . . they don't last alone for very long."

"I'm sure that's true of Jurgen."

"I think by your voice that you hope Christophe will wait for you. Don't you?"

Annaliese shook her head. "He'll go home. He hated Munich; I saw it on his face often enough. Someday, maybe— if I know I won't hurt his faith—I'll find him again back home. If it isn't too late."

Meika smiled. "He'll wait in Munich, at least for a little while, where you knew each other best. If it's meant to be."

Annaliese studied Meika a moment. As friendly as they'd been in the first few days after Annaliese had arrived in Munich, they'd never spoken about faith. Even such a statement as that—*"if it's meant to be"* . . . Did that mean Meika thought there was some design to life?

She wondered what Meika would think if Annaliese told her it was God Himself who'd brought her to that church the night before. In the light of day, it sounded ludicrous even to Annaliese—evidence in itself that she was far from believing what Christophe believed. He probably wouldn't doubt God could and would do such a thing, even for someone like Annaliese who'd turned her back on Him.

But even as she pondered those things, she wondered why it should matter what anyone else believed about politics or God, including Meika or even Christophe. Would someone else's doubts or convictions define hers?

"Last night," Annaliese said, reaching over the gap between their chairs to touch the Maltese's silken fur, "after Jurgen said what he did about my beliefs mimicking others', I only knew I wanted to be alone. I didn't want to see either one of them. I knew if I stayed in that room just up the stairs from Jurgen, it was like agreeing with him. Letting him define everything I believed, letting him think there might be some kind of future for him to keep telling me what to believe."

She leaned back in her chair. "And I knew that if I asked Christophe to help me find a place to stay," she went on, "I would be tempted to agree with his beliefs, just to be with him. So I had to go off on my own, even though the only people on the streets these days are the ones with guns. I walked along the march routes we used when I was working for the party. I went to my favorite rally corners. But somehow I ended up at St. Luke's. I don't know why; I never intended to go there. I believe—don't think me insane—God led me there."

Meika reached across this time to put a hand to Annaliese's forearm, and when the dog took the opportunity to switch laps, Meika let him. "I've done some wandering of my own since Freidrich was killed. I wandered from here to Munich because that was the last place we were happy. I didn't find Friedrich there. How could I? His body is gone, buried somewhere in France. But I did find God. His peace was more real to me in my pain than I'd ever imagined in happiness."

Peace. A word that had replayed in Annaliese's mind repeatedly, ever since her first moment of prayer the night before.

Annaliese stroked the softest fur, just behind Schatzi's ears. "Thank you, Meika."

"But I haven't done anything!"

"Oh yes, you have. So much. Thank you for taking me in, for listening and not judging. For being my friend." She laughed and drew the pet close for a hug. "For sharing Schatzi."

"I'm glad you've come." Meika winked and accepted Schatzi back. "But I suspect neither one of your gentlemen are glad you left. They both care for you; no doubt they'd both welcome you back and hope to work out the differences later."

Jurgen would at least welcome her as his partner, and Christophe would welcome her as . . . what? If she couldn't be what he needed, equal in faith, a partner in making the world a better place, not working against one another but side by side . . . if she couldn't do that, be all of that, then it was better if she never saw Christophe again. For his sake and for hers.

28

Sudden pounding echoed like gunfire, even though Christophe knew the sound came from a fist at the door. Ivo's little sister shrieked when her mother scurried behind Christophe and Ivo.

Ivo answered, letting the door open only as far as one massive shoulder allowed.

"Leo!"

Barely waiting for the door to open wider, Leo suddenly stood in the small room, a room that served as parlor and bedroom, too, at least for Christophe since he'd left Leo's home three weeks ago. Ivo shared one of the two other bedrooms in the flat with four younger siblings, but Christophe had chosen the floor in front of the fireplace instead. No sense waking all of them with his restless sleep.

"We need you, Ivo!" Leo said in place of a greeting. He thrust a newspaper at Ivo. "Our numbers are in the thousands, but we need every man we can get—ones we can trust to guard Jurgen and Leviné. Are you ready to return to service?"

Weeks of tension left by Eisner's death and the scattering of the assembly had made the balance of power precarious, anyone and everyone grabbing what they could. Spring in Munich—the first since the armistice—flowered no peace.

Leviné's Communists had proved their intentions in a battle at the Marienplatz. Christophe had once taken pride that during the entire four years of the war, not a single street battle had been seen on German territory. That was no longer true; now it was Germans killing Germans in their own homeland.

Christophe had refused to participate, even though many of the men at the warehouse had looked to him for leadership. Ivo had been slower to decide but knew his disability made him weak. So they'd ended up hiding like anyone else who refused to fight. Day after day since the battle between Communists and tattered government forces began, they stayed off the street, keeping clear of roaming armed men from either side. A growing number of Communist soldiers might not look at them suspiciously due to their working-class clothing, but it was safer just the same to keep out of their way. Either fight for them or fight against them—there were no neutrals on the streets anymore.

Christophe received the paper from Ivo, reading claims of the new Communist regime.

"We need every man," Leo said to them. "Government forces in Berlin are trying to gather the free corps—calling themselves the White army—to abolish us, and the Socialists are building an army of their own. We'll join with them against the free corps if we have to—"

"And turn on each other to see who will win after that?" Christophe asked. "The Socialists or the Communists? When you used to be Socialist yourself?"

"Yes! Now is the time to be rid of the voices who don't agree. Are you with us again? For the future of your families? for the future of the world?"

Ivo was already shaking his head. "I can barely shoot a gun;

you know that, Leo. What use would I be in street fighting the way it is now, with so many guns? I was only good to scare away thugs. And drive the truck."

"You can take a bullet, can't you? For Jurgen, for Leviné? They can't so much as leave the privy without protection—and if the free corps make it here, we'll need every man we can gather. They're already at Dachau. We need you more than ever."

"No, Ivo! No," his mother called from the shadows. "All of that is behind you now."

Christophe looked at Ivo's mother. She'd been more than relieved to take them in when the fighting had started, telling them both how worried she'd been when Ivo was involved with the Socialists—even though they'd never used guns, they threatened their use often enough. The Communists under Leviné had proven an entirely different sort since seizing the power left vacant by Eisner's death. But Jurgen had joined with him anyway.

"I'm sorry, Leo," Ivo said. "Not this time."

Leo looked as if he might say something, then held back. He looked at Christophe, but only for a moment. Then he turned to the open door. "If you change your mind, we're at the warehouse. All of us have moved to the barracks, where it's safer."

"Leo, wait," Christophe called. "Have you heard from her? from Annaliese?"

Leo shook his head. "No." He started to leave, then paused, putting a hand into one pocket. "But here. This came to the house for you. Before we left, a week or more ago."

Christophe nearly leaped at it, seizing the envelope extended his way, a return address scribbled in the corner. Düray!

But his breathing stopped, his throat tight. Not Annaliese at all. Her parents, from their old home in Braedon. Though new to him, it was obviously an old letter, for surely they'd sailed by now.

"Thank you," he said, the words barely audible.

Leo left without another word.

Christophe exchanged a glance with Ivo. He didn't look any sorrier than Christophe felt to see Leo gone.

Then Christophe went to the light above the table, seeing the envelope had already been torn open. He unfolded the contents and read the script from Annaliese's mother, tidy, small handwriting.

It was dated weeks before, at the end of February. He skimmed the words.

> *. . . and so we're still here, for how long I do not know. Herr Düray remains too weak to travel, but he gains strength a little every day. If only our Annaliese were here, it would surely give him the medicine he needs.*

Christophe read the letter twice, confused, before realizing Frau Düray must have written another letter first, one that had no doubt been lost in all of the city's chaos. Annaliese's father . . . too ill to travel. So they were still here, in Germany?

Perhaps *that* was where Annaliese had gone!

29

"But you can't go back to the city!" Meika's voice was high-pitched, piercing the calm of the morning.

Annaliese held up the newspaper, having searched as she did every time they received news from Munich. She tracked events all over Europe, in Russia and Austria or anywhere. And there it was—Communism had taken over Hungary weeks ago. The paper was that old!

"This is what they were waiting for, Meika. It's supposed to spread, like a huge red wave. The Communist revolution has already begun. I must go!"

Meika waved her hands as if to erase Annaliese's words. "All the more reason for you to stay here! Besides, you said Christophe wouldn't stay in the city, that he would go home. If you go anywhere, you ought to go there, not Munich. At least it'll be safer in the rural towns."

She shook her head, already convinced. "But what if he's still there, waiting for me? looking for me?" She wrung her hands. "I have to find him—it's my fault he's in the city at all. I should have told him where I'd gone. Why didn't I?"

Annaliese paced, involuntarily raising one hand to the sudden ache in her forehead. She must make plans. "If he isn't at the flat, or if Leo and Jurgen don't know where he is, then I'll go home and see if he's there. But I can't go all the way home without stopping in Munich first. The train will take me seven blocks from Leo's. Not so very far a detour." She wondered if Meika heard the fear behind her words.

Annaliese would have hurried away, but Meika ambushed her at the doorway and caught her by the hands.

"Are you sure, Annaliese? very sure that this is God's leading and not something you think you ought to do to prove to Jurgen you know what you believe now?"

"I've done nothing but pray since the moment I saw the article this morning." She drew Meika close, praying for strength with each word. "God will be with me no matter where I go. I know that now. These weeks of learning from each other, from God's Word itself, from your church, haven't been wasted. I've been praying for direction, to know when I would be ready to find Christophe." She pulled back, holding Meika's face between her palms. "That moment is now. I'm ready to tell him that his faith is my faith. I can claim that now, on my own, without having him think I've changed only to gain his love."

"But to go to the city . . ."

"God will keep me safe. Somehow, Meika, I know Christophe's there. Waiting for me." She drew her friend into another hug. "Be happy for me." Then she turned away, calling over her shoulder, "And pray!"

Christophe tried the gate but it was locked tight. Looking through the bars, he knew such noise would alarm the dogs, yet there was only unexpected silence.

He wished he could see the house from where he stood, but even with the trees holding barely more than a promise of spring, the wood was too thick and the distance too far. Backing up, he looked down the road, noting the height of the fence in comparison to the sturdiness of the iron gate. There was no easy foothold on the gate, but he'd scaled higher walls than this from the depths of a trench.

First he would make sure there were no dogs.

"Hey! Hey!" He shook the gate and the lock rattled. Then he waited.

Nothing.

He frowned, myriad thoughts going through his mind. The letter had been weeks old; perhaps Herr Düray had made a quicker recovery than expected. Perhaps Annaliese had been the right medicine, as Frau Düray hoped. Perhaps they'd all sailed together and were already gone.

He was tempted to walk into town, to see what anyone knew. He'd been in such a hurry to get here that he'd come straight from the train, half-expecting Annaliese to somehow spot him and meet him at this very gate. What he should do was walk back to town, make some inquiries. That would be the sensible thing.

Instead, Christophe threw his bag over the gate, shifted his rifle behind him, grabbed a bar from the gate, and put his hand atop the brick, pushing the tip of his boot to one corner of the gate's frame. Then he catapulted himself over.

No dogs.

Nonetheless, he didn't waste any time getting to the front door of the mansion. He rapped with the knocker, and it echoed as if the place were empty. He waited.

He knocked again. Waited.

At last he took a few steps back, assessing each window,

wondering if he should make his way around to the back to see if there might be a gardener's cottage, some other place where a caretaker might reside.

He might have done just that, but movement from one of the windows caught his eye. There was someone inside, though reluctant to answer.

He knocked again and called out, "It's me, Christophe Brecht. Frau Düray! Come to the door."

He wasn't at all sure it had been Frau Düray, but it had certainly been a woman. The hand pulling aside the lace curtain was small, the shadow behind it slight. Surely not Annaliese, or she would have let him in already.

"Frau Düray!" He announced his name again, pounded once more.

Then he heard movement. Someone was standing just behind the door.

"I'm looking for Herr or Frau Düray," he said through the barrier. "Or their daughter, Annaliese. Are they here? Can you tell me where they are?"

"Go away," the voice said. A woman's, as he'd suspected, but unfamiliar. Young.

Then he heard a commotion, another voice from farther away that he couldn't quite make out. The girl behind the door called back that she wouldn't unbolt the door for anything. And then she said his name.

A moment later the door flew open.

Frau Düray stood there, fully dressed and yet not quite herself. Circles surrounded her eyes in a grayish brown that made her appear older, tired. She clutched at the collar of her gown, which, he noticed now, was wrinkled as if it hadn't been pressed at all.

"Christophe!" She nearly fell against him, her arms tight around his neck. "Oh, you've come! Thank God. Is she with you? Is Annaliese with you?"

She pulled away to look around, past Christophe, around the doorway, over his shoulder. Only to step back, pressing her stomach with one hand and the collar of her gown again with the other as if the pain of disappointment was too great to bear.

But her greeting hadn't been the one he wanted, either.

"So . . . she isn't here," Christophe said gently. "I'm sorry. I've lost her—but I think she's safe. She left the political group she was working with weeks ago, when they went Communist. She left of her own free will, without any trouble."

Frau Düray looked so desperately unhappy, he rambled on to assure her. As they went inside, he talked about how Annaliese had been working for the hope of Germany, and she didn't want to be found just yet, that was all. She thought her family gone, or he was sure she would have come here.

Movement caught his eye and he let his voice fade away. A door opened, not from the parlor but from what he'd thought was the dining room. Upstairs, too, he noticed a set of shadows that hadn't been there a moment ago.

Like uncertain children coming forth after the call of authority, one by one people appeared from behind other doors and hallways. Old and young, men and women. One woman even held a little lapdog, which yapped the moment she untied a string from around its snout.

Without a word, Christophe looked at Frau Düray.

"Friends from the city," she said softly, "and . . . friends of friends."

In Munich, anyone unwilling to "fairly share" with those of

lesser means had been ousted from their homes under threat of being shot, allowing those from the proletariat class to take up any excess room. But he hadn't expected this in the countryside.

He leaned closer to Frau Düray. "Is anyone . . . forcing you to alter your living arrangements?"

She shook her head. "They've fled the city to come here. I don't blame a single one after the stories they brought with them." Then she smiled. "Truly, it's been a blessing. So many brought provisions with them, and we've been able to share. Sharing is easier when it's voluntary."

"I came as soon as I learned you hadn't sailed in February. How is Herr Düray?"

Frau Düray looked up the stairs, and for the first time Christophe saw past the others. There, at the top, stood Herr Düray. Leaning heavily on a cane, half his face drooped in an unnatural frown, yet dressed as neatly as he always had.

"Who is it? Edith—you are . . . here? Vera?"

"I'm coming, Herr Düray," the servant behind Frau Düray said as she held her black skirt out of the way and hurried up the stairs.

"It's Christophe Brecht, Manfred. He came to tell us about Annaliese."

Frau Düray took Christophe by the elbow with one hand and with the other smoothed her hair back and out of the way, pulling a ribbon from her pocket and freeing her hand to tie her hair away from her face. "Come into the parlor, Christophe, where we can talk. Vera, bring Herr Düray along, please."

There was a different smell in the mansion, of dust and shut-in air, of musty clothing and old food. Of dampness, too, and he saw why when he stepped into the parlor. Laundry lines hung from the chandelier, hidden evidence of those living inside this mansion. Christophe had smelled far more unpleasant scents, but it was so unexpected that he swiped at his nose, hoping to brush it away.

"Is there coffee, Vera?" Frau Düray asked in her old voice, and if Christophe would've closed his own eyes to the barrenness of the room, to Frau Düray's appearance, closed his nose to the staleness of the air and the odd placement of the laundry, he might have believed everything was all right from the assurance in her tone.

"No, Frau Düray. But I believe there's tea." She handed Herr Düray off to his wife.

"No tea for me," Christophe said. "I don't want to take what you have."

"There is enough. Serve it in here, Vera."

There were no knickknacks left, no vases nor piano, no side chairs nor occasional tables upon which those knickknacks once rested. But the painting was still there, an image of days long gone for the Düray family. And the two sofas still sat opposite one another, a small table in between.

Christophe's gaze settled for a moment on Annaliese in the portrait, reminding him with a twist to his gut how deeply he missed her.

Herr Düray shuffled toward the sofa, one hand on his cane and the other still on Frau Düray. He was clearly impaired, perhaps even blind, though he did look as if he were peering Christophe's way.

"So where . . . ? My . . . my Ann-liese?" Herr Düray's voice was gruff and garbled, as if he were trying to talk with a mouthful of marbles.

Christophe waited until they were settled, then took a seat opposite them. "I'm afraid I can only tell you where Annaliese isn't," he admitted. "She won't be found in any familiar place in Munich. I've searched everywhere. Then—" he pulled out the letter he'd received from Frau Düray—"when I received this, learning you were still here in Germany, I came hoping to find her here, with you."

"And you can see she isn't here," Frau Düray said. "We'd hoped you were still with her."

"Yes, I'm sorry. She must believe what I believed, that you'd already sailed. I'm sorry to hear of your illness, Herr Düray."

"We cope," he said. "With . . . God's help."

"Herr Düray is much stronger than he was," Frau Düray said with a smile. "He's gaining more strength every day. And more of his vision. We thank God for his progress."

"I can see," Herr Düray protested.

But Frau Düray shook her head, something he clearly did not notice. "He sees light, and he does have a small window of vision."

Vera came in with the tea and set the tray in front of Frau Düray before disappearing again.

"I apologize for the state of the house," Frau Düray said as she poured. "It's been so hard on those who've lost their homes." She looked toward the doors that opened to a dining area, evidence of the state of affairs. The hall and rooms were empty now, others having given them privacy, but her face was grave.

"What happened to the guard and the dogs?"

"When people started coming from the city, the guard left. He said he wanted to join the revolution." She handed a cup of tea to Christophe. "I suppose it's just as well he's gone. His dogs might well have eaten poor little Freddie. That's Frau Traugott's dog. We have children here now, too. I don't think I'd have wanted them around those dogs."

"There was no one else to hire, to take his place?"

Frau Düray shook her head. "While our friends fled the city, workers flocked to it. But what could we do, except offer what we have anyway? We heard stories of the banks having all of their cash removed, of factory owners shot down and anyone who wasn't Communist taken to prison. We planned to be gone by the time the Communists came all the way out here . . . but to look at us, you would think us already set upon, wouldn't you?"

She seemed to want his affirmation, and he nodded. It was true, except for her clothes. Wrinkled silk was still silk.

"We've let all of our help go except Vera, who does her best, but there is too much to do."

"More help . . . come," Herr Düray said, "if she would pay."

"It's true we're being careful with our money," Frau Düray said as she sipped her tea. "America will be expensive if Manfred cannot work for a while, even with help from our friends there. We've had to be frugal for the time we have left here. Fewer workers means higher wages."

"You still intend to sail, then?"

"Of course. We can't stay here. I won't live a prisoner in my own home. Another ship sails next week, and we plan to be on it now that Manfred is walking again."

Christophe said nothing, wondering if America would be more forgiving than Germany itself for the results of the war.

"You must tell us everything about Annaliese and how you came to lose track of her. She's safe? Are you sure?"

He nodded because he'd been able to convince himself of that by the grace of God. So he told them everything, in the hope of convincing them that Annaliese was safe.

And praying he was right.

30

For the first time in her life, Annaliese wished she could wear trousers and carry a gun. Clearly that was the only way to wander through the streets of Munich these days. A city she hardly recognized.

The train hadn't even entered the center of the city and she'd been forced to walk, starting in one of the more fashionable neighborhoods she hadn't seen the likes of since visiting Munich with her parents years ago. Once she reached the interior of the city, she saw only men with guns. The few civilians visible wore working-class clothing, as she herself wore. A woman in peasant dress, a scarf holding down her hair, went into one of the most elegant homes on the block—not even bothering to use the service entrance. She walked up to the front door, looked over her shoulder at Annaliese as if in defiance of a challenge, then went inside without even knocking. As if she owned the place!

Annaliese hurried through the neighborhood. She felt as if she were the last woman on any street of the city, and though no one seemed to take note of her—except, perhaps, from behind curtains at their windows—tension followed every step. She wanted only to find Christophe and then leave as quickly as she'd come.

It wouldn't be long before she came to Leo's house. She walked briskly, praying all the way. Her heart pounded heavily, in stark contrast to her feet, which fairly sailed along.

These were the very streets she'd walked with Christophe, so safe at his side. The thought made her wish he were here right now. Made her hurry her steps even more.

She rounded the corner of the street where Leo lived and saw another group of men, each armed, laughing and patrolling as if they were still at war. *How is it that men are still at war—within Germany?*

Annaliese slipped quickly onto the nearest porch to wait until the men passed. She crouched into the corner behind an old flower box, praying they moved along without stopping.

The voices neared, along with the clop of their boots, the rattle of their rifles.

Then they moved away.

She peered out to be sure they were well down the street, then resumed her pace toward Leo's. It wasn't far now.

"Hey, hey!" The voice pitched her heart in a lurch. She quickened her step.

"Look there."

"You walk too fast," another voice called.

She kept walking, sparing only a quick glance over her shoulder. She should have waited until they'd turned the block. Why hadn't she? How foolish!

The whole bunch of them was turned around, heading now in her direction. Stinging fear shot from her soul outward, ending in sharp prickles at her fingertips. She didn't know how many there were—she wouldn't spare another glance—but guessed there to be at least a half dozen. A small crowd indeed, but a crowd just the same. She knew the danger of such a thing, when all one had to do was incite the wrong action. One became all in a crowd, none to blame for whatever they chose to do together, or so they might think.

"What is your name?" another called.

She kept her eyes focused ahead, never slowing her pace. *Lord . . . please . . .*

"Stop, comrade *Fräulein*! We're all comrades!"

One of them trotted around her to stand in her path. She skirted past.

"Stay with us a little while, *Fräulein*," said another.

"Yes, it's lonely in the streets these days."

One of them pulled the hat from her head.

Her brain screamed to run, and her feet would have followed. But there were too many. One woman fettered by a skirt couldn't escape a half-dozen armed men.

Her heart hammered her chest so loudly she was certain they could hear it. *Oh, Lord . . . please . . .*

"Give me my hat," she said, astonished at the assurance in her own voice. Surely God *was* with her.

The one with the hat laughed. "For a kiss."

Another stepped forward between Annaliese and the man who'd whipped the hat from her head. "Hey! Do you know who she is?"

"Of course I know who she is. A pretty *Fräulein*. What more do I need to know?"

The one who'd stepped between them turned in a flash, grabbing her hat so quickly from the other that he instantly lost his grip.

He faced Annaliese, handing the hat to her. "You're Annaliese, aren't you? You used to speak on the corners with Jurgen? And in the beer halls, too!"

From behind her, someone repeated Jurgen's name, and she thought a couple of them took a step backward, away from her.

"Yes, I'm Annaliese." She put her hat on again. "I'm going to see Jurgen right now."

"Then you're going the wrong direction. Don't you know where he is?"

She pointed down the street, in the direction of the house he'd shared with Leo.

But the man in front of her shook his head. "No, he's at the barracks with us now. It's safer." He bowed, then tipped his hat at her as if they stood in the parlor of any polite home in the city. "My name is Odovacar Schmidt."

Someone laughed again, this time louder than before. "No, *Fräulein*, his name is Popoff."

Suddenly, where they had been a menace a moment ago, they were all just boys not any older than she. "I know where the barracks are, Odovacar," she said, "but it's far from here. Ten blocks, at least. Is anyone still at the house down the street? Huey? Bertita? Christophe?"

"I think Huey still lives there with Bertita, along with a lot of others now. They live with the people, *ja*? But someone tried to kill Jurgen on this very street. It was bourgeoisie, certainly. Tried to shoot him outside his home!"

Her breath caught in her throat. Christophe could easily have been with Jurgen. He still lived there as far as she knew. "Were bodyguards with him? Was anyone hurt?"

"No, no one was hurt."

More laughter. "The bourgeoisie can't shoot!"

Odovacar extended an arm toward Annaliese. "I'll take you to him. Jurgen has been living with the men ever since, for protection. Until things settle down, at least."

"And the others? Ivo? Christophe?"

"They've left the barracks, both of them. A shame to lose Christophe; he was the best I've seen with a gun. He taught me everything I know about this one."

With his free hand he held up the gun from his shoulder as if it were a toy. She wished it were.

They started walking and Odovacar, or Popoff to his comrades, set a leisurely pace.

"Wait until you see the barracks, *Fräulein!* There are enough of us now, between our men and Leviné's, to keep the whole city safe—even from the free corps, should they be foolish enough to try getting rid of us. Any more men and we'll burst through the walls."

He smiled then, such an innocent, friendly smile, in utter contrast to what she feared only moments ago. She could almost smile back. For the first time since leaving Meika's, Annaliese felt a measure of safety. Maybe it was relief that the men wouldn't harm her, or maybe her senses were right—she was closer to Christophe than ever. He might not be at the barracks, but he was here . . . somewhere. And she meant to find him.

The air was cool but not cold, the sky blue, the trees beginning to bud. Birds sang from the branches. With six armed guards around her now, Annaliese noticed that spring had arrived in Munich.

⸙

Christophe closed the cover of his haversack, the clothes Vera had washed for him now neatly tucked away. Wrinkled, since it appeared Frau Düray only used the hot press for Herr

Düray's clothing, but clean. After an extra day at their crowded mansion, it was time to return to Munich. Annaliese had to be there somewhere; either that or he would find someone who knew where she'd gone.

He would stop at his home to retrieve a set of his old clothes, those he'd worn before he went off to war. Without a doubt bourgeoisie-class clothing. And he would ask Frau Düray to provide something for Annaliese. Just asking made him feel hopeful; he would prepare as if he was certain to find her.

He looked around the near-empty room he'd used. It was the one spot they'd kept empty, in hope of Annaliese coming home. It was as sparsely furnished as the rest of the house, offering only a bed. Still, Christophe left the bedroom with a touch of regret. Somehow, knowing it had been her room, her bed, had been enough to keep the nightmares away. Last night he'd enjoyed the first uninterrupted sleep in months. Years.

He found his way downstairs, hearing young voices along the way. Children laughed from one of the rooms, evidently enjoying living conditions that provided ample playmates. The women, too, hadn't seemed all that inconvenienced. He'd seen a half dozen chatting over a sewing project last night. The men, however, had mostly been absent.

He found Frau Düray in the parlor with two other women, but when he neared, she stood to greet him.

"I wonder if I may talk to you alone, Frau Düray?" he asked.

She agreed, then led him from the room to a small door opposite the parlor. She withdrew a key from her pocket, unlocked the door, then led him inside.

The room was a small office, with only a desk and one chair left and a landscape painting of the Bavarian Alps on the wall that seemed conspicuous under the circumstances. It likely hid a wall safe.

"You said yesterday that you still plan to sail. You still have the means to do that, then?"

She nodded and looked at the painting as if to confirm what he'd guessed. Their resources were tucked away.

"Do the others living here know?"

"No, Manfred and I thought it best to keep our circumstances to ourselves."

"Good, that's very good."

She smiled. "But I trust them. And God, too. It's Manfred who worries about what might happen, even though he's starting to trust God again."

"It does no harm to be cautious."

"Christophe, do you think we should wait to sail? Do you think there's hope she might come home?"

He wanted to tell them yes, that surely she would be home soon. But they would be better off away from here, away from Communist troops eager to conquer, away from the hunger, away from the fighting that somehow, even after the last four years, their fellow Germans couldn't give up.

"No, Frau Düray. Don't wait. You should go. I'll bring her to America if I can."

She smiled, then went to the desk and withdrew paper and pencil from one of the drawers. "This is the name of the ship we're sailing on. And this is where we'll be staying in America. Although Annaliese would know, I think. We're with our old friends the Kemp family in Baltimore."

Christophe accepted the information but made no effort to quit the room. He shuffled his feet. "Frau Düray . . . there is something I want to ask you."

"Yes?"

"It's . . . about Annaliese." He wanted to add Giselle's name, but at the last moment his courage failed him. "I wanted to ask if you could supply me with a change of clothing for her. Her clothes were gone from her room."

"Yes, we've packed her clothing in trunks. They're kept next to the ones we've packed for ourselves. When we leave . . . if she isn't with us, we'll entrust everything to Vera, who will be the only caretaker left until our friends can go home. Things are bound to settle down, aren't they?" She sighed, not waiting for an answer. "It is much to ask of an employee, and one so young as Vera. She is smart, though, and when things improve, she'll work with our lawyer to see about the sale—of the factory, too."

He had no doubt they would compensate the maid for such a task—and probably generously, too. But the wrinkle on Frau Düray's forehead proved she wasn't entirely convinced Vera was the best liaison between them and their lawyer.

"Even if it takes me longer than I expect to bring Annaliese home, I'll see that Vera isn't overwhelmed with the responsibility. Don't worry."

Frau Düray seemed as near a smile as to tears just then, and he wished he knew how to rid her of every worry, especially those about Annaliese. But he couldn't imagine how to make such real worries disappear; he could only think to bring her attention back to his questions.

"When I find Annaliese, I don't know who will be in power anymore. We both fit into the working class now, and that's safest for the moment. But if government troops take over, not a working-class person—man or woman—will dare be seen if a White army gathers here in Bavaria. Red troops won't have a chance, and a government army might assume anyone in the working class would be sympathetic to Red troops, if not fighting for them. So she needs to be able to dress to either class, depending on which army is in power. I'll stop at home for a change of clothes, but I hoped you'd have something for Annaliese."

"Of course! Anything to keep her safe." She started toward the door and he knew his chance to ask something else would be lost if he let her go.

"And there is one more thing."

She stopped, turning to him. "Yes?"

He shifted his weight from one foot to the other, readjusted the gun hanging from his shoulder. He knew if he was to be at the train in time, he must speak now or hold his tongue— maybe forever. If Annaliese's parents sailed next week, this could be his last chance to find out the truth.

"Did you know that Giselle was receiving letters from a soldier who wanted to desert the army? that she stored those letters inside envelopes belonging to letters from me?"

Frau Düray folded her arms. Her brows dipped and the corners of her mouth went tight. "I burned those letters, every one of them. How did you know about them?"

"Annaliese saw the letters. She thought I'd written them."

"Oh! I'm sorry, Christophe. If she's been under the impression that you had any part in what Giselle did . . ."

"I was able to explain it to her. But you knew they weren't from me? How?"

Frau Düray looked from Christophe to the door, as if deciding whether or not to talk about a subject she clearly did not wish to address. Then she unfolded her arms and faced Christophe again.

"Two years after the war began, Giselle joined the German Red Cross. I wouldn't let Annaliese, insisting she was too young. Giselle went off on her own, and there wasn't a day that passed that we didn't worry over her. And then last spring she came home. She'd been sick, and they sent her home because she couldn't meet the demands of her duty."

She looked ahead as she spoke, no longer at Christophe. "But she'd changed, our Giselle. I suppose seeing so much death, so much suffering, was bound to change her. And . . . she was in love."

She folded her arms again as if she were chilled. "I found one of the letters from the man she fell in love with. It explained why she'd changed. He was full of hate for the war, for those he blamed for keeping it going. The Kaiser, of course. Hindenburg. I hadn't meant to read it. Vera had found it, folded, inside the pocket of a dress she was laundering. Once she read it, Vera thought I should know what it said. I confronted Giselle about the letter, asked her to stop corresponding with him, even to stop thinking of him."

Frau Düray hesitated, still staring ahead. "For a while I thought she'd agreed. But she received more letters. At first I thought them from you. I know that's what Annaliese believed." She smiled, but it was a sad smile, without a trace of happiness in her eyes. "Annaliese always did have a special place in her heart for you. I think she was jealous of Giselle, being closer in age to you. Having your friendship."

How different their lives would have been if he'd noticed Annaliese's interest in him, if their friendship had been able to bud through the years of the war. By the time he came home, they would already have known each other . . . and she would have been all grown up.

"Giselle picked up the mail in town and must have begun switching the envelopes so none of us would know. The last letter she received from him said if she really loved him—"

"She would do something to help end the war, to bring him home."

"Yes, that's right. And then, when Giselle did what she did—starting that fire . . ." Frau Düray brushed away a tear rolling down her cheek. "Manfred didn't know she would go back inside. He saw her, you know. It haunts him to this day. He saw her run from the factory; then he saw the flames. When Giselle spotted him, she tried to hide from him. She ran the other direction—too close to the factory. She was hit by debris from the explosion."

She raised unsteady fingertips to her forehead. "Here. She was hit here. You wouldn't have thought it had even hurt her, if you'd seen her face. She was lovely, right up to the moment they closed the casket."

Then she looked at Christophe again, as if she'd been away for a moment but was back now. "Manfred has forbidden me to talk about it, even to Annaliese. He blames himself for what happened; he didn't want Annaliese to blame him too."

"And yet she left home anyway."

Frau Düray nodded slowly. "I thought she would come home. I didn't know she'd read those letters or that they had anything to do with the reason she left. They must have made her hate her father too, the way they made Giselle hate him. And me, too, a little, I think."

Christophe approached Frau Düray, taking one of her hands in his. "Annaliese went to Munich to see if she could make a difference—to make Germany a better place. One without armaments or war, one where everyone took care of everyone else."

"I wish the world were a place such a dream could succeed."

"So do I."

Christophe let go of her hand, taking up his haversack again, alongside his gun. He only needed bourgeoisie clothing for Annaliese, and then he would go.

Frau Düray turned back to the door as if she'd read his thoughts. It was time for him to leave.

Christophe asked one last question. "Do you know what happened to him? the boy who wrote the letters, who started so much trouble for Giselle? for Annaliese?"

"After Giselle was . . . gone . . . she received another letter from him, so I read it. It was full of the same hate, the same demands for her to do something. He'd deserted his post, refusing to fight anymore. He didn't know what had happened to her, and he wanted Giselle to meet him. Two weeks later I received another note meant for Giselle, written by a soldier who knew him. He said that the boy was shot—by a German officer, for desertion of duty. Executed without a trial, so the letter said."

She put a hand to her mouth but words came out anyway. "God forgive me, his was one death I didn't mourn."

31

Annaliese barely recognized the warehouse. Bunk after bunk formed close and tight rows, filling every possible spot. She'd always thought the warehouse too large for the dozens of men Jurgen had once convinced to follow him. Now it was far too small.

There must have been hundreds of bunks now, and nearly as many men present, of all ages and sizes. They had only one thing in common: each of them had at least one gun. She swallowed hard, hoping Odovacar had been telling her the truth. If Jurgen wasn't here . . .

Like a breeze through this forest of men, word spread that there was a woman among them. Some of them were in various stages of undress, a few of whom hurried to grab their shirts while others called to her invitingly. She held on tight to Odovacar's arm and stared straight ahead, trying to see nothing at all. He patted her hand, and from the side of her vision she thought his chin a bit high, his smile too wide. Obviously he enjoyed this prize he'd brought back.

"Didn't I tell you the warehouse was full?" Odovacar asked. "And this is just one barrack. We have men collected all over the city! Just like this."

The news made her shiver. No wonder the streets were empty. People couldn't even go out to hunt for food or jobs anymore with so many guns about.

There was a makeshift tent in the center of the cement warehouse, and it was there Odovacar led her. Anyone within earshot might have known something was going on in the barrack. Between whistles and invitations—both friendly and unsavory—the noise and energy had undoubtedly shifted the moment she stepped inside.

Before Odovacar could call out for someone in the tent, one flap was flung open. Leo stood there, a curious glance from right to left, until passing Odovacar to settle on Annaliese.

"Anya!" He simultaneously reached for her with one hand and with the other held back the tent flap. "Jurgen! Come quickly."

Then Leo pulled her closer, not in an embrace but to pull her past him and, as soon as Jurgen appeared, to bring them together.

Jurgen's smile was warm and familiar, his arms safe amid such an overcrowded collection of men.

"You've come back," Jurgen said, and she could only call him astonished. "To me!"

Then he moved closer for a kiss, but she turned her face so it landed on her cheek. Let others think she was only modest, but there was more than one reason she kept him from her lips. Those were reserved for another—and Jurgen's were the last lips she wanted to touch.

"Can we talk? Maybe . . . somewhere else?"

Leo still held part of the tent flap, which he now opened wider. "Come in, Anya. Come in."

Jurgen nodded, and he searched her face, as if looking

for something he hoped to find. Even so, his brows gathered apologetically. "I'm sorry, but Leo's right. This is home for now, all I have to offer. Come in."

The inside of the tent was dim and cluttered, although the two cots weren't nearly as snug as those surrounding this interior enclosure. They were joined at an angle in the corner, the opposite ends holding scrawny pillows. The warehouse had smelled of dirty cots and unwashed bodies, and the same odor was here but lighter. Spring hadn't reached the warehouse, even here. Clothes were piled in one corner, a stack of books in another, next to an oil lamp. A bucket of water sat on a small, round table off to the side, next to a pitcher and two glasses, and a large bowl with soap and towel nearby. Neither Leo nor Jurgen appeared to have shaved in several days. She was surprised, even in the muted lighting, to see how much gray speckled Jurgen's face. Far more than the trace of gray in the light hair on top of his head.

"Leo—"

Jurgen had only to say his name. With a promise to bring back food, Leo said he would return . . . in a while.

"Will you sit?" Jurgen extended a hand to one of the cots. It was littered with a rumpled blanket, discarded clothing, and an open book, all of which he swept aside.

"No," she said, still standing. "I can't stay, not here. But I didn't know what else to do, except come to you."

He reclaimed one of her hands. "Annaliese, don't you know you are always, *always* welcome in my life?"

"But I'm not—that is, I'm not . . . in your life. I only came . . ." She let her voice drift away. Even in light of her anger at him—the state of the city was at least partially his fault, wasn't it?—it seemed cruel, having seen the eagerness with which he'd looked at her face, in her eyes, for something she couldn't give.

She looked at the cement floor instead of at him, at the stains that speckled the surface beneath their feet, spots of oil or some chemical or something else from the days the warehouse had been used for whatever it had been intended. "I came hoping you could tell me where to find . . . Christophe."

The hold on her hand went momentarily limp; then he squeezed it before letting her go altogether. "I see."

"Do you know where he is?"

He stepped away, facing the tent flap that Leo had closed behind him instead of looking at her. "No. He left shortly after you did. I haven't seen him since."

She suddenly wished she could sit but knew she couldn't, not here. Her limbs were weak, her mind awhirl. How foolish she'd been to leave Meika's . . . and yet, what could she have done? She had to find Christophe; he would never have found her there.

Outside this tent were hundreds of men, and beyond this warehouse thousands more. Armed. Where could she go without protection? without help in finding Christophe?

She stepped closer to the tent flap, which put her closer to Jurgen. Before she could reach the opening, Jurgen pulled her into his arms.

"Are you sure, Annaliese? very sure you want him, not me? I know I can't give you all of my attention right now, but soon, when this is over, I can devote myself only to you. You'll be at my side to help the people, helping me to guide them, to take care of them. Isn't that what you've always wanted? To help the people?"

"Yes, that *is* what I wanted. But not the way you've—"

He cut off her words by putting his mouth to hers. She wrenched away, pushing at him, but he was too strong. His beard scratched her skin, poking into her. "No . . . Jurgen . . ."

Jurgen released his hold, stepping back as if surprised by his own actions. He put a hand to his face, rubbing once, letting the palm scrub his chin and cheeks, to pull back on his own hair. "Forgive me. It's . . . it's this place. This stinking . . . prison. All these . . . men. . . . They want too much of me, all the time wanting me to assure them, to lead them." He sent her a half smile. "I was carried away at the sight of you. Forgiven?"

Hands now clenched in fists, she glared at him. "Even if I still wanted you in that way, I'd have gotten over it when you abandoned everything we worked for together. Never once did you ask me what *I* believed, Jurgen, or even consider I might have an opinion of my own—one that might be different from yours. And now look at the people you said you wanted to help. The city is in worse chaos than ever, people cowering in fear while men prowl everywhere with guns!"

If he'd been surprised by his own actions, he seemed no less surprised by her words. "It's necessary—and sooner or later it would have come to this. Don't you see? It's for their own good, in the end. When everyone is truly equal, they'll thank us even for this. . . ."

She turned away, wanting nothing more than to leave. She'd heard enough of his idealistic dreams, and now none of them made sense. But the same thought as a moment ago struck again. Where would she be safe? Traveling through the streets of the city alone? Should she return to Meika's? What about Christophe? She couldn't leave Munich without him.

"I'll go, then," she said softly, but tears stung her eyes as the words slipped past her lips. Because she didn't know where she would go.

He said nothing, only watched her take the last step to the tent flap, his arms now folded across his chest. She couldn't keep her hand from trembling as she pulled the flap out of her way. She must walk through that legion of men by herself, without Jurgen or Leo or even Odovacar. And then out to the street. God help her, she had no choice. Stiffening her shoulders, raising her chin, clenching her fists, she filled her mind with the same plea that had seen her safe so far: *God, help me; God, help me . . .* then took a step beyond the opening.

Only to feel Jurgen's hand on her arm, pulling her back inside. "Annaliese! This is madness. Of course you can't leave alone. Even to go back to wherever you were hiding away, you'll need an escort. I don't even know how you came here— or where you want to go. Where have you been? Where will you go?"

"I—I don't know exactly."

She meant to say she would find a place, tell him that she could take care of herself, that she would be fine. She might even tell him God would provide a place for her, although she knew Jurgen wouldn't welcome her choice of faith any more than he'd welcomed her choice of Christophe.

Instead, a shudder ran through her she couldn't control. Jurgen was the last person whose help she should want; his attempt to kiss her made him barely any better than those just outside this tent, those who'd ogled her from the moment she walked in.

But he'd stopped himself, and foolish or not, she was grateful to him for that. She would have to trust him.

She wanted nothing else than to be away from this place

with all these men, away from Munich altogether, where guns ruled and society was shut down. But why should she depend on God to keep her safe when *she'd* been the one to make such a foolish decision, coming back to Munich when it was in such a state as this?

She covered her face, her palms instantly wet with her tears.

Jurgen's arms came about her again, only this time more gently. "Then you'll stay here," he whispered, "where it's safe."

Christophe gazed at the passing countryside, at the trees dressed in their newest green of the season, at the evergreens standing in contrast, taller than ever. He recalled the forests in France, those that had once been as thick as Germany's. But they'd destroyed the land's garment that God had provided, replaced it with bodies and graves.

Something out the window in the distance caught his eye. So far off he doubted others looking toward the same spot had noticed anything out of the ordinary. A moment later the landscape swelled, and even he was unsure what he'd seen.

Except it was somehow familiar. A cluster of uniforms that, try though they might, did not entirely blend in with the landscape. Troops. In uniform. Free corps? Perhaps . . . but he couldn't be sure. It wouldn't be the first time his imagination had gotten the best of him.

He settled back, intent on resting at least for a few minutes. Tonight would probably not hold much rest, not back in Munich.

They were still miles from the city and it would be dark soon, but even so the train slowed its speed. He thought nothing of it at first; the train always slowed around one curve or another. Yet when he looked out the window again, he saw there was no bend in their route, nor any nearby hills to navigate. They were slowing for no apparent reason.

Grumbles sounded here and there from those taking up seats in the half-empty train car, but soon enough an uneasy silence settled over them. Even here in second class, no one could be sure who was safe anymore.

A conductor came through the cabin door, assuring everyone they would soon be traveling again and not to worry.

Christophe followed him to the back of the train car.

"Are there troops up ahead?" he said, just loud enough over the rumble of the train pulling forward to be heard by the conductor.

He turned to Christophe, an expression of surprise on his face. "Why do you ask such a thing?"

Christophe shrugged, and the gun on his shoulder rattled against the back of an empty seat.

The conductor, an older man, glanced from the gun to Christophe, then patted his shoulder. "The war is over, my friend."

Christophe shook his head. "Not here."

The conductor gave a single, sad nod, then said he would find out why they'd slowed so mysteriously. He walked back through the car, toward the front of the train.

Christophe took a seat once the train started moving at a greater speed again, and since he had his pick of several empty ones, he chose to sit near the front vestibule. For several minutes he watched the door to the cabin ahead, no longer bothering to look out the window. Until he heard another complaint from behind.

"They've switched tracks," someone said, loud enough for all to hear.

The surprise around him gave way to panic before Christophe had even moved to the seat behind him, one that held a better view of the land they passed. The claim was correct; they'd switched tracks and were no longer going east, toward Munich. They were headed south, toward the Alps, and Switzerland.

32

Annaliese barely tasted the bread. Not that it was tasteless—certainly in the past couple of years she'd been served worse. But even if it had been the finest bread the best German baker could produce, she wouldn't have enjoyed it.

She was trapped. Jurgen and Leo were right. Until they could find a safe place for her, she was stuck where she was. Amid several hundred men. And two right in front of her.

"What about the house?" she asked. "Huey and Bertita are still there, aren't they?"

"There is no room left," Leo said. "We're no different from anyone else suffering at the hands of greedy capitalists. Before we left to come here, we willingly opened our doors to those who've been taken advantage of. You missed quite a lot, Anya. Even now, Leviné is implementing our fairness goals, despite what the remnants of the last republic is trying to do against us. Do you know the bankers removed every bit of the cash from their vaults? Even the plates for banknotes. They've shut off the supply of food, too. But they'll see. We'll prevail because we have the numbers behind us. The people."

"All of the people, Leo?" she asked quietly. "Maybe the

bankers were trying to protect the people who'd invested in them."

Jurgen swiped at his mouth after a drink from his cup. "Anya is a bit peeved at us, Leo. We haven't taken the time to share with her how our thoughts and goals have grown, so she isn't entirely with us. Yet." He looked at Annaliese. "It's the natural progression of society, what we have in mind. Capitalism is for children, for greedy, self-centered infants who haven't yet learned to share. The future will be better, Annaliese; you'll see. For all of us."

She looked at the bread still in her hands, considering his words, but not about capitalism. Was that all he'd heard her say, that they hadn't shared *their* beliefs enough to convince her? What about listening to hers?

For a moment she considered answering him, posing questions, having a discussion about what really was best for society. But she knew it would do no good. Jurgen was only good at speaking, not listening. Instead, she asked, "If they shut off the supply of food into Munich, then where . . . ?"

Jurgen finished what was on his plate. "Confiscated from those who've always had too much, from right here in Munich. It was the least we could do."

Annaliese thought of the woman in working-class clothing who'd gone into the aristocratic house in the neighborhood where she'd been made to get off the train. *As if she owned it,* she recalled thinking.

Evidently she did. The people owned it all now.

"I doubt everyone will accept fairness if it's forced on them."

"There will be an adjustment period, of course. New ways take time to settle in. But they'll see. It's best for all of us."

She thought of her parents, of how hard her father had

worked. She'd hated him for turning to armaments, but before that he'd produced metalwork for tools and parts other manufacturers used. To produce things everyone needed, from coffeepots to toys.

Annaliese had allowed herself so little thought of her father, but now thoughts of him came freely. A day had come when someone with a gun could tell him he must follow new rules. There was no longer any private property, only public. No one family should profit any more than another. In essence, her father's talent, his risk and ingenuity, his labor, would be rewarded no differently than the least of those who worked for him.

Didn't the Bible talk about such things? that the least would be greatest; the last, first? Perhaps God liked some of the ideas Jurgen and Leo and Leviné wanted to implement. Greed *must* be a sin.

But was it really greed that drove men like her father? Had he really worked so hard in order to cheat others? Giving what he'd worked for to those who hadn't worked for it at all— for whatever reason—made less sense to her now, seeing it in action. Throwing people from their homes, confiscating their goods, had never been her idea of fairness. She'd only wanted to make sure everyone was given the same opportunities, no matter how people dressed, whom they knew or didn't know, how they spoke, or what they looked like.

She'd only wanted to level the opportunities, not level results from those who put forth different efforts.

Jurgen caught her eye, and for a moment she was tempted to speak her mind, try convincing him away from what he obviously believed. He gave her one of his old, familiarly charming smiles that he must believe she would still welcome, and almost reflexively she wanted to give him one in return. Automatically, like the way she'd once taken on his beliefs. How naive she'd been.

"Leo," she said softly, "I would like help finding Christophe."

He stopped chewing. He looked from Jurgen to Annaliese, then back to Jurgen. "I thought . . ."

"No." Jurgen glanced again at Annaliese and to her surprise he didn't appear annoyed, or even surprised, that she hadn't waited for him to bring up her request. For the first time, he looked as though he wanted to do something that wouldn't serve him—but wanted instead to see her happy. "She's chosen Christophe, not me. And because we love her—both of us, you and I, Leo—we'll help her. Won't we?"

"Well, I . . . I don't know where he is. How would I? He left that night some weeks ago. We haven't seen him since."

Jurgen frowned at Leo. "I thought you spotted him once when you were rounding up more men that day. Didn't you tell me you gave him that letter? the one that came from Annaliese's parents?"

Annaliese looked at Leo. "There was a letter from my parents? Was it for me?"

Leo shook his head. "No, it was addressed to Christophe. It seems he came to Munich to find you—to stay with you—at their request."

"Yes, that's true. So . . . you read the letter?"

Leo had the grace to look momentarily embarrassed. "Yes, we thought the content might tell us where either you or Christophe might be so we could get the letter to one of you."

"And where is the letter now?"

Leo stood, taking his empty plate and reaching for Jurgen's, then placing them on the corner of the table. "Now that you mention it, Jurgen, I do recall having gotten rid of it. I was going door-to-door, scrounging up every last man for help. I did spot Christophe. I remember now. He was with Ivo, I think."

Annaliese stood. "With Ivo? Where?"

"Here in Munich. More crowded than ever, I thought at the time." He turned back to them, away from the table where he'd left the plates. "It was his mother's flat. You recall, Jurgen, we used to visit there when Ivo first joined us."

Annaliese ignored Jurgen's nod and faced Leo. "Will you take me there?"

Jurgen came up behind her, stroking one of her arms. "Leo will send someone for Christophe, to bring him here. Won't you, Leo?"

She could go to Christophe. She could go right now, this very moment. "But—"

Jurgen was already shaking his head, hushing her. "It's too dangerous, Annaliese. You can wait for him here." He sighed. "Soon things will be better. When our ways have been accepted. Then the streets will be safe, even for babies. You'll see."

Christophe jumped off the train when it slowed as it reached the station of a village in the foothills of the Alps. Here he was, miles out of the way. He knew he wasn't the only one inconvenienced, but he was probably the only one who would dare go against the orders of the free corps army and travel the rest of the way to Munich by foot.

All of Munich must be surrounded by troops from other parts of Germany—or soon would be. He'd learned from the conductor that White troops, loyal to what was left of the ravaged but official German army, had already been fighting the Red Communist army in Dachau, north and a bit west of the city. That was why the train had been diverted, to keep clear of what was certain to be another battle—unless the Communists in Munich surrendered their arms without a fight.

He shifted his pack onto his back, keeping the rifle easily accessible, along with the pistol in his pocket. It was late already, but he would have to find a place to sleep somewhere along the way. Spring had brought weather warm enough to use heaven as a roof once again, and for that Christophe gave thanks.

Even as he begged God to help him find Annaliese—if she was still in Munich.

33

Annaliese scrubbed at a stain on the cement, wishing she could banish her worries the same way she could banish the smell. She wondered where some of the men had gotten enough vodka to make them vomit. Maybe it wasn't alcohol at all that had infected them the night before. More likely it had been fear.

Men. Confined, bored, tense. Waiting. Probably much the same way they'd been in France for the past four years. Thank God she'd been too young to be expected to do this sort of work then—or worse, as a nurse having to tend wounds and blood.

A bang sounded from somewhere and she jumped from knees to feet. She stood staring at the door, fully expecting armed men to reappear—who knew from which side of this conflict. But nothing happened. The door didn't even open. The bang could have been anything, but whatever it was, it wasn't an attack on this building.

Since the men had left that morning, only their tension remained behind. Leo and Jurgen and a handful of men around them, serving as guards, inhabited the warehouse now. Word had spread like morning birdcalls that a White army had been gathering around Communist Munich, that the men behind the red flags must defend the city, defend their dreams for the future. For the hopes of everyone of lesser means.

Annaliese told herself to be sorry they'd marched off, knowing if there was to be a battle, some undoubtedly wouldn't return. But the moment the warehouse cleared except for the scant remnant, she'd breathed her first easy sigh since her arrival the morning before.

Yesterday she'd waited eagerly for Christophe to come to the warehouse. She'd taken a chair outside the tent, opposite ones that Jurgen and Leo sat in. She'd let them talk about the battles that had taken place in the past weeks. How Leviné had taken charge of the councils, how easily he'd gathered an army of ten thousand men to guard Munich and protect its newly proclaimed Communist state. How he'd had anyone voicing resistance to the new regime arrested. They talked, too, of the tragedy of those who'd already died in street battles when men loyal to the Communist ideals clashed with those who didn't see the future as brightly and clearly as Leviné and those like Jurgen.

But she'd barely listened. She kept looking at the door, each and every time it had opened.

Never once did Christophe's familiar outline enter.

It wasn't until well past dark that the men sent to find Christophe returned, telling Leo that he'd been at Ivo's but wasn't there anymore. He'd left Munich, but Ivo knew neither where he'd gone nor when—or if—he would return.

So all night Annaliese had planned how she would leave. She would ask Odovacar to take her to the train station in the morning. If she could find a train to take her outside the city, she would go home. Surely that must be where

Christophe was now. Little wonder. Munich was another battle site these days, and she knew he'd had enough of that. At least he must be safe, far away from whatever threatened to explode inside this city.

But shortly after dawn, before she could even leave the tent, Odovacar had been summoned along with the rest of the men. She'd nearly burst into tears. And then she'd prayed. She must wait, and wait she would. The moment she could get away, though, she would say good-bye to Munich and not look back.

In the meantime, she scrubbed.

Christophe slipped to the edge of the marching army, an army he knew only too well. Not a single one of them asked him any questions. They looked no farther than the make of his rifle and the cut of his boots to know he was one of them.

The outskirts of the city were deadly quiet, as if it had been evacuated. He knew it hadn't been. Outsiders might not be gaining easy access into Munich, but he hadn't seen a mass exodus, either. They were there, hiding away in their homes, in much the same way so many French had hidden when Germans had marched through in August of '14.

That it was Germans hiding from Germans wrenched his stomach. How had this happened? Hadn't they had enough, the same way he'd had enough? When would it be time to stop fighting?

Christophe had killed his last enemy, and neither these men nor the ones on the other side should be called that. He had no intention of adding any more faces to his nightmares.

But he marched anyway because it was the only way to reach the last place he'd seen Annaliese.

He stared ahead, wondering where he would be today if Frau Düray hadn't asked him to go after Annaliese. How else would he have found a way to care about what went on here in Munich, except through Annaliese? Without her, would he have cared enough to hope for a better future for himself? for anyone?

He couldn't be sure. He knew he'd always wanted something better than this, and now he couldn't imagine a future—a better future—without Annaliese.

He wouldn't fight for Communism or Socialism, no matter what, and he doubted Annaliese would expect him to.

But he *would* fight for a future with her.

34

"They're here! They're in the city!"

The sentry, a boy who couldn't be much older than thirteen, shouted his message the moment he'd opened the door, then ran toward the tent in the center.

Annaliese stood but did not join them. So the battle had begun. She wondered how long it would be before this battle was near enough to hear. She looked around, questioning if she should flee this spot that was obviously a place meant for soldiers, not civilians like her, or non-Communists like her.

But the same thing that kept her here last night kept her here again. She had no place else to go.

God save her. God save them all.

❧

The stench was the same, the grunts and cries, the quiver of light from firing guns, the pale faces around him—paler still after they fell.

Christophe never drew his weapon, not even when men around him started falling. The one on his right was dead already; he knew that from the severity of the wound to the

man's head. But another to his left and then another in front . . .
The one nearest he checked for a pulse at the neck, finding it
despite the blood soaking his shoulder and arm.

"Hold on, soldier," he said in his ear. "I'm going to take
you to safety."

Christophe pulled the man to conceal him behind a stack
of chairs at what must have been an outdoor café. The man
was still conscious, though stunned, and his gun fell away the
moment Christophe clasped him around his chest. He left the
weapon on the street.

Then he went to the other man who'd fallen and did the
same, first checking for a sign of life and finding it—weak.
More blood, unconscious, certainly more grievously wounded
than the first man had been. Christophe grasped him beneath
the arms, pulling him in another direction, to what he hoped
was a flat between the shops. A flat where someone lived.

The door was locked, as he'd expected, but a kick to the
knob had the frame splintered in no time. Screams pierced
his ears, although he saw no one, not even in the shadows of
the unlit room.

"There is a man here," he announced to whoever had
screamed, "a man needing care. He can't hurt you."

And then, taking with him the man's weapons, Christophe
left the soldier unarmed, hoping whoever lived in this shop-
keeper's home would see to the needs of a man who might
otherwise die—a man who'd come to defend the rights of bourgeoisie shop owners.

He returned to the street. Men collapsed and blood spurted
and Christophe, like so many stretcher bearers he'd seen doing
the same, went from wounded to wounded. He gave aid where
he could from the bandage roll in his jacket—the last one the

government had issued to him the year before, something he should have thrown away long ago but had carried with him anyway, like a habit he found too difficult to give up.

Unlike the last battle he'd fought, Christophe was unable to tell the difference between these fighting armies—White or Red, none carried flags, and some on both sides wore a German uniform. Christophe didn't care; he helped whom he could as an angel would. And surely angels were there, a shield between Christophe and the bullets sailing around him.

"Wounded here!"

Annaliese heard the cry and without thinking drew near. She'd heard the gunshots—hollow and short, like firecrackers in the distance. A fighter from the street stumbled over the threshold, dragging a man beside him until the guard at the door rushed to his aid. Between the two of them, they hauled the injured man to the nearest cot, where Annaliese met them. She had neither training nor equipment, not even a single bandage, but surely she could do something.

She nearly vomited at the sight. He was not merely pale but white, limp and unconscious. So much blood, so wet and shiny, still streaming from the side of a boy who looked even younger than Annaliese herself. What could she do? What could *she* do to save anyone from such a wound?

The fighter who'd brought him had a good deal of the man's blood on his own hands and shirt. "His name is Shultz. You'll help him, *ja*?"

Annaliese found herself nodding even though everything inside told her she was less than adequate to meet such a task.

The fighter was already turning away, leaving her alone at this boy's side. Not even the guard who'd helped move him to the cot stayed near. He returned to his post.

She ventured another step closer but was afraid to touch him for fear of doing more harm than good. "Shultz?" How absurd to say his name as if to ask his permission or his help in assessing what to do for him. But she was too stunned to do anything else.

Movement beside her banished her stupor.

Leo stood there, a frown on his face. "There's nothing we can do for him." Then Jurgen, who was a few paces behind, joined them. Leo turned to block him from the sight. "The fight must be nearing if they're close enough to bring wounded here instead of the hospitals. Let's go."

Annaliese couldn't imagine where Leo would take Jurgen. Back to the tent? That hardly offered any protection, not even with the half-dozen guards left behind. They were all as fragile as this boy bleeding to death in front of them.

But Jurgen wouldn't let himself be pulled away. He looked beyond Leo's shoulder, at the man who even now seemed to be melting into the cot beneath him. Jurgen stepped closer, closer even than Annaliese stood, and bent over the boy.

"You're not alone," he said, laying a hand to his forehead, smoothing back curly hair. Then, without turning to Leo, he added, "Aren't there any supplies here? bandages? iodine?"

"Come away from there, Jurgen," Leo said. "What do you think you can do?"

Resistance to Leo's coldheartedness made Annaliese braver than she'd been a moment ago. "Pull away his jacket, Jurgen. Maybe the blood makes it look worse than it really is. I'll see what I can find for bandages."

"You're both fools," Leo said. "If they're fighting close enough to bring him here, we could be attacked at any moment. Jurgen, come along *now*."

"And go where?" He was already working on the jacket, ignoring the red discoloring his fingers as he freed each button. "If I'm going to die in this fight, Leo, I'd rather do it helping someone than hiding. So if you're not going to help Annaliese, get out of the way."

Annaliese didn't wait for Leo's response. She ran through the narrow aisles, calling out to the men who guarded the doors, others who lingered around the tent where Jurgen and Leo had been.

"Medical supplies!" she called. "Are there any here?"

The men at whom she'd directed the question, those in front of the tent, only looked at one another with as much of an inquiry on their faces as she must have had on her own. She turned when one of the men at the rear of the warehouse called out.

"We have bandages—here." He held up what looked like a toolbox, green and metal and hopelessly small. No bigger than a breadbox. What sort of army was this, without any medical supplies? Had they expected this revolution to be as bloodless as the last? With countless armed men filling Germany?

She called the guard forward, taking the box from him. At least it must have something in it because it was heavier than she'd expected. Then she hurried back to the injured man's side.

Jurgen had the wound fully exposed now, but she couldn't tell the size for all the blood. She pulled open the box, spotting white bandages, gauze to soak up the blood, and cotton cloths and rubber gloves. Too late for Jurgen to use those now, but she handed him some gauze. She found a small bottle of iodine and one of alcohol, taking them out but pushing aside things she knew they wouldn't dare use: thread, needles, and tubes of some sort.

God help her, she wouldn't simply hand over such supplies and be of no use. If one more young man was brought through those doors, she would use these supplies herself and not cower in the effort.

❦

Christophe pulled yet another man off to the side of the street. He'd forced himself to leave those who were dead or near dead, knowing there was nothing to be done for them. But this man was sitting up, having been struck along the side of his head, obviously dazed but fully alive. To leave him in the street would be to invite someone to finish him off.

Christophe shoved him under the shelter of a storekeeper's awning, then moved away, intent on getting to the next who might need him.

"Wait . . ."

Christophe turned to the man, surprised by the clarity in that single word.

"Don't leave me . . . not without a gun. I can't find it. I lost it."

The soldier's rifle was still slung over his shoulder. Christophe shifted it to the man's lap. Then, without another word, he continued his mission.

❦

Tear sheets for bandages. Apply pressure to the wound to stop the bleeding. Tie a tourniquet. Dab iodine—vicariously wincing because the boys upon whom she performed the services were unconscious and couldn't wince for themselves.

Man after man was brought in, so many even Leo was shamed into helping. Even he could hold gauze to a wound. And then, amid the new smells, the groans, and the growing number of cots in use, Annaliese's most fervent prayer was answered.

A man entered on his own two feet, this one neither carried nor coerced. He toted a bag and claimed he was a doctor but needed to say no more than that before Annaliese asked him what to do.

"You'll direct me to the ones I can help," he said as they walked. "Monitor those who are brought through those doors. The ones who come in on their own, cussing or angry, can wait. The ones carried in, delirious and barely able to call for their mother—those I cannot help. Take me to the ones who moan, *Fräulein*. It's them I can help."

And so she did as directed, praying all the while to categorize the wounded as she'd been assigned. From afar, she watched while he performed any miracle he could while guards were commandeered to the duty of holding patients down for surgery. She heard the ping of bullets removed from wounds, dropped into a pan. She saw a guard hold open a grievous wound with a long silver instrument so the doctor had two free hands to explore. She saw men faint; she saw men die. And some, she saw survive.

The steady stream of fighters pouring in from around the city soon had the men in the streets either retreating or surrendering. Though it was difficult to tell one side from the other, surrender was clear enough in the relinquished weapons, the lifted arms, the growing silence.

Once Christophe learned there was a makeshift medical station set up in the back of an empty garage, he'd carried men there one by one.

He didn't count the minutes or the hours the battle raged; instead he counted the men he'd helped.

Twenty-three.

Only when the bullets ceased and more men came out to help the wounded did he realize the significance of the number.

Twenty-three was the number of men whose faces haunted him at night.

There, at the threshold of the garage-turned-hospital, without caring who saw him, Christophe fell to his knees.

35

Annaliese brushed her forehead with the top of her wrist, only vaguely aware that the influx of injured men had gradually diminished. The needs before her went on, even though another doctor and three nurses were there now to perform more expertly what she'd attempted to do before they'd arrived.

But there was water to be fetched, cotton cloths too precious to be discarded that had to be rinsed for use again, utensils to be cleaned in antiseptic. She did what she could, still too dazed to think about having acted as a nurse upon living souls who'd deserved someone with far more training than she. Hours passed before she spoke to anyone about something other than a task at hand.

Odovacar was brought in, wounded. He'd donned a helmet he'd taken from a fallen man only moments before a bullet ripped through it. Nonetheless the impact had knocked him out, leaving his forehead bloodied and his mind disoriented. The doctors and nurses were still busy with more-severely wounded men, and so as soon as she could, Annaliese went to his side to clean his wound, though he soon fell unconscious again.

She returned to him some time later, after a doctor had

seen him. "I don't think it would've been all that glorious in France after all, *Fräulein*," Odovacar said to her. He held on to her hand as if he couldn't bear for her to leave him. "It's been only a couple of battles for me, and I've already had enough."

She looked around the barracks, thinking she would easily trade its newly acquired stench of death for the smells she'd tried banishing earlier. "I hope this will be the last of it."

But somehow she wasn't convinced of that, and neither, she thought, was Odovacar. She looked at him again and saw a tear slide from one eye.

"We're losing, *Fräulein*. Our men are scattering—there are too many on the other side."

She pressed his hand in hers. "Someone must win. Maybe if the guns can be put away, we can go back to the idea of giving voice to the people—through voting."

He offered a weak smile. "I should be too young to agree with such a dull solution to Germany's troubles, but the last few hours have aged me."

The mention of politics made her think of Jurgen and Leo, neither of whom she'd seen in quite some time. Certainly not since the first doctor had arrived. Her gaze went to the tent.

"They're not in there."

The observation had come from the man in the cot next to Odovacar. He was wounded in the leg, sweating and restless but fully alert.

"Jurgen?"

"I saw Leo take him out that way." He aimed his chin to the back door of the warehouse.

"Probably to safety," Odovacar offered, looking sympathetically at Annaliese. "You needn't worry about him if Leo is with him. He'll make sure Jurgen is taken care of."

"Then he'd better get him out of Munich altogether," the other man said. "If the Whites stay, they'll kill him—or any one of us who worked with Leviné."

Odovacar looked from the man to Annaliese, his eyes considerably wider. "Maybe all of us right here."

A shudder crossed her shoulders, but she shook it away. "They can't possibly kill everyone who supported the Communists. Once order is restored, things will settle down again." She gently pressed his hand, still in hers. "You mustn't worry, Odovacar."

If only she could heed her own advice.

The worst of the battle might have passed, but Christophe knew the streets were anything but safe. He fit in well enough with the free corps troops still roaming the more affluent parts of the city, but because of his familiarity with so many men connected to the revolutionaries, he could safely walk into Ivo's neighborhood too.

It took several moments for Ivo to come to the door, and even then he only opened it wide enough to pull Christophe inside, then shut it tight behind them.

"Is the fighting over?"

Christophe shook his head. "I don't know. The free corps are still spreading through the city. I heard the Communists in Dachau fell yesterday, and from the number of men I saw with the Whites here, I don't think the Reds will last long."

From the corner, Ivo's mother prayed a quick and audible prayer—about saving them from either of the armies. Christophe echoed the thought.

"It's best if everyone keeps hiding," he said to her. "I'll try to find provisions . . . but everything is still in chaos."

Ivo shook his head, mumbling something about having flour that would last, but his face was still far too solemn. "I need to tell you something, Christophe," he said. "Leo sent someone here yesterday, looking for you."

"Why?"

Ivo took a seat and waved a hand for Christophe to sit at the table too, but he didn't. "He invited you to the warehouse because Annaliese is there. With Jurgen."

"With . . . ?" Now he did step closer and grabbed Ivo by the collar. "What do you mean, *with* Jurgen?"

Ivo pried loose his shirt. "Sit, man, sit."

Christophe paced. She was at the warehouse? Right now? The last time he'd been there, it had been full to the brim with men. Why would Jurgen have brought her there, of all places? "Tell me exactly what the messenger said, Ivo."

"He told me Leo gave him a message that Annaliese had been away for a while, but she'd returned to Jurgen."

Suddenly Christophe needed the chair he'd refused before. He fell into it as if one of those bullets that had so miraculously missed him on the street had found him here.

But something didn't make sense. He eyed Ivo again. "Why seek me out to tell me she chose Jurgen? I would've found out, sooner or later. As soon as I found her on my own."

"Maybe they wanted you to know she is all right."

Christophe shook his head. "I don't think it was kindness that made Leo want to tell me she'd returned."

Ivo shrugged. "Leo has always protected Jurgen. Maybe he's doing that now so you won't come looking for her to confuse her again."

Christophe pushed himself upright so violently that the chair behind him wobbled on its legs. "I won't believe she chose him," he said. "Not until she tells me to my face."

And then he went back out to the streets.

36

Gunfire pushed Christophe toward the shadows. He wasn't sure the bullets had been aimed at him, but he was sure the streets weren't safe for anyone yet.

The street outside the warehouse seemed a common destination. Trucks and soldiers were drawn to the same entryway Christophe approached, and orders were shouted for some of the wounded to be carried out to an ambulance truck.

Even as soldiers scrambled to follow orders, Christophe heard the words he'd dreaded. These wounded were to be taken either directly to a commandeered prison or to the hospital nearest the police barracks. Apart from a sniper or two, it seemed all of Munich was slipping under the White army's control.

Newly placed sentries wouldn't let him inside the warehouse, but even from the threshold he saw more than a dozen cots still full. Off to one side, a doctor performed what looked like emergency surgery, similar to the kind Christophe had seen closest to the front. Behind the doctor, men moaned, slept, or called for one of the nurses in the narrow aisles. He scanned those women, but none were familiar. Not that he'd expected to find her with a nurse's apron on, anyway.

Nor did he see Jurgen or Leo, and for one awful moment he wondered if they'd been taken into custody already. Sentencing Leo and Jurgen for crimes associated with the Communist activity was one thing. But Annaliese? Would she be considered guilty because of her association with him?

He approached one of the sentries again, this time at the door rather than the wide delivery entrance, where the trucks awaited their imprisoned cargo. "I'm Major Christophe Brecht," he said. "I'm looking for a woman who was here earlier. Not a nurse."

"A revolutionary?"

He shook his head. "No. She only took shelter here."

The soldier scanned the large room, which was only half-full even with all of the activity. "Look around, Major, but I think there are only nurses here. The rest are men."

Christophe stepped inside, but even as he did so, he realized the risk. Should any of the men he used to train in this very building recognize him as a comrade, he would be taken captive as a Communist and be unable to prove himself otherwise. Certainly no one in the White army could vouch for him.

So he stayed behind the cots, out of the line of vision of the men closest to him. Which brought him closer to the doctor who was just finishing with a wounded man. His hands were soaked red, and when he went to dip them in a pan, he saw it was already crimson.

"I need more fresh water here!" The doctor held up his hands, scanning the area much the way Christophe himself was doing. "Where is she? She was here a moment ago."

Christophe felt obligated to answer, being so close by. "It appears all of your nurses are tending other patients."

"No, not a nurse. A girl. She was helping. She just brought me these instruments." His gaze returned from wandering the room and settled on Christophe. "But she's gone. What are you doing? Can you lend aid here?"

"I . . ." He nearly refused, intent on finding Annaliese. But if he were going to ask about her, perhaps it would be easier to coax an answer in exchange for aid. He took the tin bowl of water and dumped it in the nearby sink, rinsing and filling it with more water.

"Did you say you were helped by a girl?" Christophe asked. "Was she about this height?" He raised a palm to his own shoulder. "Pretty, blonde hair?"

"Yes, I suppose. Here, I need these put in fresh antiseptic." He handed Christophe a tray of blood-soaked surgical tools. "There is more in that bag, beneath the sink."

Christophe took the tray of instruments, but as he returned to the sink, he looked again around the room. If she wasn't here now, surely she had been here not long ago. And might return.

⁓

"Here, in here."

Annaliese, hearing the hushed voice call from the shadows, was at first hesitant to heed it. But Odovacar, who countered his dizziness by leaning on her steadiness, headed in the direction of the man who'd spoken.

"No guns."

Odovacar slipped the rifle from his shoulder, handed it to Annaliese, then leaned against the wall instead of against her. She looked around, wondering what she was supposed to do with it.

"There." A single hand, extended in the lusterless moonlight, accompanied the voice. It pointed behind her. "Lift the lid."

Two tin barrels stood near the brick wall at the back of the alleyway. She discarded the gun in one, repositioned the lid, then rejoined Odovacar.

They'd been running in their best rendition of a drunken race since sneaking out the back of the warehouse, almost three blocks away, after the Red sentries had abandoned their posts and new soldiers took their places—all without a shot fired.

She thanked God no one from the White army descending on the warehouse had seen them go, or surely they would have been stopped. She wasn't entirely sure the White army would believe she was without ties to the Communists. Even *she* couldn't convince herself of that. No ties to its politics, that was certainly true. But to those who'd advanced it? Maybe they would think her guilty enough.

She hadn't quite believed it was safe until now.

A priest opened the door wide enough to let them both inside. "We can give you food and shelter for only a few days at most." The solemn priest had a circle of gray extending from the temples to the back of his head, giving the impression of a halo. He looked at Annaliese. "You know, of course, that you cannot stay?"

She glanced at him, startled. Where else could she go? Back to the barracks, taking a chance on being arrested? She looked around. There was no one else in sight.

"Couldn't I stay . . . even here, in the corner, out of sight?"

"I have no loyalties to either side, but the men I have downstairs are Red. Twice I've had to turn away White soldiers looking only for a roof over their head. It wouldn't be safe to have you stay, and I cannot take you to where I'm hiding the men."

She would have argued if any words came to mind, but she had none. She wouldn't endanger others because of her own hopelessness.

"I only came to help my friend," she said, and Odovacar nodded even as he leaned against the wall.

"Say your farewells, then. Quickly."

"You'll be all right here," she assured Odovacar, then hugged him. "I will pray for your safety."

He looked at her curiously as if wondering if she'd been sincere or said it only for the benefit of the man of God waiting to take him away. She smiled and hoped he read her candidness.

"Maybe it's only the wound to my head, or maybe it's that I'm headed to the cellar of a church, but I think I'll join you in that praying, *Fräulein*."

The last thing Christophe wanted to do was act as nurse to those who might finger him as one of their associates, and yet he found himself with little choice if he wanted to wait for Annaliese's return—if she returned. There were more than a dozen men he'd trained to use a rifle taking up cots, but thankfully for Christophe—unfortunately for the men—most were unconscious. The rest never looked his way.

But he soon doubted she would return. If Leo had his way, he would have spirited Jurgen to a safe place, most likely with Annaliese at their side. What Christophe needed to do now was find that safe place.

Christophe looked around again, deciding it was no use to wait. If she'd been here within a half hour, she might still be nearby.

He went to the back of the warehouse, saluting the soldier who stood guard, then walked outside and into the darkness.

The night was quiet, deathly so. Evidently neither the White nor the Red army thought itself firmly in control, since neither side took the risk of assigning patrols. The only men Christophe came across were gathered in huddles outside a beer hall two blocks from the warehouse.

He approached cautiously, holding up his hands, introducing himself as a Major in the German army. He was welcomed immediately.

"Come off the streets, Major! Have some schnapps."

The invitation came with a decidedly Prussian dialect, so Christophe chose his words carefully, making sure he gave no clue that he'd been born right here in Bavaria. "I'm looking for someone who was working for Leviné, the Communist leader. His name was Jurgen. Do you know if he's been arrested yet?"

"Maybe he's one of the dead! We shot eight of them at the municipal building in the first wave of the attack."

"Do you know names?"

The soldier shook his head, then took a long drink from the mug in his hand. "Wait until morning. Whatever leaders are left will be rounded up; you'll see."

"And shot!"

Christophe turned away to continue his hunt.

"You'd best stay with us, Major," one of the men called from behind him. "We haven't arrested all the revolutionaries yet."

Christophe kept walking, sticking to the shadows, traveling a wide radius of the warehouse, looking for anyone or anything that might give him a clue as to where Leo had taken Jurgen. He wasn't sure where else to go, what else to do. Clearly it was useless to roam the streets. He found himself tracing a familiar path, not far from Leo's house, and then going there. He climbed the porch, recalling how many times he'd seen Annaliese in this very spot.

No one answered when he knocked. It was late and he knew the city was fearful, but when he tried the door, he found it unlocked. A quick search inside showed the door to Leo's flat open—and abandoned. Evidently whoever had lived here lately hadn't waited for the White army to find out it was a home connected to revolutionaries.

The moon peeked out from behind a cloud just then, drawing his eye to the chair by the window. For a moment he was there again, sitting in that chair, having awakened from a nightmare to Annaliese's soothing voice. She'd told him she still trusted him to keep her safe, despite all the war had forced him to do.

Keep her safe . . . If only he could. If only she hadn't left him, he'd never have stopped trying to do that very thing.

Then he remembered her kiss, and his knees went nearly as weak as they'd been that night.

Nothing would stop him from protecting Annaliese—not the White army or the Red. Not even Jurgen. All he had to do was find her.

37

There was little left to eat, just a bit of dried bread and hard cheese. But to Christophe it was a banquet. He sat in the dark at the table in Leo's kitchen, his rifle beside him, a pistol in his lap. He had no intention of taking another life so long as he lived, but he didn't plan on being overtaken by either of the warring armies that might visit this home.

Noise outside the kitchen door sent him to his feet, pistol in the palm of his hand. The light was dull and he saw nothing, but he trusted his ears.

Stepping closer, he stood within the shelter of the door's arc in case someone should choose to come inside. Slowly the doorknob twisted. Christophe held up his gun, bracing himself against the wall. The door opened quietly, and in one quick movement Christophe slammed it behind the intruder.

"Huey!"

The man stood with his hands up high, a look of such horror at having a gun aimed his way that Christophe nearly wanted to laugh. He lowered the weapon.

"I thought the house was empty," Christophe said. "Are you and Bertita still living upstairs?"

He shook his head, breathing heavily from the scare. "Not exactly."

Christophe pulled out a chair for the other man, smiling now in hopes of restoring calm for both of them. "What does 'not exactly' mean?"

"Everyone's in hiding from the Whites. I came inside to see if it's been ransacked—to see if the White army has made the connection to Jurgen yet. If they know to look for him."

Heart thudding more heavily now than a moment ago, Christophe leaned over Huey. "Are you with him?"

"And Leo, too. They're safe—and will be even if we can't win against the White army."

Christophe nearly grabbed him. "And Annaliese?"

Huey shook his head, bending away from Christophe. "We left her at the warehouse. She'll be all right. The Whites have no reason to arrest her. She hasn't been with us since the change to Leviné."

"I was at the warehouse and she's not there! Why did you just leave her, without any protection? Where is she now? Did she have a place to go? Do you know where she is?"

Huey bolted to a stand as if under attack once again. "It's for her own good that we left her, Christophe. Jurgen is in hiding, and if the White army catches him, they'll shoot him—and maybe anyone with him, too. Is that what you want?"

Christophe took a step back, still clutching his pistol, then shoved it into his pocket. "No. I just want to find her."

Huey put a hand to his shoulder. "Don't worry; two people looking for each other are bound to find one another."

"Two people?"

"Popoff told me she came back to find you." He grinned.

"He heard everything that went on in the warehouse. Everyone did."

"What are you saying? That she came to the warehouse . . . for me, not for Jurgen?"

Huey laughed. "Leo said he sent someone to fetch you for her, but you never came. Then the battle broke out. What kept you away from her if you're this eager to be reunited?"

Christophe gripped the back of the nearest chair. "I wasn't there to receive the message." His gaze went back to the door, seeing only one thing: the danger that was out there. And Annaliese in the midst of it.

Huey went to the door. With a hand on the doorknob, he faced Christophe. "If I see her, I'll tell her you're looking for her. But I would return to Ivo's if I were you. It won't be safe in this house for long, once the Whites hear it was a Communist's home."

Christophe nodded. "I'll be gone in a few minutes." He put a hand to Huey's arm, delaying his departure. "If you do see her, bring her to Ivo's. I'll be there every night until I find her. I'll spend every one of my days searching—so I can get her out of this city."

Annaliese hurried past the spot where she'd first met Odovacar when she'd returned to the city; even now the memory came with a remnant of fear. Just two blocks to go and she would be at Leo's. No matter what she found there, it would be safer than these streets. Though they were empty, each sound she heard, each sound she made, echoed back to her with tension.

There it was, Leo's tall town house. As she stepped closer,

the moon reappeared and her shadow reached the very spot where Christophe had once stood when he'd thrown pebbles at her window. Her heart twisted at the memory.

There was no sound, no light, no indication at all that anyone still lived here. Probably they were hiding behind locked doors and closed curtains, in the dark so they wouldn't be noticed. Just like everyone else in the city. She put her ear to the door. No noise whatsoever.

Slowly she opened it, seeing immediately that Leo's flat was open. The moon lit the abandoned room through the lacy curtains at the front window. The couch was blissfully free of anyone's presence, inviting hers—though she couldn't help but wish by some miracle to have found Christophe there once again, sleeping as he had been the night he'd woken and kissed her.

The house felt empty in its utter silence. Had they fled, fearing the White army would find out this had been Jurgen's home?

It didn't matter why they were gone. Perhaps it wasn't safe for her here, either, but she would take the risk for one night anyway. She sat on the couch, wondering if some of Christophe's nightmares might visit her, too. The last couple of days provided enough material for her own bad dreams, at least for as long as she remained here in Munich.

She would try leaving the city tomorrow, if the trains were running. She would go home. Surely that was safer—

A noise from the kitchen stopped her thoughts. Was that the scrape of a chair on the floor? Her heart shot to her throat. Perhaps she should have checked the other rooms to be sure she *was* alone.

There was a pillow at the end of the couch, the very pillow

that had looked so small and uninviting beneath Christophe's head. She pressed it beneath her palms, welcoming it to steady her hands, but then abandoned it. She tiptoed toward the kitchen.

Though she heard nothing now, Annaliese was unwilling to convince herself what she'd heard had only been a product of her own nervous tension. She must be certain or she would never find rest.

Christophe stopped at the kitchen door. Had that been the creak of a floorboard? He'd been sure no one was in the house, and Huey had as much as confirmed it. Certainly an invading army—even a domestic one—wouldn't be so quiet.

He should leave. He looked out the kitchen window again, intent on following that gaze and resuming his search for Annaliese. Whoever was left in this house was welcome to it.

But curiosity got the best of him. If someone *was* in the house, he wanted to know who. He withdrew his pistol once again from the folds of his pocket and took two long, silent strides to hide behind the kitchen door.

Nothing. Silence. Perhaps he'd been mistaken. Nerves were bound to do that, conjure danger, even a noise that didn't exist.

He put a hand on the door that used to swing so easily. With a flat palm, he put gentle pressure on the center panel. But it didn't budge.

Annaliese pushed but the door wouldn't move. Had someone blocked the swinging portal to the kitchen? But why? Unless there was someone there . . . right on the other side of this door.

She should run.

No.

She had as much right to be here as anyone else, no matter what laws Communists had imposed about abolishing property rights. Leo had invited her to use this roof for as long as she needed it. And she needed it tonight.

But if it was a man on the other side of that door . . . One man alone might be harder to fight off than a houseful of peasants only looking to stake a claim.

She withdrew her hand, and the door slowly opened. She turned in an instant, sprinting along the quickest route toward the front door.

"Wait!"

But she didn't. She dashed through the dining area, around the couch in the parlor, almost made it to the door.

"Annaliese!"

She stopped instantly at the threshold, afraid to let herself believe she'd recognized that voice. When she turned, he was already there, pulling her into his arms, saying her name over and again as if he needed assurance that it was Annaliese just as she needed to believe it was him.

When Christophe's lips came down on hers, she wasn't sure whose tears she tasted. His or her own.

38

They sat close together on the couch, Christophe's arm around her, her hand in his free one. And incredibly, she welcomed him. More, she seemed to crave his touch—his kiss—as much as he craved hers.

He knew they should go soon—return to Ivo's, which was more secure—but it was nearly impossible to break away from her nearness. And there was something he wanted to ask that wouldn't wait.

"Annaliese," he said slowly, as if they had no place else to go, nothing more urgent to do than enjoy one another's company, "why did you leave without telling me where you were going?"

She shifted to look him in the eyes, taking her hand from his to stroke the side of his face. "Because I thought it was best—for you."

He reclaimed her hand. "For me? How can that be? Don't you know I've been in love with you nearly since the moment I came to that party office? There you were, instructing the artist on how to paint a propaganda poster . . ."

She smiled. "It's because I've been in love with you, too. I wasn't sure I would be good for you—because of our differences."

"We'll talk about that. Perhaps we'll find we're not so far apart, after all."

"Yes! That's exactly right. It may not have been true before, but it's true now. There is so much I want to share with you—and learn with you—about God. It won't be the challenge you might have expected before I left. Oh, Christophe, God is so real to me. I couldn't see that here; there were so many things in the way. Except you." She kissed his mouth quickly, her eyes happy and somehow grateful. "He drew me to Him through you, but even you were in the way for a little while. I didn't want to mimic what you believed. I wanted to find out for myself what is true."

If Christophe had thought himself dreaming a few moments ago, it was no less true now. Nothing could be further in this moment from the nightmares he suffered on this very couch.

❧

Though Annaliese had considered more than once how she would tell him why she'd left Munich without a word, she searched his face for signs of understanding. He couldn't be allowed to think for a moment that she'd wanted to hurt him or that she'd been uncertain how she felt, that there had ever been any real competition between him and Jurgen. Nor could he doubt her faith was as real as his now.

"Christophe," she whispered, "if you love me as you say you do, there is nothing—absolutely nothing—to stand in our way. No one else, no politics, nothing."

"You don't know—you can't—how many times I've prayed for this. For us." Then he kissed her again, letting his lips linger gently. "You don't know how I wanted that one kiss we shared in this room to be only our first."

"Of many," she added.

He pulled away before she wanted him to, only to grab both of her hands in his. "Yes, the first of many, but not here. I need to get you out of this city. We'll go to Ivo's and stay there until I can get both of us on a train to the countryside. It'll be easier to travel if we change into the bourgeoisie clothes I've brought—a dress for you from your home, a suit for me."

"From my home?"

He nodded. "I was there yesterday. With your parents."

Her heart, so overused from dancing and soaring since the moment she'd seen his face, bounced again. "My parents! I thought . . . I thought they'd sailed."

"They still intend to go," he told her with a frown, "but they've had a postponement. It's your father, Annaliese. He's been ill."

Her heart now fell to her stomach. "Is it serious?"

"He's much recovered. His speech remains a bit unclear, and his vision . . . Your mother says he can see, a little. And now that he's walking . . ."

She leaned away, covering her face with her hands. "I've been so unfair to him, looking at everything from only one side. Cruel, even." She thought of her grief over Giselle's death, how she hadn't considered its impact on her father or the guilt he would feel. Guilt that wasn't entirely his. Giselle had been wrong too.

Christophe put a hand on her back, drawing her close again. "There will be time enough to make up for that."

"Not if they're still sailing. There is so much I would say, to explain . . . and to understand."

"There would be time for that if we went to America with them."

She looked at him. "Leave Germany?"

"I'm only asking you to consider it, Annaliese. I think both of us should. You want to leave Munich because of how dangerous it is. The rest of Germany is in just as much trouble. Maybe if we left . . . at least for a while . . ."

Annaliese sank back into the couch, still close to him. She stared straight ahead. Leave Germany . . . after all she'd tried to do with hopes of making it better? after Christophe had fought four *years* in its name?

But then, seeing the window, she knew even now they were in danger of anything from being arrested by the free corps to becoming victims of the revolution, at the hands of one side or the other.

"Do you want to leave Germany?" she asked him. "You've sacrificed far more than I have for this country, after fighting all these years."

She saw he wasn't looking at her, either, but straight ahead at the same dark view from the window she'd considered herself.

"I thought they wouldn't want to fight anymore," he whispered. "I know that I don't. And yet they do, out there. I want to leave it behind me. The guns. The fighting. I never want to touch another gun so long as I live. But I'm not sure Germany will let me do that if I stay."

"But this is home."

He slid one of his hands around hers. "Whatever we do, Annaliese, wherever we go, as long as we're together . . . we're home."

39

Ivo was happy to see Annaliese again, and because of that his mother welcomed her into the crowded flat as if she were another member of the family. It was near dawn by the time they'd arrived, and so the flat's two bedrooms were made ready for each of them.

"And for tonight," Ivo's mother said as she stood near the door of her own bedroom, the place she'd offered to Annaliese, "you'll stay in here with me. Away from the children. For as long as you need, *ja*?"

Annaliese smiled and nodded. "Thank you—so very much."

By the time Annaliese woke it was midafternoon. She left the little bedroom in search of others, passing three of Ivo's siblings in the parlor, who stared at her but said nothing, not even when she sent them a smile. She found Christophe already awake, sharing a hard roll with another of Ivo's little brothers in the kitchen. Christophe offered the spot next to him on the bench seat when Annaliese approached the table, and Ivo's mother settled bread and a cup of coffee in front of her.

"My brother says he used to be your bodyguard," said the boy whom Christophe had introduced as Klaus. He looked like a smaller version of Ivo, already sporting broad shoulders and big hands. "Why did you need a bodyguard?"

"Because some of the people in the city didn't like what I wanted to say."

"Did you say something bad?"

She lifted one shoulder. "I just wanted everyone to get along more fairly."

"Mother says we should all get along now. That we were fighting for freedom before, that Ivo gave his fingers for freedom. So we should be free now and not fight but get along."

Annaliese smiled. *Freedom*—a lovely, powerful word. So easily manipulated.

"Ivo went out to see about the trains," Christophe told her. "I was going to go, but he thought you might worry we'd become separated again."

"He was right about that." She slipped her hand into one of his to emphasize the point. "But is it safe for him to be on the streets?"

"Who could keep him home, that one?" Ivo's mother complained as she scrubbed dishes at the sink.

Christophe squeezed Annaliese's hand. "He can pass as a free corps member. Most of them are army soldiers anyway, like us."

A fracas in the small parlor drew Ivo's mother away from the sink. She left the kitchen with dripping hands and Ivo's brother tagged behind as witness, evidently to see how his mother would stop whatever misbehavior was going on.

The moment they were alone, Christophe drew Annaliese close. "I've missed you."

"Yes, me too." She laughed. "I'm glad you let Ivo go. I don't know what I would've felt had you not been here when I woke."

"I told you, Annalise. Whatever we do from now on, we do together."

It was nearly dark when Ivo returned. His mother had insisted on keeping both locks bolted and ordered a bench dragged in front of the door. By the time Ivo was let in, nearly the entire family— four siblings, Ivo's mother, Christophe, and Annaliese—stood waiting for whatever news he had of the outside city.

"The trains are running—but not on any schedule" were his first words. "People are lined up at the station, waiting just in case one arrives. When one does, it's swarmed like a dollop of honey by ants."

"But people are there? unafraid of the soldiers from either side?"

He nodded. "They're mostly bourgeoisie, wanting to get away from the fighting. The free corps isn't letting any of the working class leave, for fear a revolutionary will get away. They want all of them arrested. Or worse."

Annaliese wanted to ask him what he meant, but a glance to the younger siblings reminded her why he hadn't elaborated.

"We're working class!" Ivo's mother said.

"Which is why it's best for everyone to stay inside."

"Even me?" one of his brothers asked.

Ivo nodded and tousled the boy's hair. "Especially you."

Christophe was already retrieving his knapsack, pulling from it familiar material. One of her old suits—a favorite skirt and short jacket of light green silk trimmed with black lace circles, a frothy white blouse beneath. Only her mother would have known it was a favorite, and the thought made her more eager than ever to be home.

The suit, stockings, gloves, and small black hat were far different from the plain, sturdy black cotton skirts and serviceable white blouses she'd been wearing in solidarity with working-class women. She'd learned to do without frills and colors and soft material but couldn't deny a small part of her was eager to wear it again—especially when she knew she could take out Giselle's pin and put it on. Eagerness to do that nearly obliterated whatever capitalistic guilt might loom in her mind—something she would no doubt have to wrestle with, particularly when she saw her father again.

And that, she hoped, would be soon.

Annaliese did not want to go to bed. They had decided to wait one more day, since Ivo's investigation had included evidence of sporadic fighting—or executions. Annaliese was almost sure he knew more because she saw him whispering to Christophe later, who received whatever news Ivo shared with a grim frown.

At dawn they would say their farewells to Ivo and his family . . . and to all of Munich.

But for now, they were as safe as they could be, and Annaliese wanted to keep it that way. Christophe sat in Ivo's parlor at her side, close together on the little sofa in front of the cold fireplace. Ivo and his family were already abed, leaving them with their first real time alone since they'd arrived the day before.

It was late and she knew they would need rest, but it was obvious Christophe didn't want to say good night any more than Annaliese did.

"Ivo's mother is probably peeking out to make sure there is no mischief going on here," Annaliese said.

"Of course. We've been adopted, and none of her children are allowed to misbehave."

But to test that statement, he leaned closer and gave her a kiss, then sat back and listened. "There, we must truly be alone."

Annaliese laughed. "Having so many sons must have taught her how to stop a fight. Perhaps Germany should consult her."

Christophe looked as though he might have responded, but a tapping at the door called his gaze. She looked, too—with alarm. Everyone in the family was home, and no one called on friends, not anymore. Surely it couldn't be a neighbor at this hour.

But the tapping was too quiet to be a soldier.

Christophe stood and approached the door. He waited, saying nothing. Annaliese hoped whoever it was would simply go away. And yet . . . hadn't she been on that side of the door only a few days ago? alone and in need?

The tapping sounded again.

"Ivo . . ."

The voice was too low and raspy to know more than that it was a man's.

"Should I get him?" Annaliese whispered.

Christophe held up his hand for her to wait.

"What do you want?" he asked through the door.

"Help, Ivo. I need your help."

"Who are you?"

"Let me in. Ivo, is that you?"

The voice had gone up in volume, and for a moment Annaliese thought it familiar. But she wouldn't believe it.

"Tell me who you are, or I won't open the door and I won't tell Ivo you're here."

"I'm a friend. Only a friend. I'm hurt. I need help."

"Are you alone?"

"Yes."

Surely it wasn't . . . it couldn't be. . . . And yet . . .

Christophe moved aside the bench and unlatched the lower of the two locks without removing the chain. Bracing himself on the doorframe, he opened the door wide enough to peer out. Annaliese could see nothing beyond his broad shoulders, but Christophe quickly shut the door, unlatched the chain, and opened it wide.

In time for Jurgen to fall into him, unconscious.

Seeing Annaliese minister to Jurgen shouldn't have made Christophe uneasy, and yet watching her gently clean his wound, nearly caress his forehead with a cool cloth, Christophe wanted to snatch her hand away.

So he reminded himself, yet again, that she did only what he would want her to do as a follower of the Christ they both now served. If it were any man other than Jurgen. The man who hadn't given a moment's attention to making sure she was safe.

As near as they could tell, Jurgen had been shot, but the bleeding had stopped and there was no bullet lodged inside. It traveled through the muscle in his shoulder, evidenced by the entry and exit wounds. And it must have happened some time ago, judging by his weakness and the crustiness of the blood. Annaliese had swabbed the area without even flinching, as well as any trenchside nurse might have done.

Christophe intended to get what information he could from Jurgen, then send the man on his way as soon as he could walk. Certainly there were any number of men still willing to give him aid. Hadn't he gathered men by the thousands to follow him and Leviné?

And where was Leo, who never let Jurgen out of his sight?

"He can't stay," Christophe said. "Not here. It's too dangerous for Ivo's family."

Annaliese nodded, but her face was so solemn he couldn't guess what she was thinking. Jurgen was coming round to consciousness. Christophe stepped nearer, but Annaliese was already speaking.

"Jurgen, can you hear me? It's me, Annaliese."

"Anna . . . liese?"

"Yes, Jurgen. It's me. What's happened to you?"

"They came. . . . They found where we were hiding. They shot—at all of us." He tried a smile. "The jacket . . . the one you gave me. It's ruined."

Christophe stepped beside Annaliese, bending closer to Jurgen. "Where is Leo?"

"Leviné . . ."

"No, Leo. Where is Leo? and Huey and Bertita?"

"They left me, all of them. Leviné—arrested." He barely had his eyes open, bloodshot and rimmed with red. A stark contrast to the pastiness of his skin. "Will use a firing squad on him; that's what they say."

Christophe thought he might be right about that.

"What about Leo, Jurgen?" Annaliese asked again. "Where is he?"

"I . . . don't . . . know. We were given away. Free corps came. . . . Leo . . . he and the others fled before the first shot. Leo left me there."

"He *left* you?"

Her voice was as incredulous as Christophe felt. Leo? A coward, after all.

Jurgen closed his eyes again, and Christophe faced Annaliese, who stood in front of him.

"He'll have to stay until morning," Christophe said. "I'll go and tell Ivo, and we can take him somewhere else before we go to the train station. Go to bed, Annaliese."

"I can stay up with you. His wound might be infected."

"I'll be here, right on the floor next to him. Don't worry."

He didn't like his own tone, filled with more irritation than sympathy, and so when she smiled, he didn't expect it.

"You're a good man, Christophe Brecht."

He accepted her kiss then but knew he didn't really deserve it.

40

"He's been hovering over you as if you were the one with a bullet hole through your shoulder instead of me."

Jurgen's observation of Christophe was true, but Annaliese wasn't about to complain. She'd just changed the bandage on Jurgen's shoulder, and for the first time since last night, Christophe had left them alone. Ivo kept his family in the kitchen, well away from their visitor.

Jurgen looked beyond her, at the kitchen door, where Christophe had disappeared with the soiled bandages. Leaning closer to Annaliese, he claimed one of her wrists. "Annaliese, I know you're planning to get out of the city. I want you to take me with you." The pressure on her wrist increased. "I should say, I want you to convince *him* to take me with you."

She might have answered—given an instant refusal—except Christophe had already returned. Jurgen let go of Annaliese's wrist as if it had turned hot enough to scald him, something Christophe obviously didn't miss. His gaze sought hers as if to make sure she was all right.

"There is something Jurgen wants to ask of us, Christophe." She kept her eyelids lowered, in case Christophe read too soon how she felt about what Jurgen would ask.

Christophe turned his attention to Jurgen, waiting.

"Are you still planning to leave the city?"

Christophe nodded.

Jurgen looked from Christophe to Annaliese, then back again. "I would like to ask you to let me come along."

Christophe folded his arms on his chest, but his eyes never left Jurgen. "Do you know what you're asking?"

Jurgen nodded. "I know it would be difficult. I know you have reason not to care for me. . . ."

Christophe stepped closer to Annaliese and pulled her farther from the couch on which Jurgen sat, as if to protect her already from what he wanted. "You were a member of Leviné's council, Jurgen. You, as much as he, gave the order to the Communists to take over this city. To cast people from their homes—"

"Yes, to give shelter to the homeless."

"To raid the banks—"

"How else could we govern, without money to right society's wrongs?"

"To arrest anyone who didn't agree with you—"

"To make the streets safe."

"To *execute* members of the most prominent families of Bavaria—"

"That was Leviné, not me!" He leaned forward as if he would rise but didn't. "They said he was doing what the Bible taught—the very book you tout!"

The words silenced Christophe, surprising Annaliese, too. "What do you mean?" she asked.

"They said there was a story in there about a husband and wife who weren't sharing properly, as others were. They were living in perfect Communism, those people! But not this husband and wife. God struck down the two who only pretended to share what they had. Leviné—or someone with him—said no one should object to carrying out an example God set, for those who refused to share."

Christophe stepped forward. "So the Communists are God, now? They decide who is to live and who is to die?"

Jurgen shook his head. "No! It's only what someone said."

"And you did nothing to stop those executions."

"It's true, he went too far. And so they'll shoot him for it! But not me; I didn't authorize any of that. I wanted only freedom—for all of us. Freedom to live in fairness."

Christophe bent over Jurgen with a look in his eye Annaliese hadn't seen since the night she'd awakened him from his nightmares. "Don't," he said, his face only inches from Jurgen's. "Don't speak to me about freedom. You want to tell everyone what to do, like a father of little children who don't know what is best for them. To decide what to take from some and what to give to others. That isn't freedom. Not the kind I fought for."

Jurgen looked away. "I know you've never believed in helping others the way I do."

"*Helping* others! With guns? With decisions they have no part in?"

Annaliese wanted to hear no more. Everything Christophe said made sense, and she agreed with him. But for all Jurgen's faults, she'd never doubted his sincerity. The answers weren't as easy as either man might think. She wished they were, because if she could condemn Jurgen for what he'd done—and maybe she could—then she might not have been able to hear the urging God was placing on her heart this very moment.

"Christophe, we must help him. You know that, don't you?"

Her question was gently spoken, certainly not with as firm

a tone as either of them had used. Yet it was loud enough to catch both men's eyes. They stared at her, one in astonishment and the other with hope.

"Do you know what you're saying? what you're risking to help him?"

"I don't believe he would've ordered anyone to be executed, Christophe. Do you really believe that of Jurgen?"

Christophe took a step back, turned away, rubbed a hand through his hair. "No," he said at last, over his shoulder.

"Then we have to help him. Only God should decide whether or not he's to die, not the free corps."

Peace flooded Annaliese's soul the moment she uttered those words. In this, she knew she was right.

41

"We can't wait another day," Christophe said to Annaliese. They sat across from one another, having just finished breakfast before the sun had even risen. Ivo and his mother were at the table as well, but the children were still asleep in their room, while Jurgen lay in the parlor. "It's dangerous to have him here, and if you want to see your parents before they sail, we need to hope a train can take us out as soon as possible."

Annaliese nodded; she knew he was right. They had no choice—no easy choice. Jurgen was barely recovered from his wound; they'd already delayed their departure another day for him.

"Let's tell him."

She took up a cup of coffee and some bread for Jurgen, then followed Christophe into the parlor. Ivo and his mother came along.

"What is this?" Jurgen asked with a smile. He was fully awake, sitting up on the sofa. "All of you to deliver one man's breakfast?"

Annaliese gave him the hot coffee and hard bread.

"When you are finished with that," Christophe said, "we're leaving. It isn't safe to wait any longer. You'll have to walk on your own, possibly all the way to the train station if the streetcars aren't running. When we're there, if there is a fight for space on the train, you'll have to fend for yourself. I'll do what I can, but Annaliese is my first priority. Do you understand?"

Jurgen nodded.

Christophe still stared. "I want you to fully understand. If you are recognized, neither I nor Annaliese will protect you. We won't give our lives for you."

Jurgen's gaze lingered on Annaliese. Christophe's words were harsh, but she also knew they were true.

Jurgen sipped the coffee. "Perhaps it is better out there today. Last night was certainly quiet. Maybe the trains are running more regularly."

"That's true," Ivo's mother said, "about the streets." The room Annaliese shared with Ivo's mother overlooked the street, and being near a corner, they had a wide view.

"It only means the free corps are fully in control," Christophe said. "They will be no help, and we won't be armed."

Jurgen frowned. "Not armed?"

"They're not likely to allow rifles on anyone but their soldiers, and I won't risk being suspected."

He'd already shared that part of the plan with Annaliese, but she'd guessed it had as much to do with his unwillingness to take another life as the risk in being identified as a revolutionary.

"But I thought—since you have military-issue boots, a military rifle—you would present yourself as a free corps member. Perhaps I, too—"

"We have no way to act out such a charade if we're questioned at the train station. No orders, no names, no information

334

at all that I could present to prove I'm one of them. So we will go as bourgeoisie."

Annaliese fully expected Jurgen to protest this as well, but he waited silently for Christophe to continue.

"I have a full suit for myself, and I will give you the shirt and the hat I meant to wear with it. You'll have to go without a jacket. The stain is too deep on yours, even if the bullet hole can be sewn shut. But the weather is warmer today. Perhaps no one will think it odd if you go without."

"And you, Annaliese?"

"I have the proper clothing."

"We're going to change now," Christophe said. "Ivo will bring the shirt to you. Do you understand everything I've said? Are you strong enough?"

He smiled and leveled his gaze at Christophe. "I'll have to be, won't I?"

Christophe did not reply. He glanced at Annaliese, then left the room.

❧

Christophe led the way from Ivo's house, heading south under a sky that showed only a promise of morning.

"Shouldn't we go the other way?"

But Christophe didn't reply to Jurgen's halfhearted inquiry. He could see the man kept up well, better than Christophe would have expected. He didn't trust Christophe, though, and that was something Christophe had little intention of trying to change.

In fact, Jurgen was right. Heading south was not the most direct route to the nearest train station. The shortest walk would take them through the heart of the neighborhood they all knew best—where those of lesser means lived. Instead, by going a few blocks out of their way, they could travel through a more fashionable neighborhood. No one expected to be able to hire a taxi these days, but if one was to be found, it would be found in that neighborhood, not their own. At the very least, the streetcar was there.

And as intended, the clothes they all wore fit the upper-class neighborhood, not this one.

If he had allowed himself to look at Annaliese for more than a moment, he would have let his admiration show. She nearly looked like the Annaliese of the family portrait, even down to the onyx pin at her collar that winked light at him. Lovely. Happy, but as worried as he was about what this day might bring.

Despite all her worries, despite knowing there were thousands of men in this very city who wanted not just to arrest the man at her side but to execute him, Annaliese allowed herself a moment of enjoyment over the feel of the silk. In the past few months she'd told herself such luxuries went with greed, but she had to admit she'd missed some things she used to take for granted. Wearing Giselle's pin reminded her that some of the things of this world really were lovely.

It was one of the things she would have to reexamine now, through the new lens of faith. When did enjoying the gifts God provided become something other than just that? something self-serving . . . even idolatrous?

She wanted to cling to such thoughts—mundane ones

and serious ones, too—about God and faith and Christophe, thoughts even of her family, of the voyage her parents would soon take, of Christophe's suggestion they might sail themselves. Not that she could really leave Germany, but knowing Christophe would do whatever it took to keep them safe, including leaving their home, made her trust him all the more. She wanted to fill her mind with anything but what might happen until they were free of this city.

She would have been worried even without the added complication of having Jurgen with them. He kept up without complaint, as if he weren't still recovering from a bullet wound and the loss of so much blood. He stared straight ahead, looking almost the part of an upper-class gentleman if one didn't look too closely at the weave of his pants. His shirt, however, despite the wrinkles and that it was a trifle taut across the shoulders, was of the finest quality, embroidered on the pocket with the letter B. It would be difficult to see that and still think him anything but well-to-do, especially with the elegance of his face and the color of his eyes that the hat barely hid. Annaliese had never thought his face fit the look of a peasant, and in Christophe's shirt her assessment was proven correct.

Her gaze most often went to Christophe. He looked every bit the Christophe she'd known before the war, the one who was never late to church, who was always polite to her and to her family. He was more handsome than ever in the suit he'd worn on Sundays, and he certainly fit the part of a gentleman. The shirt he wore now was one of Ivo's best, and although it was of inferior quality to the one Christophe had given Jurgen, there was nothing about it that seemed out of place with the higher-quality suit covering it.

He'd left behind his knapsack, two guns, and the rest of his battle garb. Klaus had helped shine his boots, so that unless one looked closely, they blended in with the suit as well. They did the same for Jurgen's old shoes.

The day was uncommonly clear and warm for so early in the spring. And as expected, the streets were mainly quiet. Service on the streetcars was indeed sporadic, but they were able to catch one after a few blocks of walking. Christophe paid for all three of them. Whether because of the early hour or the condition of the city, there were several empty seats. She and Jurgen took spots next to each other, and Jurgen sank to the leather cushion with closed eyes, as if more relieved than he wanted to admit about being able to sit at last. Christophe stood next to them, one hand on the back of the seat, the other on the leather strap dangling from above.

Annaliese barely noticed the avenues they passed. There was little to see, anyway, except closed shops and old, tattered pamphlets rustling along the gutters. Even here, in such fine neighborhoods, the old flyers reminded her of all the words she and Jurgen had used trying to convince others their way of thinking was right.

She closed her eyes to all of that now. Instead, she prayed. It wasn't until she felt the streetcar slow at the curve just before Munich's main train station that she looked around again.

The wide, cobbled avenue was busier than the rest of the city had been. There were even a few motorcars parked, as always, just outside the station entrance. Because the hour was early, the gaslights above still had a glow about them, but they were dulling in comparison to the rising sun.

There were soldiers here too, milling rather than marching. Christophe led Annaliese and Jurgen away from the streetcar, but instead of keeping away from the nearest knot of soldiers, he walked up to them.

"Do you know if the trains are running on schedule yet?"

His voice was strong and bold, not a trace of the nervousness that ran through Annaliese—and, no doubt even worse, through Jurgen.

All of the soldiers studied them, but only one spoke. "They are running, but not on schedule. Have they ever run on time here in Bavaria?"

The men behind him laughed.

Christophe led them on their way, and the soldiers let them go.

"Was that wise?" Jurgen asked, once they stepped inside, among the columns of the station. His voice was terse, a little breathless. "Calling attention to ourselves?"

Christophe didn't look at him. "Better to act the parts we're hoping to fill instead of letting them confront us first. We're bourgeoisie, grateful for them, remember?"

The station wasn't nearly as chaotic as Annaliese feared. People walked about, and in between them a few soldiers wandered with bayoneted guns. They were like fish with great stingers swimming through the station, stopping now and then but questioning only people who were dressed to lesser means. "Where are you going?" she'd heard one soldier ask. "What have you been doing in the past few days?" Followed by a search for any weapons.

She was glad, then, that Christophe had shown the restraint he had in leaving behind his own weapons.

The largest groups were found at the ticket booths. Christophe chose a line behind an older couple at one of the two open counters. The woman's hat was adorned with a tall feather, the man's fedora trimmed with a miniature version of the same.

"Have you been waiting long?" Christophe asked, so friendly they could have been going to Oktoberfest rather than standing near streets still tense with remnants of a suppressed revolution.

"Just a half hour or so," the man said.

Christophe smiled. "It promises a fine day."

The woman nodded, then glanced at Annaliese, who tried to think of something to add, to pretend this was just any other day, but not a single word came to mind. She smiled in place of furthering the conversation.

Jurgen stood behind them, but Annaliese guessed they weren't even sure he was part of their group.

"It could be much worse, young man," said the man in the feathered fedora. "Between the few trains the Allies left us and the chaos the Communists have caused, those of us allowed to keep a home might all be confined to it."

The woman at his side nodded again, her nervousness betrayed by the quickness of her movement. "Yes, we always go to the countryside at this time of the year. We've already delayed it a week."

"So I said this morning," the man added, "that we won't wait another day. And here we are."

A pair of soldiers passed by, and Annaliese watched but only peripherally. She kept her gaze on Christophe instead; he might be listening to the woman in front of them as she talked about their home in the country, but his eyes followed the nearby soldiers.

She nearly jumped when Jurgen's arm brushed hers. It was barely a touch, perhaps unintentional, yet there was something in his eye that made her fearful just the same. He was staring at the soldiers too.

Then they passed by, taking no notice of anyone. She wondered if it was her imagination that her own sigh of relief was echoed by Jurgen.

The line they were in to purchase tickets did not move, and annoyance replaced whatever relief she felt at not having a soldier around. They had relative peace, relative safety, so she must squash any impatience. She wished only to be invisible, and in particular that Jurgen would be invisible too.

Christophe encouraged the mindless chatter from the couple in front of them by asking questions, and they both seemed eager enough to talk. Anything to make it appear as though life were normal.

By the time the line began to move, Annaliese had had ample opportunity to study the growing crowd around them. She was convinced they weren't the only ones hiding something. A good number of those around them looked every bit as nervous as she felt.

When finally they had their tickets and walked toward the trains, the station was busier than ever. She didn't know if that was good or bad. Certainly it was good that people felt safe enough to leave their homes, but bad because she feared a train—whenever one arrived—might be rushed with passengers. Ticketed or not.

"You—you there. Halt."

Annaliese's heart plummeted just as Christophe took her hand in his while Jurgen, now clutching her arm, tightened his grip. But when she turned in the direction of the call, she saw the soldiers were addressing a man dressed in the garb of a worker.

Christophe led them on, even as familiar questions echoed from the iron rafters. "Where are you going? What have you been doing the last few days? Do you have a weapon?"

The man's answers were too timid to be heard.

Evidently the docility of his demeanor made no difference. A moment later Annaliese saw him marched off with a gun at his back, under arrest.

Christophe watched the man being taken away, knowing all he would have to do was whisper Jurgen's identity in the ear of any one of these soldiers and Jurgen, too, would be hauled away.

But bringing attention to Jurgen meant bringing attention to Annaliese, and that he would not do.

The closer they came to the tracks, the noisier it became, even without a train in sight. The platforms teemed with people carrying their own luggage. He scanned the area, knowing they would have to fight for a place closer to the track to have even a hope of boarding.

He held Annaliese in front of him, directing her by the shoulders which way to go. Jurgen was close at her side. Christophe's height allowed him to see farther above the crowd, but they were jostled all the way.

Soon, though, they had inched and pressed and squirmed their way as near to the rails as they were likely to get.

Christophe noticed the stares first. They seemed to be looking at Annaliese—or just beyond her. He followed the gaze, seeing Annaliese was as bewildered as he.

"Look—look at him!"

Then he saw Jurgen on her other side. The pure white of
the shirt Christophe had given him was stained with a shock-
ing red; the assault of the crowd had evidently battered his
wound open. Between the size of the blotch and the paleness
of his face, it was a wonder the man still managed to walk.

Christophe slipped out of his jacket and put it around
Jurgen. Then he pulled him along, supporting him with one
arm, the other around Annaliese. He guided them beside the
edge of the track without backing away, as far down the platform as the crowd permitted.

Was it his imagination, or was there a whisper rippling
through those around them, even here? A crowd of strangers suddenly seemed to be connecting. A crowd that Jurgen
might once have charmed with his poetry and passion. But
Christophe saw suspicion in the glances closest to them, in a
finger pointed at Jurgen.

Whispers about recent fighting sounded from here and
there. The victors were the only ones patrolling the streets
now, one reminded another. The losers were in hiding . . . or
trying to flee.

Christophe made sure Jurgen's wound was well concealed
and prayed as never before that the whistle of a train might
miraculously sound.

But it did not.

The murmurs grew louder, the crowd closer, as if everyone
wanted to see what kind of wound the man sported. There
was no place left for them to go; they were as far down the
platform as it allowed.

Christophe could hide the blood, but he couldn't hide the
paleness of Jurgen's skin, the increasing sag in his stance. He
adjusted the tweed hat, lowering it a bit to cover more of

Jurgen's face. He was drooping by the moment, his eyelids falling shut. He stood now only because he leaned against Christophe. Without him, Jurgen would surely fall.

Then what Christophe had prayed for sounded in the distance. The brakes, the steam, the whistle. Though the train was still beyond sight of the platform, Christophe knew his first moment of optimism, even as the whispers from the crowd around him grew louder.

"That man is bleeding." The accusation was repeated so often it became an echo of itself.

"Bring a soldier here!"

"For help?"

"A wound from a battle!"

"Probably a bullet!"

"Then he must be—"

The word they all feared rang from every direction. *Communist.*

Even as the train neared at last, Christophe caught Annaliese's eye. He could protect Jurgen, or he could protect her. She must know which he would choose.

And yet her gaze, so full of compassion, was on Jurgen. Not on Christophe. He couldn't tell her, over the hue and cry of the accusing crowd, that he would stay by Jurgen's side if that was what she wanted. That he would push her aboard if he had to, that he wouldn't let the crowd have Jurgen's red blood.

Because he knew if he failed Jurgen, he failed her.

The huge shadow of the locomotive pulled in behind Annaliese, and at that moment the crowd turned its attention there. Everyone scrambled forward, intent on getting aboard.

Christophe pushed Annaliese forward even as he tugged Jurgen along. Over his shoulder he heard another whistle, a different kind, from a free corps soldier fighting through the swarm of those who a moment ago were intent on fingering Jurgen. Now they had abandoned their cries in favor of getting aboard.

He saw Annaliese trip on the silk of her skirt, saw the hem tear when someone else caught it as they stepped onto the car's iron stair. Someone behind him pulled at Jurgen, who was like a rag doll between them. He was fully unconscious now, falling first one way and then the other.

Christophe heaved him up like a child, Jurgen's feet dragging, blood seeping from beneath the jacket now, dripping down to warm Christophe's hand.

Up one step, just behind Annaliese. Then another.

They were on board but pushed from behind through the vestibule ever deeper into the car.

Left with no choice, he took up a place behind Annaliese through first one carriage and vestibule, then another, until she was stopped on the other end from as furious a force as pushed from behind. Another set of passengers had gained access to a carriage farther up the track.

"In here," he called to Annaliese, who had taken only two steps past the lavatory.

Christophe tried to reach the handle, but Jurgen was too heavy to free either hand. Annaliese pulled the door open before the crush of the crowd made it impossible.

Christophe slipped inside, wanting to pull Annaliese in too. But the space was too small.

She shook her head. "I'll stay right here." Then she closed the door before he could say another word.

Even this seemed too much of a separation, with her on the wrong side of the door. Christophe settled Jurgen on the closed toilet seat and tried the door, but it wouldn't easily budge. The crowd must be too thick.

"Annaliese?"

"I'm here! Don't worry."

He couldn't stop himself from doing just that. Yet Jurgen needed attention. Christophe pulled the jacket away from him, seeing the red stain was worse even than on the platform. There was little to do about it except try stopping the flow, using the shirt itself. All he could do was pray—and listen through the door to make sure Annaliese was all right.

42

Annaliese tried not to stare at those around her but glanced surreptitiously anyway, trying to guess which were the faces of those who had accused Jurgen on the platform, if any of them were still nearby. Had the frantic crush to board the train separated her from those who had suspected Jurgen of being a revolutionary? Or were they too relieved at having found a place on the train to worry about him now?

Most faces turned away when her glance fell in their direction; they were pressed too tightly, and the indignity of desperation left little pride even in her own heart. But she still had to know. Were there any accusers around her or not?

The train lurched forward and her heart leaped with hope. But then the wheels scraped to another stop, only to lurch forward again.

And then to stop once more.

Annaliese could barely see through the narrow openings of the throng between her and the window. When she caught sight of a free corps officer on the platform, her breath stopped.

But all he did was stare at the train; those who'd cried accusations and suspicions at Jurgen were no longer at his side.

She looked around. That meant they were on this train.

Perhaps ready to point the finger again if they were assured it wouldn't endanger their spot.

With her back smashed to the lavatory door, Annaliese refused to budge, refused even to look at those around her now. She closed her eyes and prayed the train would move away from the station.

She wished she could see Christophe now, if only to glimpse his face, his eyes, to catch some kind of hope from him, even if it was nothing more than a shared wish for it. A shared prayer, the assurance that God was with them. But she knew he needed to wait in silence, and she mustn't allow anyone the use of this lavatory.

The train sat still for so long she began to fret they would never move forward. It was so crowded, and in such close quarters, the air soon staled. Few people spoke, only a mumble now and then. Barely a single complaint made it through the unease.

"Is there someone in there?"

Annaliese ignored the question, spoken by a man trying to make his way through the crowded aisle of the train car. She pretended she hadn't heard him, only held on to the latch behind her back even tighter.

"Is there anyone in this lavatory?"

Annaliese stared straight ahead.

Another man, one who had held a place so close beside her that his shoulder was pressed to the same door she held closed, tilted his face toward her. He wore the white suit and straw hat of a gentleman, and of all of those around them, he appeared the least flustered with the delay or the jammed space.

"I believe this gentleman—and the soldier behind him," he said, "are addressing you, *Fräulein*."

Heart pounding so loudly in her ears she wasn't sure she would be able to decipher what anyone else said, she looked past the man in the white suit to two others squeezing through those pinched into the train car with them.

"My husband is using this lavatory," she called when they stopped in front of her. How easily the lie passed from her lips under such desperation. "He's ill. Please leave him alone."

Voices rose around her.

"I saw her with him—the man with the blood."

Several others around them nodded along.

"It was a wound!"

"If her husband is in the lavatory, he must be the one with the bloodstain."

"He must have been fighting in the revolution. How else would he have become wounded like that—with so much blood?"

The soldier held a gun across his chest. "Ask your husband to come out here, if you please."

"I—I don't know if he can."

"Please, if you would allow me to help?" said the man in the white suit beside her. "I need to use the lavatory anyway."

"But—"

Annaliese's protest went unheeded the moment the door opened from the inside. There was Christophe, unable to open the door very wide for the press of people around them, particularly the man in the white suit at Annaliese's side.

"If you please," the man said. Then despite Christophe's attempt to stop him, he moved out of the way for the door to open farther, pulling Christophe out and forcing himself into the lavatory, effectively switching their places.

Christophe stood at her side, dressed in the once-white

shirt that he'd loaned to Jurgen, which was now irreversibly stained in red.

"There it is!"

"See all that blood!"

The soldier had little room to point his rifle anywhere but straight up, yet his intention to use it was clear enough. "You will come with me."

Christophe looked as confused as Annaliese felt. The man in the white suit was inside the lavatory—with Jurgen. And hadn't said a word. Surely Jurgen wasn't strong enough to overpower him?

"Why should I come with you?" Christophe said, snapping Annaliese from her own confusion. They had no choice but to take advantage of whatever time Jurgen extended them, and Christophe was clearly acting the part she'd set up a moment ago. He leaned heavily against the door, shrouding his eyes with what looked like heavy lids and drooping his shoulders.

"I told you he is sick," Annaliese said. Now she was glad she'd said such a thing. "He's coughed up so much blood—he's terribly ill. We're going to the country, to the doctors at the sanitarium."

A rumble originated somewhere in the crowd, whisper of a new threat. *TB.* What else could cause someone to cough up so much blood?

First one seemed to withdraw; then from the other side another moved away, then another, allowing more room between Christophe and the crowd.

But the soldier was clearly skeptical. He remained standing where he was, right in front of Annaliese and Christophe. "Coughed up that much blood?" he said. "I don't think so."

For good measure Christophe coughed again, and with his

hands already stained from holding Jurgen, it might have convinced Annaliese herself had she not known the truth.

"You will remove your shirt," the soldier commanded, attempting to shift his rifle but not succeeding in lowering it enough to be of any real threat.

"This is a public place," Christophe protested weakly. "Half disrobing might . . . upset some of the ladies."

"You can do it here, or you can do it in the presence of my other officers. I will place you under arrest if there is a wound beneath that shirt."

Christophe tried to unbutton the shirt but fumbled with mock frailty. Annaliese helped him free the last few buttons and then he removed the shirt. He held up his arms, even turned around, proving the blood did not come from a wound on any part of his body. There was a smear of blood on him from the shirt itself, but with a clean corner he wiped it away.

The soldier looked at the man who'd brought the accusations, whose face was beginning to take on a pallor of its own.

"It was very confusing on the platform," he said slowly. "We all saw the blood. It looked as though—we heard no cough. We thought perhaps . . . he had been shot."

The soldier told the man to mind his own business, then faced Christophe once more, this time with a smile.

"I can see from your boots you were in the army. Where did you serve?"

"On the Somme."

Annaliese smiled broadly. "Yes, he was a Major and served our country bravely."

She added a glare over the soldier's shoulder, aimed at the man who had tried to have him arrested. How bold the ruse had made her, when she should still be quaking in her own shoes.

But it was only the truth, what she'd said about Christophe. He had served their country bravely, and if anyone deserved freedom, it was he.

⌁

Christophe watched the soldier make his way from the train, while the others who'd accused them backed away as far as the confines allowed. He sent a glance Annaliese's way; then with another cough to emphasize his role, he prepared to return to the lavatory, to see what Jurgen had done with the man in the white suit.

He tapped on the door.

A moment later the man came out, the sleeves of his suit coat splattered with blood. The look on his face was a mix of fear and annoyance. "You've left the lavatory entirely unusable. Look! Would you look at my clothes? I don't doubt this man has some kind of horrible disease that might kill anyone who uses that lavatory."

His words renewed murmurs of TB as he made his way to one of the newer spots left open from a crowd now eager to give them any room that was left.

Then the train began to roll blessedly forward.

"I suggest you are the only one to use that lavatory," he said with obvious affront aimed Christophe's way, "until the conductor has a chance to clean it. But who can find a conductor on this train? None to be found, I'm sure of that. No room!"

Exchanging a glance with Annaliese, Christophe tried hiding his astonishment, and then he went back inside the lavatory. Jurgen was there, fully conscious, still sitting on the closed toilet lid.

"What happened?" he whispered to Jurgen.

"I was about to ask you the same."

"The man who was just in here with you," Christophe said. He knew the question was absurd even as he had to ask. "Didn't he . . . see you?"

Jurgen nodded. "He said he was from Berlin, that he worked with Leviné and was trying to escape Munich."

"Did you know him?"

Jurgen shook his head. "I never saw the man before today."

Christophe knew Communists were fleeing Munich faster than rats from a sinking ship, so he didn't doubt the story. It was one thing to help Jurgen get away, but altogether different to help anyone else. He was relieved the other man didn't need his help—and had, in fact, helped them instead.

Not that Christophe held much hope that the free corps would act mercifully if either one were caught. Not with their guns ready to spread their own form of justice.

He leaned against the closed lavatory door, feeling the rattle of the wheels beneath them. All he wanted to do now was get Munich—and really, all of Germany—behind him.

43

Annaliese kept guard over the lavatory door. She had no intention of moving, no matter who showed an interest in using the facility. Not that anyone did; TB was as frightening as the influenza. The man in the now-stained white suit occasionally smiled her way but never said another word.

She knew they wouldn't be safe leaving the train—at least with Jurgen—until most of those who had boarded with them were gone.

How far could the others travel? Germany was only so big.

The train was unable to take on more passengers within the city limits and so it crept through all the outlying stations without stopping at all.

At such a slow pace, the train ride seemed to go on forever, even beyond the city. After the first few stops without a soul departing, Annaliese began to fret that no one would disembark, and they would be trapped indefinitely aboard this awful carriage. Christophe trapped in the confines of a lavatory with Jurgen, and he without any help.

Gradually, though, the train began to lighten its load of humanity at countryside stations. From where she stood, she had only a scant view but knew they would soon come to Braedon, where she and Christophe had grown up.

She also knew they would have to pass it by.

And so they did. She sent only a fleeting glance in its direction, and she heard nothing from the lavatory, though certainly Christophe had guessed from the time spent on the train, even at this snail's pace, that they must have passed their destination.

Before much longer the man in the once-white suit departed, tipping his hat her way, then disappearing through the vestibule exit.

She watched a pack of original accusers share a meal at midday, guessing them to be part of the same family. They were well dressed: two women, three men, a youth. Though the women didn't wear much jewelry beyond earrings and a few rings on their fingers, she could tell they weren't only acting the part of the bourgeoisie; they were authentic. They mostly ignored Annaliese, which she welcomed. She didn't want any attention at all.

Seeing them eat made her own stomach twist with hunger, surprising her. She had no desire for food. How could her body hint at an interest in such a thing when the remnants of a crowd who'd been only too eager to accuse Jurgen were still around?

Furtively she studied those other faces left who might have been witnesses. Most had already departed, each taking with them one small piece of the burden from her shoulders.

Another man caught her eye beyond them, one she hadn't noticed earlier. He was alone and sat staring out the window, not looking her way, not paying attention to anyone on the train. Had he been part of the crowd on the platform?

Certainly he hadn't boarded recently; he might have come from another, more crowded train car. She couldn't be sure.

At last the family departed, a full hour past Annaliese's home village. She looked around at those who were left. Everyone had a seat, and there were even a number of empty ones now.

The man she'd noticed was still aboard. He was finely dressed, his pants of dark linen. Were his shoes just tattered by the effects of the war, or were they castoffs from someone else? Were his clothes a disguise, like Jurgen's, to present himself as bourgeoisie when in fact he was another escaping Communist?

She wished there were some kind of code, some way to find out, some way she could inquire that would let him trust her enough to answer the question. Because if he was no danger to Jurgen, they could get off at the very next stop.

As if in answer to her unspoken thoughts, the man stood to disembark. Good; that meant they could get off the train at the stop after, once he was gone.

She watched him open the door to the vestibule. But to her dismay he merely went on to the next carriage.

The train stopped to let other passengers off, then slowly started its journey again. She looked out the window to see who had been left behind on the platform and saw a handful of people. But not that man.

She tapped on the door, and Christophe opened it just wide enough to see her face.

"No one is left who boarded with us," she whispered. "There was a man here, but he's gone to another carriage. I think he's still aboard."

"If he doesn't see us, we can get off at the next village.

Jurgen needs a doctor—I can't stop the bleeding. I don't think we should wait any longer."

She nodded. They would have to take the chance. She saw that Christophe wore the bloodstained shirt, but he'd covered it with his jacket. If Jurgen was still bleeding, that would be two shirts with stains, making it all the harder to escape notice.

As the train slowed, the speed of Annaliese's heartbeat picked up. She tapped on the lavatory door just as Christophe opened it. Jurgen was there, pale but alert, his blue eyes flitting nervously about. He wore the unstained shirt, though even now a small spot was forming.

"Walk out with him," Christophe whispered. "I'll follow in a moment."

Jurgen walked steadily enough at her side with nothing more than the lightest of touches to her forearm. She pulled open the door to the vestibule; then as the slow train stopped altogether, she stepped down to the platform before waiting for a conductor to appear with a step.

She looked back to see if Christophe followed, but to her horror she saw instead the other man, the one who might have boarded with them in Munich.

"Come along, Jurgen," she said quietly. "There is a man behind us we'll want to avoid."

He stepped down behind her more agilely than she would have expected considering the extent of his injury and loss of blood. But in spite of that, a shadow closed in behind them.

She continued to lead Jurgen, who stumbled once.

"Wait, please." The man's voice was cool, calm. Close.

Annaliese acted as if he were nothing but a pest following them, an overeager follower from one of the crowds they used to draw. Sometimes members from their crowds would get too close, would separate themselves from the rest in hope of capturing some of their essence, some of the magnetism that had drawn them and so many others.

The shadow grew taller, closer. She felt it in the swirl of air closing in around them. Jurgen stumbled again and the stain that had been the size of a coin a moment ago spread larger. Annaliese accepted some of his weight, helping him along.

"You were there," the man said, still too close. "In Munich."

Annaliese refused to acknowledge the words, refused even to look at him.

"You were with Leviné."

At last Annaliese looked back, not to confront the man but in search of Christophe.

"You were with him when he ordered them shot. For no other reason than that they were wealthy."

Her eyes still searched for Christophe. There—he was just getting off the train.

But something else caught her eye, taking her breath away. The man was so close behind them, and he had a gun.

"Christophe!"

He surged toward them, but not before the gun went off. Jurgen stumbled at her side just as Christophe pounced on the man behind them. His gun went off again, but Annaliese saw that this time it had been aimed at the sky.

The first bullet, however, had found its target. Jurgen leaned against her, into her arms, even as from the corner of her eye she saw Christophe wrestle the man who had fired, kicking away his gun. Another man rushed from the station house to help Christophe subdue him.

Behind her, the train shot steam and sparks, then chugged away, oblivious.

Annaliese could support Jurgen no longer, so together they sank to the platform. He stared at her as if all he could see was her face, smiled as if there were no pain. "You made me a better man, Annaliese. For a little while, anyway." Something pulled at his face, a pain from a wound she couldn't see, though the evidence of the new wound bathed her hands. "But it doesn't matter . . . anymore."

Tears heated her cheeks as his blood heated her hands. "No, Jurgen! You'll be all right. We'll get a doctor—"

Christophe appeared at their side. "She's right, Jurgen. They're sending for a doctor right now."

Jurgen's gaze found Christophe. "I think . . . I think I will be seeing that God of yours before a doctor can get here."

"No, no!" Annaliese said. "Don't give up. You mustn't. . . ."

Jurgen looked straight up, past both Annaliese and Christophe. "He was right. I was with Leviné. I could have stopped him, maybe. I could have rescued some of the bourgeoisie he murdered. But I didn't."

Annaliese leaned even closer so that he was forced to look at her again. "You didn't cause it, Jurgen," she told him. "I know you wouldn't."

"Tell that . . . to God . . . on my behalf."

And then he closed his eyes.

44

Annaliese walked with Christophe at her side, her hand in his. They'd barely spoken since seeing to Jurgen's body, entrusting him to the local authorities. She and Christophe were as vague as they needed to be about how the murder had taken place, explaining that Annaliese had merely helped him from the train and the other man had come up behind them. She squashed the betrayal in her claim of not knowing Jurgen, and yet she told herself she really didn't, not anymore. The Jurgen she knew wouldn't have stood by and allowed innocent victims—even capitalists—to be shot for no reason. The shooter had been taken away in custody, and she would let that man identify Jurgen. They had left their names and addresses, but with homes in Braedon, Annaliese hoped to be spared anything that had happened in Munich.

They'd also been quiet during the wagon ride Christophe had been able to arrange that took them nearly all the way to Braedon. She guessed he hadn't been as stunned by Jurgen's death as she had, but she welcomed Christophe's solemn sympathy in the touch of his hand, the crease of his brow, the way she knew he silently prayed when he bowed his head and closed his eyes, opening them only to look at her.

Soon their walk would end at the mansion her parents occupied. Christophe had told her they weren't alone there anymore, that they'd taken in a number of bourgeoisie from the city. She was glad of that, even though she would have preferred a more private homecoming. A quiet place to ask her father's forgiveness.

The gate to the mansion was in sight now, the boundary to the home her parents would soon leave behind.

"Thank you," she said quietly to Christophe as they walked.

"For . . . ?"

"For coming after me." She was glad when he stopped, taking advantage of their last moments alone to bring her into the circle of his arms. "And for not giving up on me. I'm not sure I would have been so persistent for someone like me had I been in your shoes."

Christophe smiled. "There is a verse in the Bible, one I would like to read with you many times in our lives ahead." He kissed her before adding, "It says love *never* gives up."

Then he took her hand again, with the other pulling a key from his pocket. "To the lock on the gate," he told her. "You can thank your mother for sparing us a climb over the wall. This key used to belong to the guard."

Inside the gate, they walked down the lane toward the mansion. Annaliese looked at the house that she'd hated, knowing its luxury had played a part in sending her away. But right now she imagined nothing more than those within it. Her mother was here. And her father.

No sooner had she finished the thought than the front door burst open. There, not walking but running in spite of a gown that limited her gait, was her mother, coming toward her with open arms.

Annaliese ran too, and in a moment they embraced more tightly than they had since she was a child. "Mama!"

Christophe stood by and with a sob her mother pulled him near, the three of them clasped together.

Then Annaliese saw beyond them. At the doorstep was her father. His impairment was instantly noticeable, but when he called her name, she thought nothing could sound more lovely.

Epilogue

"Are you sure you won't come with us, Annaliese?" her mother asked. "You need not even pack—it's done for you. It wouldn't take Christophe long to gather some of his belongings. What could be more exciting than a honeymoon in America?"

Annaliese threw a glance at the last trunk to be carried out the door, knowing most of the ones that belonged to her waited in the library, where they had been since her mother had packed them. She'd opened only one trunk since returning, but it could easily be collected and added to her parents' belongings, which were right now being transported to the carriage outside for the first leg of their journey to America.

The houseguests had already bid their good-byes, amid grateful tears for having housed them in such a time of need. But now they had disappeared, allowing the last of the family farewells to take place in private.

Annaliese slipped her hand back into Christophe's. Her husband. "I'll keep my trunks handy," she said, "and once everything is settled here—the factory, the houseguests, the house—we'll come. At least for a visit."

That would have to be enough. Even now, as her father stood nearby, leaning on his cane, she almost wished she could accompany them.

But as eager as she was to restore her relationship with her father, it was probably best to allow more time for forgiveness—on both sides—to take hold. It had been two days since she'd come home, two days of happy reunion with her mother, including a wedding as hasty and exciting as any of those that had taken place before the war. Both she and Christophe had wanted to share the occasion with them, so the decision not to wait had been simple. Yet these couple of days had only allowed a gradual easing of awkwardness between Annaliese and her father.

Besides, there was much to be done here. The guests were already looking for other accommodations, but no one knew how long that might take. The government might be ousting Communists at that very moment, but it could be some time before Munich was safe again.

All of Christophe's holdings had to be settled too, making it impossible for them to leave Germany even if Annaliese were fully convinced she wanted to. It was hard to leave a place she'd struggled so fiercely to help mend.

Her mother took them each by the hand. "I know you want to make a difference, and I admire you for that. But don't ignore what's best for you. It isn't getting easier to live here since the war ended; it's only been harder. Think of your children, should God bless you with some." A new thought seemed to surprise her. "Oh! And as your children's grandmother, don't I have a right to want them safe? and within reach to love?" She squeezed Annaliese's hand. "Promise me you'll do what's best for them, even if that means coming to America."

"It's time to go, Edith," her father said from the threshold. His vision truly must be improving from what had been described when Annaliese first returned. Already he was walking toward the light of the open door.

They followed him outside and Annaliese's heart fluttered

as for the first time she seriously envisioned the possibility of going to America. How could she face the prospect of having children without her mother nearby to help? She knew Christophe was ready to leave Germany; Nitsa was already in America, and he was likely even more eager than Annaliese to see his sister again.

Maybe—someday—she could leave. If she were ever convinced she'd really helped their homeland toward a better future.

She hugged her father and then her mother, losing her own battle with tears when her mother lost hers.

"We'll come," Christophe said, taking his turn to hug Annaliese's mother. "Have I ever failed to bring your daughter to you?"

Annaliese wished she could laugh, grateful for Christophe's promise. But when her parents disappeared inside the carriage and it rolled down the lane, all she had were more tears.

She waved even though they surely could no longer see her.

"We'll see them again," Christophe said gently, pulling her close. "One way or another."

She nodded. It didn't matter how much time passed until then, no moment could be more painful than this one.

They'd barely made it to the porch before sounds of another carriage slowing at the gate drew her attention. She waited for it to pass, but the sound stopped altogether. Then she heard someone alight, followed by the bark of a dog.

"Were your parents expecting more guests?" Christophe asked.

"Not that I know of."

"Let's see who it is, then."

When Annaliese was close enough to see the driver, dressed

in a uniform that was somehow familiar, excitement bubbled in her breast before she even knew why. Where had she seen that emblem, the one that tied his employer to a fine home in a village several miles east of Munich? And was that dog's little yap somehow familiar?

"Meika!" Annaliese let go of Christophe's hand, hurrying past the coachman. She rushed to the side of the carriage, pulling open the door just as Meika and Schatzi nearly tumbled into Annaliese's waiting embrace.

"You—you're here!" She laughed when Schatzi wiggled between them, alternately licking Annaliese's and Meika's faces. "Oh, I'm happy to see both of you! I have so many things to tell you." Annaliese pulled herself away just as Christophe came up behind her, and Schatzi issued a firm, high-pitched bark. "If only you'd come yesterday—you could have been witness to our wedding. Meika, this is my husband."

Meika extended her hand while holding Schatzi away from him with an apologetic smile. "I'm afraid he doesn't like men. He's quite the ladies' dog." Then she eyed Christophe with an approving nod. "So you're Christophe. Yes, Annaliese described you well enough for me to have pictured you correctly. I'm glad you were able to find one another. It's why we came to Braedon, to make sure Annaliese made it safely beyond Munich. I was so worried about her!"

Christophe put his arm around Annaliese. "For good reason. You've probably heard about the fighting there."

Meika nodded again, but Annaliese put a cautioning touch to her friend's shoulder before petting Schatzi again. "You shouldn't have risked traveling. If I'd known you were on your way, I'd have been the one worrying. Why didn't you take your motorcar? It would have been faster."

"We would have, but my driver said he was afraid we wouldn't be able to find fuel. So we took the coach and stayed clear of the city. Up until a little while ago, we had quite an impressive escort—a contingent of free corps, patrolling the roads."

"Probably hunting fleeing Communists," Christophe said.

"They made me feel entirely safe," Meika said. Then she turned back to the open door of the carriage just long enough to pull out a folded newspaper. "Accounts of the battle are in here. But there is something else, Annaliese. Something I wanted to show you. The moment I saw it, I knew I shouldn't ignore the prompting to come see you."

She handed Schatzi to Annaliese, then unfolded the paper on the floor of the carriage at the open door. Meika ignored headlines that Annaliese glimpsed about street battles, turning to a page nearly buried in the back. At last she found what she was looking for and refolded the paper so the article was displayed.

"Look here—you're quoted in the newspaper!"

Confused, Annaliese glanced between Christophe and Meika, clutching the dog closer. "I'm quoted?" She swallowed hard. "Not linking me to Jurgen?"

"No, he's not mentioned at all. Look, it's from the German Women's Association and they talked about your pamphlet! They quote you directly, about how at long last women have a voice, and that such sentiments should be noted around the world. As far as America! Do you know women don't yet have the vote there? At least not from coast to coast. It's to be brought up again in their Congress any day now, and this writer goes on to suggest their government should read *your* pamphlet to see why it makes sense to use the talents and insights of the female half of any population."

Annaliese cast Christophe a merry glance, exchanging with Meika the newspaper for Schatzi. She'd been so focused on German politics that she hadn't realized women had no voice in America's ballot boxes. What a transition the world had ahead, now that women were finally being heard. Even women in the wilds of America. How exciting would that be, to help with such a change?

Perhaps she could! American women weren't so very different from German ones, were they?

Christophe's wink told her he was already following her line of thinking. And his English was so much better than hers. . . .

Author's Note

The setting for this novel is a volatile and complicated time in German history, one I attempted to share from a simple affection for history rather than scholarly authority. My hope is to present a glimpse at the conditions in Germany following the Great War, a time that served as the foundation for so many of the horrors that followed. There are, without doubt, many facets of that time in history left out of this story. For those omissions, whether intentional or otherwise, as well as for any misinterpretations of this time period, I offer my sincere apologies and a hope that the characters did their job to entertain.

There are, however, a few factual details mentioned in my story that I found interesting and wanted to elaborate on:

- Kurt Eisner and Eugen Leviné were actual historical figures, and both played prominent roles in Germany's history at this time.
- Kurt Eisner's assassination left the Socialist regime in disarray, providing enough chaos to inspire Eugen Leviné to attempt a Communist revolution in Bavaria. During the course of the revolution, Leviné accused a number of wealthy, prominent citizens of Munich of being counterrevolutionaries, succeeding in murdering eight of them by having them shot. After his arrest by the free corps, Leviné was sentenced to a firing squad and died crying, "Long live the revolution."
- The free corps ushered in their own reign of retributive terror, matching and in some cases surpassing the damage the Communists had done.

Writing this story reminded me how deep the passion for politics can run, particularly if the values and freedom of an individual are threatened. It also reminded me that a public voice can make a difference if we don't lose hope. At the very least, the challenges of this time and place in history prompted me to pray more often for our own country and its leaders and to be thankful that we have avoided such horrors because our government is of the people, by the people, and for the people.

About the Author

Maureen Lang has always had a passion for writing. She wrote her first novel longhand around the age of ten, put the pages into a notebook she had covered with soft deerskin (nothing but the best!), then passed it around the neighborhood to rave reviews. It was so much fun she's been writing ever since.

She is the author of several novels, including *Pieces of Silver*—a 2007 Christy Award finalist—*Remember Me, The Oak Leaves, On Sparrow Hill, My Sister Dilly*, and most recently, the Great War series. She has won the Romance Writers of America Golden Heart award, the Inspirational Readers Choice contest, and the American Christian Fiction Writers Noble Theme award and has been a finalist for the American Christian Fiction Writers Book of the Year award and the Gayle Wilson Award of Excellence. She is also the recipient of a Holt Medallion Award of Merit.

Maureen lives in the Midwest with her husband, her two sons, and their much-loved dog, Susie. Visit her Web site at www.maureenlang.com.

Discussion Questions

1. At the beginning of the story, Germany has been defeated and the soldiers are marching home. What do you imagine they were thinking and feeling at that time, and what do you imagine the waiting families might have been thinking? Have you ever faced disgrace or defeat? How did you respond?

2. Jurgen's initial message is a cry against tyranny and a desire to end inequality, but he compromises his ideals when they no longer seem feasible. How do you think someone as idealistic as Jurgen was able to cross a line from wanting to serve society to wanting to control it? In what areas are you tempted to compromise when it's difficult to achieve your goals?

3. Does the separation between Annaliese and her parents have more to do with their beliefs, or just a lack of communication? Is it possible for family members or friends who hold different beliefs to still be close to one another? What does it take to make that sort of relationship work?

4. Frau Düray asks Christophe to go to Munich in search of Annaliese. Do you think she did the right thing, or should she have accepted her daughter's independence? How have you seen parents respond when their children rebel? What are some constructive responses? destructive responses?

5. When you've been in a crowd or part of an audience, have you ever been aware of the audience uniting as one

large element, wanting to enjoy/agree/approve of the speaker or performer? How did you respond? Did your emotions and energy change after the crowd dispersed?

6. Is there an appropriate balance between an idealistic society that shares all things in common and the work-and-reward system of capitalism? What are the merits and failures of both ends of the spectrum? How much should people depend on the government? Should individuals, churches, and private charities assume more of the burden?

7. When Jurgen asks how a loving God could let war destroy the world He created, Christophe responds that God gave us the ability to choose, and He won't take back that gift just because we make a bad choice. Do you agree with Christophe's response? How would you have answered Jurgen?

8. Leo is the power behind Jurgen. Have you ever known, or known of, anyone who is happy to be working behind the scenes, avoiding the attention or accolades but pleased when the one they've chosen to support receives such things? A teacher? A relative?

9. Christophe has qualms about Jurgen's agenda. Was it ethical for him to remain and help train Jurgen's fighting forces anyway? How would you have handled the task that Leo and Jurgen assigned Christophe?

10. Some of the Socialist ideals appear to offer freedom— from the restrictions of government, of religion, of

nationalism, even of marriage. How do these ideas agree or disagree with your own view of freedom?

11. At one point, Leo states that the masses will allow almost anything to happen unless a gun is pointed directly at them. Do you agree that the populace is easily swayed? How involved should people be in politics? How involved do you think the government should be in the lives of its citizens?

12. How did you feel about Annaliese's decision to help Jurgen escape near the end of the story? Would you have done the same if you were in her position?

13. Even before the First World War, women of many countries had been fighting for the vote. How do you think this war influenced attitudes about the role women play in society, especially in view of the next world war that was yet to come?

14. How did you feel about Annaliese and Christophe's decision to stay in Germany at the end of the story? Did you wish they had gone to America with Annaliese's parents?

More great fiction from
Maureen Lang

A legacy she never expected.
A love that knows no bounds.

A legacy she never wanted.
A love she'd only hoped for.

Engaging the Mind.
Renewing the soul.

www.maureenlang.com

Two sisters. One committed the unthinkable.
The other will never forgive herself.